GOBBELINO LONDON & A SCOURGE OF PLEASANTRIES

GOBBELINO LONDON, PI: BOOK 1

KIM M. WATT

For further information contact www.kmwatt.com

Cover design: Monika McFarland, www.ampersandbookcovers.com

Editor: Lynda Dietz, www.easyreaderediting.com

ISBN 978-1-9160780-9-3

First Edition February 2020

10 9 8 7 6 5 4 3 2 1

For everyone
who suspects that cats have
great and secret lives.
Because they do.

CONTENTS

THAT OLD MONEY SMELL

IF ANYONE HAD ASKED HOW BUSINESS WAS GOING, I COULD have summed it up like this: currently, a very large man with a very bald head was waving a very heavy tyre iron around our office in a very threatening manner. And, our office being too small to swing the proverbial cat (and trust me, that'd better be proverbial. Cats do not take kindly to such treatment), he had already cracked the back of the rickety chair on his side of the desk, smashed one of our three remaining overhead fluorescent lights, and had come alarmingly close to my ears where I crouched on top of the rusty old filing cabinet. I bared my teeth at him, but he ignored me. Most of our clients do. All his attention was on Callum.

"I want my money back!" our visitor roared. He'd gone a quite startling shade of red, and it occurred to me that we might be saved any further trouble if he just keeled over of an aneurysm right here. But our luck was never that good. And then there was the fact that dead bodies can be

kind of tricky to explain, so it was probably better if we got rid of him in a rather less final manner.

"We did the job you asked for," Callum said again, his voice calm. He was still sitting in the slightly less rickety chair on his side of the desk, hands folded in front of him as if this were a perfectly normal client meeting – and, to be fair, it wasn't *that* unusual for us. There was a reason we only had three lights left. Well . . . two, now.

I could have told Callum not to bother though, that the cool collected approach wasn't going to work. Baldy wasn't the sort of person who listened to reason. Baldy was the sort of person you bopped on the nose then fled while he was still confused. Of course, that was a bit hard when he was between us and the door, waving a tyre iron around like he had places he wanted to insert it. Actually, given the conversation of the last few minutes, that was exactly what he wanted.

"This wasn't what I asked for!" the man bellowed. "You were meant to find out where the money was going!"

"Well, we did—" Callum started, which was evidently not what our delightful client wanted to hear.

An inarticulate roar ripped out of the big man's throat, filled with all the pain and fury of an injured animal, and he brought the tyre iron down on the desk so hard I thought the wood was going to shatter. It would have, if it had been one of those flimsy modern desks. As it happened, our desk was an ancient artefact Callum had found in a charity shop, and the floor probably would've given way before it did. All that happened were a few more scars joined the rest on its surface and Callum finally jumped out of his chair, shoving it into the wall behind him.

"*I want my money back!*"

Well, at least he was consistent. Problem was, even if we'd wanted to give the money back, we couldn't. We had this thing called rent, plus every now and then we liked to eat.

Callum put his hands out to the man like a lion tamer. "Sir, I'm sorry this wasn't what you wanted to hear. But the problem with private investigations is that we rarely turn up things people *do* want to hear."

The man roared again and flailed at the desk with the tyre iron, scattering pens, old paperbacks, a mug of tea and the folder of photographs to the floor while Callum watched with a resigned look on his face. I peered down at the photos. I was particularly proud of the one that showed the man's business partner stripped naked except for a cap of leaves and flowers – well, two caps, but let's not get into details – and being painted green by two older women in wellington boots and gardening gloves. Everything had actually been shot in video on one of those little action cameras, but I'd managed to hold position on the windowsill at the perfect angle to avoid reflection and catch the business partner's rather blissful face. Apparently being rendered moss-green, adorned with daisies and walked on as if you were a lawn was both delightful and (given the vanishing funds) a pricey business. Humans.

With the desk empty, our client paused, glaring around the room. Callum took advantage of the man's lull in hitting things and screaming to say, "I'm very sorry about this. But now that you have the evidence, you can press charges against him for embezzlement and misuse of company funds."

The man sucked an enormous breath in and screamed again, having apparently decided that was either more satisfying or more effective than hitting anything else. The woo-woo doctor upstairs pounded on the floor. For someone so into inner peace she wasn't very patient with external noise.

The man stopped screaming and scowled at the ceiling, then thumped it with the tyre iron, sending a shower of plaster pattering down on me and turning my black fur a fetching but unnatural shade of grey. I shook the dust out of my ears with a huff as Woo-Woo pounded back. Our client hit the ceiling again, so hard I thought the tyre iron might pop straight through, and for a moment it looked like we were in for some sort of cross-ceiling war, but this time Woo-Woo didn't respond. There was silence as plaster dust drifted around us, and Callum sighed.

"You … you *divot*," the man said finally. "The money's one thing. But I'm going to have to fricking *break up* with him now."

Callum stared at the man, then at me. I shrugged. Okay, I suppose I should have picked up on the body language cues between big man and the business partner, but I hadn't been looking for them. I'd just been interested in where the partner went *after* he left the office. When he didn't go home to his wife and three children, that was. Seriously. Humans really have to complicate things. Why not just get on with what makes you happy?

"Well," Callum said carefully. "I can see how that does

make things more difficult. I'm sorry. But at least you know where the money was going, right?"

Our client covered his face with one hand, the tyre arm hanging limp at his side. Callum eyed it like he was going to make a grab for it. I hoped he didn't. The NHS was all very well for stitches, but we spent a fortune on hydrogen peroxide and gauze. However, the man moved before Callum could do anything, picking up the fallen chair and setting it upright, then sinking into it with his head hanging low. The chair creaked even more threateningly than it usually did.

"I suspected," the man said, his voice muffled as he wiped his face with one hand. "But then I thought it was maybe just his family, you know? Putting demands on him. That I could have understood. Mine does that, too."

His does too? Gods. They didn't need body painters and private investigators. They needed a good talking-to regarding happiness, the shortness of life, and the pointlessness of worrying about appearances. Although, if everyone worked that one out, we'd be out of work, so maybe it was just as well.

"Unfortunately, this sort of investigation can turn up things we're not ready for," Callum said, retrieving his mug from the floor. "Would you like a cup of tea?"

The man wiped his nose. "Do you have anything stronger?"

"Sure." Callum went to the little cubby off the office where the kitchenette was crammed in, such as it was – nothing more than a sink with a cupboard above and another below it, and just enough counter space for the kettle and a one-ring electric hotplate. He fished out a scratched glass and ambled back to the desk with it and the bottle of decent whisky we kept for clients. It was amazing how often they needed a nip. I said we should charge for it, but Callum told me I had the heart of a sea snake. Not sure if that's worse than a regular snake or not.

Callum let the man snivel and drink his whisky and tell a disjointed and not unfamiliar story of love and deception and loss in stilted sentences, while he made all the appropriate noises and nodded in all the appropriate places. He's good at that. For someone who spends most of his time with a cat, he's got the whole people thing down. The man's voice got quieter and gentler and slower, and eventually he sat back in his chair, revealing a shining pink face and cheeks pinched with sorrow. He looked at the tyre iron as if not sure what to do with it, then got up a little unsteadily, holding a hand out to Callum to shake. Callum shook it, and I made a face – the big man had been wiping his nose with that paw just a moment before. And they call animals dirty.

Callum walked our subdued client to the door, which took all of two paces – our little office was sufficient, but that was probably the most you could say for it. There was exactly enough room for the desk and chairs, an armchair that folded out into a single bed (okay, so it was our home-slash-office, but who's counting) and the set of filing cabinets where I kept my souvenirs, and which I felt lent us quite the air of legitimacy. Callum thanked the man for choosing G & C London for his investigative needs, patted him on the shoulder, and let him out before clicking the lock over firmly, for all the good it would do against even a small child with an ounce of determination. Then he gazed around the room, sighed, and started picking up the mess off the floor, tutting at a book that had spat pages all over the place. But I mean, what does he expect? He buys them in bulk at car boot sales and in the reject boxes of libraries. They're tatty and old and I'm surprised he hasn't caught something nasty from them yet.

"So what's next?" I asked.

Callum finished stacking his paperbacks and went to get the laptop out of the desk drawer. We'd only made the mistake of leaving that on top of the desk once. "Nothing. We have nothing."

"Seriously?"

He sighed. "Yes. Seriously."

"Should we try advertising? I feel we're not really giving ourselves the chance to achieve our full potential here."

He set the laptop to fire up, and it squeaked and groaned like an ageing hippo while he went to put the kettle on. "Advertising takes money, Gobs. We only just made rent this month."

I really wish he wouldn't call me Gobs. My name is Gobbelino, but for some reason that mystifies me, humans can never leave well enough alone. They've got to shorten it, unless your name's short, in which case they lengthen it. One of the many things about humans that make no sense whatsoever.

"How about flyers?" I asked him. "You could do that, right? Print out a bunch of ad-type things."

"I could," he agreed. "It doesn't seem very professional, though. Not very subtle for a private investigation firm."

I eyed him. "Starving seems pretty unprofessional, too."

"Fair point." He poked the computer, but it was still spluttering through its start up. "We're going to need a new one of these soon, too."

"You know I can make that happen."

"No, Gobs."

I sighed. The thing is, I'm not a supermarket-own-brand type of cat. I like top shelf. And when one is small and subtle and knows how to get into places unnoticed (or how to bribe rats with a weakness for pork pies to do it for one), it's possible to live quite well on very little cash. Callum, unfortunately, has both a patchy history with the law and a shiny new conscience. The end result is that he's maddeningly resistant to even a whiff of rule-bending. So while I may still liberate the odd tray of less-fresh-than-it-could-be white fish from the local corner shop, I keep it very much on the sly. If he finds out, he goes and pays for it with money we can't spare.

There was a knock at the door, a cheery little *tap-tap, tap-tap* that we both recognised.

"Come in, Mrs Smith," Callum called. I was 99 percent certain the woman's name wasn't Jane Smith, but who cares, right? A name's just a name, and we all have things we'd prefer to leave behind us. Besides, she makes me custard with that fancy cat-milk.

"Hello, loves," she said, peering around the door. "You knew it was me! You're terribly good at this, you know."

Callum grinned at her. "I've just put the kettle on. Can I make you a cuppa?"

"Don't mind if I do," she said, patting her mane of tight

white curls into place. She had it styled into plaited sections by her face today, with butterflies clipped to the top and flowers stuck rather haphazardly all over it. "I made far too much shepherd's pie last night, so I thought I'd bring some over. And then I thought, well, if I'm coming over anyway, I'll bring you some lunch too." She hefted a frankly enormous carrier bag onto the desk, and fished around inside until she came out with a Tupperware, stuffed to bursting. "You must be so busy chasing down criminals and so on," she continued, opening the container and setting it on top of the desk. "You can't have any time to make your own meals!"

I jumped off the filing cabinet and onto the desk, investigating the Tupperware while Mrs Smith scritched between my ears rather pleasurably. I rewarded her with some purrs then set to munching chicken hearts in gravy. The woman was a gourmet.

Callum stepped back in from the kitchenette with two mugs of tea, and Mrs Smith set a giant sandwich on crusty brown bread in front of him. "You really must let me give you something for this," he told her.

She waved a hand and unwrapped her own sandwich, which was roughly a third the size of his. "No, no. I feel so much safer having an officer of the law across the hall. And what would I do with all this food, anyway?"

Callum didn't correct her regarding the officer of the law bit. He'd tried to before, but she resolutely refused to grasp the difference between a PI and a police officer. And who were we to disabuse her?

Especially when she kept coming around with chicken hearts.

THE AFTERNOON WAS long and rainy, heavy with the promise of colder weather to come. Callum leaned back in the creaking desk chair with his boots on the desk and some battered book with a trench-coated gumshoe on the cover in his hand, flicking steadily through the pages and helping himself to chocolate digestives. I sprawled on the desk, watching the rain chasing down the windowpanes, smelling damp streets and drifting lives and silence creeping in through the single glazing.

I was glad I wasn't out there. Being a street cat has its advantages, but rainy days demand central heating and soft beds, in my mind. Or small fan heaters and malfunctioning radiators in our case, but it was still better than being out there with wet feet and one eye open for the next young tom coming in on your patch. Or worse. I'd had a rough run of things in those days. Humans can be downright vicious, but they're not even the worst of what a young cat can come up against. And sometimes even your own kind won't step in to help you out. Sometimes they do rather the opposite. Young junkie kids, on the other hand, can be the most surprising of creatures.

I don't know how long the afternoon stretched, while Callum read and I wandered the cat-paths that run between memory and meditation, my eyes half-closed against the dim day. Until something tickled me. I looked up. Callum had almost finished his book, and the biscuits were almost gone. The light outside was grey and heavy, and the air seeping in around the window frame was cold and sharp. I yawned, stretched, and pricked my ears.

There. Someone was coming down the hall. I could smell them already, a heavy floral musk of perfume washing ahead of them. It seemed at odds with the muted thud of boots on the threadbare carpets, the delicacy of the scent more suited to high heels and slick dresses. The visitor brought the breath of the rain with them as well, and, under the perfume, the strange dull reek of leather chairs and wool carpets and high, still rooms wrought in brass and dark wood.

They smelt of money, in other words.

2

MONEY FOR NOTHING

"Someone's here," I said. They couldn't be going anywhere else, surely. Not with that old money scent. I mean, I'm not saying our clients are loaded, because they aren't, but the visitor didn't smell like the sort of person who went to woo-woo doctors, or as if they'd be employing Mrs Smith's tarot-reading and crystal-ball-gazing expertise. And unless someone had a rich relative come to gloat at them, we were the only other destination in the building.

"You recognise them?" Callum put an old receipt in his book to mark his place and swung his overlong legs off the desk, already reaching for the cricket bat in the corner. *That's* the sort of clientele we have. Not old money.

"No. Someone … I don't know. Something's off." As I spoke, there was a sharp knock on the door. It was a no-nonsense, let's-get-on-with-things knock. We didn't have frosted glass in the door, like in those PI shows on the TV, because the building mixed residential and business. So it was a crappy hollow door like any other, not even a peep-hole to check on things through, and the knocking was clear and immediate. For no reason I could explain, I suddenly wished Callum had locked it again after Mrs Smith had left, and that we could just sit here still and silent, unanswering, until the unseen visitor gave up.

"Come in," Callum called, giving me a puzzled look. I was a bit puzzled myself. The fur on my spine was rippling like the visitor was bringing a terrier in with them, and my nose was full of the sticky musk of that perfume even before the door opened. It felt like it was clawing its way down my throat and through my sinuses, drowning everything else, swallowing every other scent. I didn't like it, *really* didn't like it, but I couldn't have said why any more than I could have said why pickled eggs fill me with horror.

It's a thing, okay? And I will never understand why Callum insists on having them every time we go to the pub for curry night. The results of that particular combination are truly disastrous in a small office, too, which does nothing to endear them to me.

The handle turned, and we both stared at the door as if expecting something monstrous to jump through. I've seen plenty of monstrous things. Callum has too, in fact, but what we saw in the early days he probably put down to withdrawal or a bad trip or something. We don't talk about that stuff. Some memories are best left where they are.

Callum does see things other humans don't, though. He has magic in his skinny bones somewhere, and he accepts a talking cat without question, as well as the fact that the only reason other cats don't talk to him is that they've got nothing to say. And while we don't seek them out, when certain other aspects of magical Folk surface, he just goes with it. That kind of says everything that needs to be said about his level of comfort with the – for humans – unusual. And probably quite a lot about his ability to fit into normal human society, too.

But it wasn't a monster at our door, which should have felt like more of a relief than it did. It was a woman with rain beaded in her thick dark hair and a dubious look on her face. She looked at the sign on the door, which proclaims *G & C London, Private Investigators*, in gold lettering on a black plaque. It's *classy*. Callum got it in return for helping a printer move house. Although, admittedly, it looks a bit out of place on the stained door with its splintered, roughly repaired bottom (another unhappy client kicked it), and might give people a slightly skewed impression of our base of operations. Her gaze shifted from the plaque to Callum, who still had one hand on the cricket bat, and to me sitting straight upright on the edge of the desk.

"Mr London?" she said. "Gobbelino London?"

"Callum," Callum said.

"I was told to look for Gobbelino London," she said.

"He's my partner," Callum said. He refuses to call me boss, even though I'm blatantly the senior figure around here. "*Business* partner," he added, rather unnecessarily, I thought.

She obviously realised she was dealing with the *junior* business partner, because she said, "Can I talk to him?"

"I'm afraid not," Callum said. "Gobbelino doesn't deal with people directly. He's very reclusive."

"I see." She sounded unconvinced, and looked again at the plaque, as if to reassure herself she was in the right place. Callum shoved his paperback under a flyer for a car boot sale, which wasn't exactly a great leap upward in the image we were projecting.

"We work all cases together," he said. "Whatever you tell me, you tell him."

True enough, since I was sitting right there, breathing that heavy perfume and trying to get the hair on my back to calm down. It wouldn't. My tail was starting to go now. Why? She was right there in front of me, just some human in skinny jeans and a quilted coat who'd slipped with the perfume bottle. Maybe she forgot to shower this morning or something. She didn't look like the sort of person who forgot much, though.

She sighed. "Alright. I suppose." She came in, closing the door behind her, and glanced at me again. For just a moment I thought her eyes were *wrong*, then the thin grey light of the afternoon outside hit them and they were perfectly human, blue as … something blue. Periwinkles, or whatever. Or is that a kind of shellfish? I don't know. I'm not good with flowers. Or shellfish, although I like a nice mussel when I can get one.

"Please have a seat," Callum said, waving unnecessarily at the sole chair on her side of the desk.

She did, inspecting it before she sat down like she thought there might be the previous occupant's bodily fluids still decorating it. Rude. We might run a slightly rough ship (through no fault of our own, I might add), but it's a clean one. And that one time the guy bled everywhere we replaced the chair, anyway. And it was totally not our fault.

"How can I help?" Callum asked, steepling his fingers. He probably thought it made him look serious and mature, but it just made him look like he was about to play that kids' game – you know the one. Here's the church, here's the steeple, down it comes and crushes all the people. Or whatever. Although probably no one plays that anymore. You lose track over the course of a few lifetimes.

The woman folded her hands in her lap. Her jacket was open, and the jumper underneath looked soft and expensive, like it'd pill under your claws and collect cat hair like mad. It made my paws itch. "Are you sure I can't talk to Gobbelino?"

"This is how we work, I'm afraid, Ms …?"

"Ms Jones will do," she said. Callum didn't question it. Lots of people don't use their real names when they come in. No skin off our chins. Or tongues, whatever. We're interested in who the customer pays us to be interested in, not the customer themselves. So she could call herself the High Ruler of the Purple Ascot Ponies and we'd still take the case. She glanced at me again, her face expressionless, and I returned her gaze flatly. "Alright," she said. "I was told Gobbelino London was the one to talk to, but if this is how it works . . ."

Callum opened one of those big yellow notepads, put her name and date at the top of a page, and said, "Whenever you're ready."

She sighed. "Something has been stolen from me. A book. A family heirloom."

"Valuable?"

"To me, yes. Very much so."

"Any idea who might have taken it?"

She tapped her fingers on the back of her other hand. "My ex-husband. There's no way anyone else would have known where it was."

"So you'd like us to confirm he has it?"

"I want you to get it back."

"Um." Callum bounced the end of the pen on the notepad. "Request he give it back, you mean?"

"No. I don't want you to talk to him. In fact, I explicitly forbid you from making contact with him. I want you to steal it back."

Callum and I exchanged glances, and I arched my eyebrow whiskers slightly. She *explicitly forbade* us? A) weird, and b) no one forbids a cat anything. It just doesn't work. That's like a law of the universe. Although my tail was still so pouffed out it was starting to ache, which gave me an uneasy feeling that if anyone could forbid a cat something, she might just be able to. Somehow. I wished I could get through the stink of that perfume to what was underneath.

Callum scratched his chin, stubble rasping under his bitten nails. "Well, we can't just go around *stealing*—" He broke off as the woman took a fat envelope out of her bag and set it on the desk, opening the top. I craned around to see, and, yeah. Stuffed with notes. My colour vision's a bit wonky, but the size said they weren't fivers.

"The book is not – and can never be – his. I want it

back. I do not wish to involve the police. I do not want to know details. And I insist that you *do not* contact him in any way. I will pay well for the inconvenience. Can you handle that?"

Callum tore his gaze off the envelope. "Ms Jones," he started, and she put another envelope on the desk.

"In there you will find details of the book, photos of my ex-husband, and specifics of where he works and lives. All you have to do is find the book and hold it for me until I contact you." She tapped the envelope of money. "This is a 25 percent deposit. The rest will follow once I have my property."

Twenty. Five. Percent. There was at least a couple of months' rent in that envelope alone. Salmon and roast chicken and clotted cream, here we come.

"That's rather over our normal fees, Ms Jones," Callum said. I glared at him. Old Ones take him. We were going to have to have words regarding the fact that sometimes overcharging is *absolutely fine*. Like, for instance, when the client *wants* to give you money. Not that it was exactly a problem that had come up before, admittedly.

She shrugged. "Call it a bonus. The money is not an issue. Getting my book back as quickly as possible is. I'd like you to prioritise this case over all others." She glanced around, and I could hear the *if you have them* as clearly as if she'd said it aloud. Rude, but accurate.

Callum didn't answer right away, and I examined the woman. She had fine features, nothing extraordinary. Long fingers with silver rings scattered on them, and small silver stars glittering in her ears. She carried herself like someone who knew she didn't need permission to take up space, and like she'd be having words with anyone who suggested otherwise. She was wearing high Doc Marten boots with extra buckles that didn't quite go with the quilted coat, which was the sort of understated casual that screamed Hunter wellies and hunting parties. Her handbag was monogrammed and cavernous enough she could have been carrying one of those yappy little dogs in it. She wasn't, thankfully. Or not that I could tell. I couldn't smell anything under that cloud of musky perfume, and it still felt like a smokescreen. Scentscreen? I sneezed, and she glanced at me, eyes narrowed. Not a cat person, clearly.

"Is there anything we should know?" Callum asked finally. "That's a lot of money for a book. Even a family heirloom."

"He doesn't sleep with a machete under his pillow, if that's what you mean," she said. "And the book's not filled with recipes for crystal meth."

Callum gave a strangled sort of snort, then managed to get himself under control. "Well, Ms Jones, you have a deal." He extended a hand over the table and she looked at it, then took it and locked gazes with him.

"Don't read the book," she said. "It will be in a wooden box, as described, so just leave it in there. Don't take it out of the box. In fact, don't even *open* the box. It's private."

Callum frowned. "Of course not."

"I mean it," she said. "I'll know if you do."

What, was she going to fingerprint the thing? But Callum just nodded and said, "No problem."

She nodded back, short and abrupt, and let go of his hand, then got up and plucked one of the business cards from the cracked holder on the desk (they were printed in neat black lettering on matte white card. Classy stuff, just like the sign. And from the same printer. It had been a *big* move, and a rather urgent one). "I'll call you in a few days."

"Is your number in here?" Callum asked, tapping the envelope. "In case we have questions?"

"No," she said, and let herself out the door, pulling it shut in a swirl of chilly, musky air. We listened to her boots fade down the corridor, then Callum went and checked she was actually gone.

"You too, huh?" I asked, trying to groom my fur back into place.

"That was odd, right?" he said, coming back to the desk and tipping the money out to count it.

"Dude, my kitty senses are *on fire*," I said.

"Any thoughts?"

"None," I said. "That perfume just drowned everything. I can still smell it. I mean, she seemed pretty well human. But that whole outfit was so … perfect. Or almost perfect. Like she was trying to look like the polo set but didn't quite have everything for it. But that doesn't necessarily mean anything. Maybe that was just her dressing down to appease the commoners. Maybe she's a rich eccentric with a disproportionate affection for old books."

"*Very* disproportionate," he said, stacking the notes in front of him. There was more there than we'd made in the last month. Hell, the last *six* months.

"Well, never look a Trojan horse in the foot, or whatever."

He frowned at the neat pile of notes. "Mouth. And

maybe. But this can't be legit, G. Not this amount of money."

"Not up to us to decide that. She wants her book back. Seems pretty straightforward to me."

He poked the money like it might bite, then sighed. "I suppose. You want some salmon?"

"Thought you'd never ask." I thought about it for a moment. "What the hell's a Trojan mouth, then?"

WE ATE WELL THAT NIGHT. Callum went out and bought fresh salmon for me, plus some cat milk and a handful of shrimp, although our neighbourhood being what it is, they weren't exactly straight off the boat. They'd probably been in the corner shop's freezer for about three years, if I was realistic about it. I didn't care. Yeah, I might have a bad stomach in the morning, but what's life if you can't spoil yourself now and then?

Callum didn't join me – he went across the hall and invited Mrs Smith out for a slap-up dinner down the local Chinese. I'd have gone, but I don't like it there. They get really huffy about me coming in, and act like I'm going to shed on the buffet. To be fair, I probably would do exactly that if Callum would just look the other way for long enough, but that's only because they were anti-cat first. Cute of him to take our dotty but devoted neighbour out, I know, but you'd think he'd have a human closer to his own age he could splash the cash on. He seemed pretty disinterested in most people, though. Fair enough. Each to their own, and more shrimp money for me. Plus, you never know how a new human's going throw out the delicate balance of a partnership.

I scoffed salmon and shrimp and fell asleep with my belly comfortably full, curled on top of the microwaveable cushion I'd liberated from a pet store last winter, promising Callum it was reject stock I'd found in the bin. It was soft and warm and glorious, and I barely looked up when he came home in a whiff of cigarette smoke and spiced sauces, and unfolded the armchair.

"Good night?" I mumbled at him.

"I went back to the buffet four times," he said, and yawned. "I ate seven spring rolls and two servings of deep-fried ice cream."

"Awesome," I said, and fell asleep again.

In my dreams, the musky perfume crept around me like a fog, yellow and poisonous, and someone walked just out of sight, their boot heels hard and dull on the tattered ground. As much as I ran, I couldn't catch them. And behind me the world crumbled to darkness.

3

THE JOY OF THE SEARCH

THE NEXT DAY DAWNED COLD AND DRIZZLY, THAT SORT OF bone-aching damp the north's so good at. Days like this, I'm never quite sure why I stick around this country. I should head to Greece, or Turkey, even Spain, something like that. Hang out on town piers with the local cats and fight over the fishing boat hauls, sleep in the sun under the bougainvillea. Of course, it's a long trek for little feet, but I could wrangle my way onto a truck or something. Cats are nothing if not persuasive.

We had breakfast at the greasy spoon on the corner, seeing as we were flush, and the young woman with the old scars of oil burns under her eye smiled easily at Callum when she set a giant mug of tea in front of him.

"How's your kitty?" she asked, scratching me behind the ears. I arched my head up into the palm of her hand. Humans love that. And, you know, it's pretty good for me, too.

"Irritating, mostly," Callum said, and I stopped arching to glare at him.

"Aw, he's lovely." She gave me a final scratch. "And I love how you take him everywhere with you."

"I don't really have a choice," Callum said. "You should see what he does if I leave him at home. Disgusting little monster."

I bared my teeth at him, and the young woman gave us both a dubious look before wandering off to fetch our breakfast.

"Well, there's just no call for that," I told him. "And you should be friendlier. She smells nice."

"I was friendly to you. Look where that got me," he said from behind his cup, and a bus driver at the next table gave him a puzzled look.

OUR DECREPIT ROVER was parked in an alley not far from the office. The best thing about that car is that no one's ever going to bother stealing it. More's the pity. If I was better equipped for car theft I'd have seriously thought about it, but of course Callum won't. Not these days. His ethics really get in the way of us living our best lives.

We walked to the car through the persistent rain, Callum in the ridiculous long trench coat he'd found in a charity shop, me darting from one scrap of shelter to the next, paws cold and nose damp, the whiffs of marks left by other toms and the scratching of rats mixing with the dull tarmac and bin scents of the back streets.

Callum opened the door and let me jump in and scoot across to the passenger side before folding himself into the driver's seat. He really is abnormally long and lanky. No one needs to be that tall.

"That coat stinks of wet dog," I told him.

"I like it," he said, pulling on levers and pumping pedals in the weird alchemy that was the only way to get the wreck of a car to start.

"I think someone died in it."

"Possibly. That'd be the only reason I'd give it up." He tried the key, and the car gave a startled cough.

"It's ridiculous. You only like it because of all those crappy detective novels. You think you're Gumshoe Pete or something."

He snorted. "Yes, he's a well-known detective and fashion icon."

"I'll pee on the damn thing. It's an embarrassment."

"It's waterproof." He fiddled a bit more and tried the key again. This time the engine started, albeit with the wheezing of an asthmatic donkey. "Good girl!"

"Why do you have to talk to the car?"

"I talk to you, don't I?"

I huffed, and he chuckled, cranking the heater up and using the sleeve of his coat to try and wipe a gap in the condensation on the windscreen.

"Where to first, then, Gobs?"

I ignored the silly nickname and said, "We may as well check out the office. Have a nosey around."

"Wouldn't it be better to take a look at his apartment first?" Callum took a scrap of paper from his pocket, squinting at the addresses he'd copied from Ms Jones' paperwork. He never took originals out of the office. We're professionals, and you just never know when someone's going to shove you in a canal or empty your pockets for you. No good having originals on you then. "He's probably going to be at work. We can't just waltz in and start poking around the place."

"Yeah, that's *if* he's at work. We go to the office, make sure he's there and going to be there a while, *then* we go to the apartment."

"We could just stake out the apartment and see if he's about."

"And he could have just gone out for some milk and be back any moment." This sort of thing is why he should just accept I'm the senior partner. I mean, really.

The labouring heater had cleared the windscreen enough that we could see the grey buildings peering back at us, and Callum shifted the car into gear, hauling on the handbrake to get it to release. "Alright. Maybe he'll just have the book out on display at the front desk, huh?"

"Now you're thinking." I settled back into the torn seat as we rattled out of the alley and onto the main road, the windscreen wipers working wearily. Callum tapped his fingers on the wheel and whistled tunelessly. The radio had been stolen before we even acquired the car, which had itself been payment for finding out who was methodically looting anything movable out of a second-hand (well, more like fifth- or sixth-hand) car yard. I did think we should have held out for one of the cars that still *had* its radio, but, to be fair, I don't think there were any. I wondered if the balance of Ms Jones' payment could get us some better transport.

OUR QUARRY'S name was Walker, not Jones, so either our patron had kept her maiden name or somehow thought we couldn't work out what her real name was. It didn't bother us. As anyone will tell you, cats have more than one name, too. Anyhow, Walker ran a dental clinic out of a little collection of shops in one of those trying-to-be-a-town-centre suburbs on the outskirts of Leeds.

Yeah, I know, Gobbelino London, but I work in Leeds. I started out in London. Stuff happened, and that's entirely another story.

Anyhow. The buildings were modern enough to lack even a whiff of character and old enough to already feel a bit tatty, but there was a fair bit of parking on the street, and Callum found us a spot across the road not too far from the clinic. We could see the door but didn't look too obvious, and even the monstrously ancient Rover didn't stand out too badly among the rather more presentable but still elderly Fiats and VWs parallel parked around us. There were some fancier cars too, but not many. Harley Street it was not.

Callum got out and ambled down the road, crossing over between cars and vanishing down an alleyway near the clinic with his hands in the pockets of his hideous coat. He wasn't gone long, reappearing with his head down against the rain and drips running off his nose.

He clambered back into the car and shook his hair out like a dog.

"*Ew*," I said, with feeling.

"There's a BMW back there that matches the plates from the file," Callum said, ignoring the fact that he'd just splattered me with rain. Rude.

"It's a start," I said. "Doesn't mean he's definitely here, though."

"Why wouldn't he be?" Callum asked, taking a cigarette packet from the depths of his coat.

"He could've gone somewhere on foot," I pointed out. "Or by Uber. Or he could have a sneaky little second car parked somewhere."

"Are we thinking he's a criminal mastermind?" Callum asked. "He took a *book*. From his ex-wife."

"A very precious and apparently valuable book. Who knows what else he's capable of."

Callum extricated a cigarette from the packet. "Yeah. You're right there. We should really be on our guard."

I glared at him. "You're not lighting that in here."

"It's raining," he said.

"So? Go give yourself cancer somewhere else."

He sighed and put the cigarette back in the packet. Filthy habit, but better than what he used to be into. "Well, the front windows are all opaque. I can't see in, but we can keep an eye on the door. See if anyone's coming or going."

"You could go and make an appointment," I suggested.

He wrinkled his nose. "I don't like dentists."

"You wouldn't have to keep it. Just see if the doctor's in."

"You go and see. You're the covert operations expert."

I clambered onto his lap and peered out the driver side window at the low buildings across the road. I can pick up a lot from both the sense and the scent of a place, and my night vision is awesome, but details in the distance aren't my thing. "Where is it?"

"That window there. Big frosted plate glass."

I couldn't even see the window except as a suggestion of different coloured wall. "Can you see any other open windows or anything?"

"Nothing." He pushed me off his lap. He says it's weird having a talking cat sat on him. But, seriously, is it any weirder than having a cat who *won't* talk sat on you? "Let's just keep an eye on things for a bit. No point rushing in there."

"This is not getting the pay cheque any quicker," I grumbled. He ignored me, scrolling through his phone as he looked for something to listen to. Not that there was much choice. Our phone was too old to hold more than a couple of albums, and too decrepit to stream it. Such are the standards I put up with.

WE SAT THERE for the next hour, arguing over the music and why he couldn't just go in and claim to have a dental emergency, or to enquire about teeth whitening or something. He kept talking about the NHS and needing to be registered, but I reckon he's never been to a dentist in his life and was just scared. I suggested as much and he suggested I could go scout things out in the rain, make sure there wasn't an easy way in through a back room or something.

It was getting boring sitting there, and his coat smelt, and he kept whingeing about wanting a cigarette, so eventually I got up and said, "Open the door."

"Why? Where're you going?"

"To the Jellicle Ball, where d'you think?"

He snorted. "Gobs, I can't see any way in. The upstairs windows are all shut, I couldn't see anything open around the back, and you can't just walk in the front door."

"Watch me."

"G, no. Seriously. Dentists are like sterile and stuff. They'll freak out."

"G, yes. Odds are they won't even see me. If they do, sure, big fuss, a stray got into the waiting room. Boohoo. No one'll connect it with our esteemed client. Or you, for that matter."

He looked at me for a moment, then shrugged. "Fine. At least I can have a smoke while you're in there."

"Outside," I said. "*Outside* the car."

"Sure," he said, and opened the door onto the steady rain.

I glared at him and jumped out.

Everyone says cats hate getting wet, like it's weird or something. Tell me, if you were wearing your favourite, most comfortable clothes, would you like to get drenched and then have to walk around dripping and cold for the rest of the day? I don't think so.

So I checked each way – road safety, kids, it's good for cats too – then sprinted across the street with raindrops rebounding from the tarmac and into my face, making me sneeze and shake my ears out. There was a small over-hang above the door to the dentist's, so I huddled in there and waited.

I didn't have to wait long. Some woman with a squalling kid shoved the door open, almost knocking me over as she went. I gave her my best evil glare, then slipped past before the door could nip shut on my tail. Inside was warm and smelt of disinfectant, and I slipped behind the water cooler to shake a bit of the damp off and eye up the room. There were only a couple of people in the waiting area – an old man wheezing tobacco and cheap mints in the corner, and a rotund woman sitting pointedly as far from him as she could get. The woman behind the desk was skinny and severe looking, her face so pinched it was as if all her flesh hung from the clip that held back her hair. She looked like the sort of person who kicked cats, so this was not a situation for charm. This was a situation for stealth.

There were only two internal doors leading out of the waiting room, and although I couldn't make out the signs on them, the fake peppermint smell from the closest suggested that was the way to the dentist's chair. The other was probably toilets or something like that.

As if hearing me, the rotund woman got up and headed for the far door, her purse clutched so close under her chin I thought she was using it as a sick bag for a moment. Then the other door flew open and a man reeking of cologne and tooth dust leaned out.

"*Mr* Abbot," he boomed, like the announcer at a funfair. "Come on in, come on in. Let's look at those dentures of yours, eh?"

Mr Walker, I presume, I thought, and scooted around the reception desk and under the chairs closest to the door before diving past the dentist into the brightly lit hall beyond. No one noticed me – cats are good at not being noticed. It also helped that the receptionist had her snooty nose stuck to the computer and big man dentist had waded across the floor to help the old man out of his chair. I nipped down the hall and into the dentist's room, and had time to find myself a quiet corner between a cabinet and a wall before I even heard them leave the waiting room. Humans are *slow*.

"Now then, Mr Abbott," the dentist was shouting as they inched down the hall. "Have you been flossing those dentures? Haha. Ha."

Cabbage, I thought, and apparently the erstwhile Mr Abbott thought so too, because his growled reply was short and unamused. Not that the dentist took any notice. He prattled and hee-hawed his way into the room, installed the old man in the chair, and parked himself on a stool next to him. I was starting to understand what Ms Jones didn't see in him.

Now that I was in the exam room, I wasn't entirely certain what I was doing there. It was kind of a risky move – a lot harder to pretend I'd just wandered in off the street if I was spotted. Not that anyone would suspect that I was, in fact, a PI, because humans are terribly human-centric in their world view, but it was whether the purpose of sneaking in (which is a pleasure in and of itself) coincided with finding out where our loud friend was hiding the book. I couldn't tell yet if he was the sort of person who would carry it with him, or stash it in a safe, or tuck it away under his pillow at home. He didn't strike me as the sentimental sort, though, so I wondered if he'd flogged it already. That would make things trickier.

But I was here now, so best make the most of it. I slipped out from my hiding spot and padded behind the dentist's stool, looking for a briefcase or a rucksack, or even some cupboards that smelt of anything other than medical supplies and plastic. But everything was metal and rubber gloves and the chalky scent of peppermint mouthwash.

There were no bags on the floor, but there was a little desk in the corner with a flatscreen on it that looked promising. Even from this angle I could see papers piled haphazardly on top of each other, files and appointment books and leaflets. There also looked to be a laptop case resting precariously on one corner. Paragon of organisational virtue he was not.

I glanced back at the dentist, leaning over Mr Abbott's noisome mouth with the thin hair at the top of his head showing. He was still booming and guffawing, and Mr Abbott was looking increasingly distressed, unable to answer due to the various metal implements sticking out of his mouth. Coast was as clear as it was likely to get for now.

I jumped onto the chair tucked next to the desk and checked to make sure I hadn't been noticed. Nope – Walker had his back to me, and the old man had his eyes screwed shut under the funky glasses they give you in dentists' offices. I scanned the desk, wondering how big this book was. Or the book box, if it was still in there. Ms Jones' details had been sketchy at best, and dimensions hadn't been among them. Was it like some dinky novelty book? Or more like a tome? There definitely wasn't a tome here. A small old hardback could be in among the mess, though. There were plenty of papers spilling across the desk, notes and flyers and invoices and bills and patient records, which seemed rather careless. There was also some sort of dancing sunflower thing with a brand on it, lots of Post-its with times and names on them, some fake teeth and a coffee mug crusted with dried foam. But no book, no box. Not on top, anyhow.

I stepped onto the mess of the desk cautiously, the papers slipping under my paws. God, the man was like a hamster. I flicked a few papers aside experimentally as I headed for the laptop case, then realised I should be able to feel the book through the paper if it was hidden among the mess. So I trudged back and forth across the desk, sniffing my way about the place and hoping I'd – quite literally – stumble across what I was looking for.

There were bloody Post-its everywhere, and they kept getting stuck to my paws, while I shook them away irritably, and sometimes had to pull them off with my teeth. They mostly said things like, *Mrs Clegg, pls call back*, with a phone number, and were proving horribly unhelpful. There were paper clips, too, that stuck into my pads, and every now and then I'd get excited and think I'd found something, only for some hurried digging to turn up a muesli bar or another Post-it pad. He had quite the fixation with them.

I'd just decided to see if I could get into the laptop bag, and was pulling a pink Post-it off my paw – *Eggs!!*, it said – when I noticed the silence. The drilling had stopped. I looked around, one paw raised and the Post-it still in my mouth, and met the astonished eyes of both Mr Abbott and the dentist. We stared at each other for a long moment, then I put my paw down, widened my eyes, and said around the sticky paper, "*Mraow?*"

4

A DENTAL ALLERGY

Now, here's the thing. Cats, as you've no doubt noticed, get everywhere, especially where we're not meant to. We take pride in it. Hanging out in library stacks or stalking hotel hallways or snoozing in your bath, even if you don't have a cat. *Especially* if you don't have a cat. It's a thing. And we have ways of making ourselves belong in lots of places, too. Places we can learn things. Pubs and shops and village halls. Downing Street. Although the pub is generally a better source of quality information, if we're going to be honest here. And humans, you know. You make it easy. You either offer us some biscuits or ignore us, because you're never quite sure if we maybe are meant to be there. You're so easy to keep an eye on.

But anyhow. We get everywhere. And that's because we can shift. Shifting's like teleportation, but it's magic, so it's real, not some sci-fi mumbo jumbo. We just step out of this world into the space behind it, the space between all worlds, the Inbetween, and step back again somewhere else. Which means that, in general, cats can get in or out of wherever we want unless someone who knows what they're doing has locked us out with runes. That, or if someone's actually physically got hold of us or caged us (the structure of a cage messes with magic. There are rules). Otherwise, *whoosh*. Now you see us, now you don't.

Only, I can't.

I mean, I suppose I technically *could* shift, but in my last life I had some complications. One of those complications resulted in that particular life being cut short by the unseen monsters that lurk in the Inbetween, snapping up intruders like pigeons gobbling just-spilled chips. And those monsters are fast, and hungry, and have long memories for scents, and they never, ever stop hunting once they have one. If I set one paw in the Inbetween, it'll probably get chomped off. So shifting's out for me. Which meant I was going to have to get out of this particular situation on my own four paws.

I went for the big-eyed look and a purr, then batted an orange Post-it onto the floor. Cute, right?

Well, it turned out neither of them were cat people. Walker lunged at me, shouting something about filthy animals – I tell you, if you want to talk filthy, I got a good look at his mouth as he charged, and his own personal dental hygiene was *not* inspiring. Mr Abbott started yelling something too, but he still had the vacuum-thingy in his mouth, and it got stuck somewhere, so his shouts turned to gargles, and he was waving his arms about so wildly he knocked the drill off the side table. Walker was still coming at me, but at the expensive sounding crash his drill made when it hit the ground he swung back with a horrified look on his face and dived to rescue it from the floor.

Mr Abbott's eyes were rolling back in his head, and the gargling had become gulps for breath – that bloody thing must've been suctioning up his tonsils. I considered saying something to Walker regarding it being better business to save his patient than his tools, but humans aren't good with talking animals. They either block it or panic, and there was more than enough panic going on as it was. I huffed, but, seeing as it was on the way out anyway, jumped from the desk to the old man's belly, swiped the suction tube out of his mouth (it was well stuck – it took a good tug to get loose), and as he drew a hefty whooping breath I leaped for the door. Thankfully it had a nice long handle, and I grabbed it as I hit the panels, dragging it down with me. The door popped open, I shot through, and I was sprinting down the hall with my ears back by the time the dentist had recovered from the shock of his precious drill being knocked over.

"Hey! *Stop!*" Walker shouted, banging the door wide behind me, and I snorted to myself. Like that ever worked on any cat, PI or not. But, as it was, I came to a skidding halt at the door to the reception area anyway. Old Ones take it – a knob rather than a handle. All smooth and shiny looking as well, no grip on it at all. I flattened my ears and backed myself against the wall, going for the small and scared look. If cute didn't work, maybe pathetic would.

"Bloody pest!" Walker snarled, and aimed a kick at me that I dodged effortlessly, giving him a disgusted glare. Who kicks a cat? It didn't surprise me he'd stolen a book.

He probably burned them, and took sweets from babies and all.

"Hey!" Mr Abbott warbled, clinging to the door of the exam room. "You leave him alone! He saved me while you were too bloody busy worrying about your stupid machine to see I was *choking!*"

"You weren't *choking.* And *stupid machine?* It's worth more than your life insurance, old man!" Walker had gone very pink, except his ears, which were an interesting shade of bright red. He looked like he couldn't decide between trying to stomp my tail or shoving the old man back into the chair.

I eyed the hall, looking for another escape route, and hoped I wasn't going to have to bite anyone. It was less the principle than the taste I objected to.

Mr Abbott shook a twisted finger at Walker. "I'll do you! I'll do you for reckless endangerment! My son's a lawyer, he is!"

Walker immediately forgot me, turning on a smarmy smile and taking a step back toward the old man. "Look, you weren't in *danger,*" he began. "Of course you weren't. And we'll get back to the exam in just one moment. Why don't you go back in and sit down, and I'll get Stella to bring you a nice cup of tea, *hmm?*"

"I almost choked!" Abbott shouted. He had a surprising set of lungs on him, given the wheezing. "That cat saved me!"

"That damn cat's how the problem started," Walker complained, and glared at me. I glared back.

"Leave the poor kitty," Abbot said. "Leave him alone!"

Walker glanced at the old man, then back at me.

"Filthy stray," he hissed, and lunged forward with both hands outstretched. I spat at him, showing him my claws. "*Ow!*"

Okay, maybe I more than showed him. Sometimes you've just got to be ruthless in this business.

"You—" Walker rushed me, kicking out with his nasty pointy shoes, and Mr Abbott shrieked at him to stop, then started yammering on about suing him again, and I dodged around them both and scooted straight down the corridor with Walker in hot pursuit. I dived back into the exam room and leaped at the window, hoping there was an easy latch on the damn thing. But no, of course not. No one ever thinks of making things kitty-friendly.

"Get out!" Walker roared, running in after me, and I obliged, legging it back to the door that led to reception and putting my tail against it. Abbott was still harping on in his wavery voice, and the dentist still looked like he wanted to take his precious drill to me.

This was getting me nowhere. Shock tactics were called for. I glared at them both and said very clearly, "Animal cruelty."

They both stared at me.

"What?" Abbott said, rubbing one ear. "What'd you say?"

"What was that?" Walker demanded at the same time.

"Animal cruelty," I repeated. "Actually, we should probably start with reckless endangerment of patients, which probably adds malpractice to the list, and *then* animal cruelty."

Walker blinked, then snarled, "Shut up, old man," evidently deciding that the velvety tones coming from the small black cat in front of him actually belonged to the hoarse old man behind him.

"Eh?" Abbott said, rubbing his throat and looking like he wasn't sure if he'd been on the laughing gas. Then the door to the reception area swung open to reveal the stern receptionist (presumably Stella) glaring at them, and two old women in the waiting area clutching their pearls. Well, figuratively. They weren't wearing pearls, but if they were, they would have been clutching them. I went from standstill to sprint in a heartbeat, shooting straight past Stella and leaping to her desk, and from there to the frosted window. I hit the glass hard and slid down it with all four limbs spreadeagled, my claws screeching loudly enough to hurt even my ears. Highly undignified, and no way of knowing if Callum was looking at his phone rather than the building, or if he could even see the shape of one small cat through the frosting, but it was all I could think of in the heat of the moment.

There was an awful lot of shouting going on behind me – the receptionist trying to calm everyone down, Mr Abbott calling *here, kitty kitty*, Walker screaming that I'd been planted by his ex to destroy him (that was an unfortunate connection, and not one I had thought he'd make), and the two ladies were demanding to be told what on *earth* was going on and did someone need to call the RSPCA?

I abandoned the window and scooted toward the ladies in their row of waiting room chairs. One screamed and kicked her legs up like I was a mouse or something, clutching her heart rather dramatically. The other, though, grabbed me and snuggled me into her consider-able – and heavily perfumed – bosom. I sneezed.

"*Doctor* Walker," she snapped. "Just what is the meaning of this?"

"That cat," he shouted. "That cat's just ruined about a thousand pounds worth of equipment!"

Trout bollocks I had. I doubted the drill was *that* fragile it couldn't stand the odd fall. Besides, he'd been the one to drop it.

"So what do you propose to do?" my saviour demanded. "Sue him?"

I was just about suffocating between the sickly perfume and how close she was holding me, and I tried to shove her away. She just snuggled me closer.

"I'll sue his damn owner for damages. And counter-sue this old fool too!" Walker jabbed a finger at Mr Abbott, who looked like he might just take a swing at the dentist rather than wait for his son to file papers.

"You pillock," he said. "That cat spoke!" He still had a drool-stained paper bib on. "It *spoke*. It's special."

"Of course it did, Mr Abbott," Stella said, and patted him on the arm. "Let's sit you down and get a nice cup of tea, yes?"

He pulled his arm away from her. "It did. And I won't let it be hurt!"

"Of course not, Mr Abbott," she said, and took his arm again. "You should sit down, though."

"I'm telling my son about this," he insisted, but let himself be put in a chair, still staring at me. "You did speak."

The lovely perfumed lady hugged me tighter, and I

wondered if biting the arms that saved might be permitted in this sort of situation. It was a terrible thing to even contemplate, but I really couldn't breathe and the wool from her cardigan was getting in my nose and making my eyes water. I wondered if I was allergic to nice old ladies, or just dentists.

"Give me the bloody animal," Walker said, waving impatiently at me. "I'll shut him in the back room until the owner turns up."

"I'm not giving you this little angel," the woman replied, giving me a squeeze that made my ribs creak. I tried to push myself away from her, but she must've been a powerlifter. There was no give whatsoever. "There's no telling what you'll do to him."

Out of the corner of my eye I saw the outside door ease open just a crack. Callum peered through the gap, rain dripping from his silly coat, and I twitched my ears at him, that being the only body part I could actually move. I hoped the twitch communicated just how desperate and undignified the situation was. He grinned, so I suppose it worked.

"Give me the cat," Walker said.

"I'm not giving you the little diddums," my lady saviour said, and I swear I heard Callum snort.

"It broke my equipment," Walker snapped. "The owner's going to have to pay."

Eh. He had to catch us first.

"Cats will be cats," the woman insisted. "He was probably scared. And I think he could be a stray. He's skinny enough."

I *was not* scared. Although this was hardly the time to argue the point.

"Fine," Walker said. "You want the cat, you keep him. But I'm going to sue you for the cost of repairs to the equipment, in that case."

Cat lady's grip loosened a little. "Well, now. He's not *my* cat, obviously. But you can't hurt him."

"You talked," Mr Abbott said, leaning closer and peering at me with sagging eyes. "I know you did."

I winked at him, and he thought about it, then grinned and winked back. His dentures were apparently still in the examination room, so it was an alarming sight.

"I'm not going to hurt him," the dentist said, ignoring Mr Abbott. "I just want to make sure I get compensation for the damage he's caused. And whoever claims responsibility for the cat is responsible for that, too."

Cat lady had eased her grip enough that I could breathe. I tensed the muscles of my legs, ready to make my escape, and she clamped me closer, forcing the air out of me with a whoosh.

Mr Abbott poked her. "You're strangling that cat."

"I'm keeping him safe," she said, half-turning away from the old man. I rolled my eyes at him pleadingly.

"So you'll pay for the repairs, then," Walker said.

"Let the kitty go," Abbott said.

"Your silly equipment's not my responsibility!" the woman snapped, ignoring the old man.

"Well, if you're saying the *cat's* your responsibility—"

"Let him go," Mr Abbott said, tugging at the woman's sleeve rather peevishly. "You're hurting him."

She released me with one arm to shake him off, her expression horrified. "I would never hurt a cat!"

I took my moment. I don't know if you've ever tried to hold a cat that doesn't want to be held, but trust me when I say normal physics doesn't apply to the shapes we can twist into, or the power we can put into our kicks. Or to the sharpness of our claws, for that matter, although I tried to be circumspect in that. She had saved me from Walker, after all. Cat lady let me go with a screech of alarm, Abbott wailed for me to stop, Walker howled something inarticulate and lunged at me, and Callum opened the door. I shot past him and sprinted across the road, hearing the screech of brakes and the thud of his long strides behind me. Someone laid on their car horn, but we both ignored it and legged it for the Rover.

Callum had started the car before he left it, and the doors were unlocked. He hauled the driver's side open and piled in as I bounded across the seats to safety, and he was already jamming it into reverse as I fetched up against the far door. Mr Abbott was waving and squeaking his way across the road, the cat lady a couple of strides ahead of him and arguing with a young woman in a Ford Ka who'd had to swerve to miss them, and the receptionist was scowling at everyone like she wanted to send us all to detention. Walker was right behind us, and he slammed his hands on our bonnet just as we shot backward, Callum stomping the brakes millimetres before we hit the car behind. I tumbled off the seat into the footwell with a squawk as he jammed the Rover into gear, and as we lurched forward again I scrambled back up to see Walker jumping away before we ran over his feet, still shouting at us, his face and ears even redder than they had been before.

We dodged the Ford Ka, barely missed taking out an old woman on a rickety pushbike who was all done up in a bright yellow raincoat (and who swore very loudly and very creatively), then we roared off down the road under the cover of the belching exhaust, clipping our wing mirror on a rubbish bin on the way.

Callum fumbled for his seatbelt. He was still grinning, and as we threw in a couple of turns down some side roads just to be on the safe side, he looked at me and burst out laughing.

"What?" I demanded. *"What?"*

He struggled for a moment, then managed to say through giggles, "Diddums."

"Ha bloody ha. It was no joke being in there, I tell you. I was almost suffocated by a woman's bosom."

"The great cat burglar strikes again."

I huffed. "And you were so much help."

"Ah well. I thought one of us should try to keep a low profile. You know, since we're not meant to have any contact with Walker." He pulled open the pot of Dreamies we kept in the doorless glovebox and put them on the seat next to me.

"No point having a low profile if your partner's squished," I complained.

"You've got pink fluff on your ears, diddums." He kept his eyes on the road while I cleaned them urgently, but I could still see his smirk. Well, next time he could do the sneaking.

5

BREAKING & ENTERING

WE PULLED UP IN FRONT OF WALKER'S HOUSE AND CALLUM turned the engine off before we could asphyxiate in the leaky exhaust. Yet another reason to liberate a better car – it made winter stake-outs problematic, to say the least, not being able to run the engine. But Callum wouldn't hear of it. *Of course*.

We stared at the building, a big detached house inside a high wall, Edwardian or Victorian or what have you. You know the type. Tall windows, high ceilings, dark stone. Spires and all that. It was divided into apartments, but they'd be of the posh variety that cost more than your average terraced house. The drive was a coil of pale gravel with a turning circle by the front doors, the grass golf-course trim and the flowerbeds mercilessly geometrical. Even the trees lining the street looked expensive. Either business was better for Walker than his downtrodden little clinic suggested, or he was having delusions of grandeur. I voted for the latter. I still had doubts that anyone could trust a dentist with teeth that yellow.

The big wrought iron gates were dripping in the soft, persistent rain, and there was no one in sight inside them. Well, why would there be? Sensible people would be home with a hot water bottle and a fluffy blanket.

"I'm not sure we should do this now," Callum said. "If we've spooked him, he could come straight back here to check on the book."

"It's still the best chance we've got," I said. "There's no reason he'd think we're after the book. I mean, a cat and some guy in a broken-down car?"

"Hey, this car did just fine," he said, petting the wheel.

I huffed. "Sure, *this* time. Next time it'll stall out and we'll get done."

"Whatever. Look, if he's nervous, he's going to come back as soon as he can, whether he's suspicious of us or not. This isn't the right time to do this."

I looked at the dreary day and considered agreeing with him just so I didn't have to go out there again. But I thought it was more than likely our only chance. I hadn't told Callum that Walker had pretty much accused me of being sent by his ex-wife, or that I'd kind of had to talk. It was enough that I'd been chased out of the dentist's office – he didn't need to know all the gory details. Anyway, I thought the odds were high Walker'd hide the book somewhere else the first chance he got, and this was the best opportunity we had to grab it if it actually was in the apartment.

"I'm wet already," I said. "May as well just get it over with."

Callum gave me a thoughtful look, then shrugged and opened his door. "Off you go, then."

I sighed. The problem with being the feline partner is that you're inherently better at sneaking that your *homo sapiens* counterpart. I mean, Callum's not bad at passing unnoticed. He's far too long and tall than can possibly be convenient, but he somehow always gives the impression of being slightly insubstantial, less *there* than others, and he holds himself in a way that means people rarely take a second glance at him. He's human as they come, but the way other humans just seem to pass him by makes him seem more like Folk. Your average human never notices Folk.

The world doesn't exactly teem with magic anymore, but it's there, and so are the magical Folk, the fauns and the dryads and the gnomes and all the rest, but humans are too interested in what's happening on their phones to notice any of it. Which kind of works in our favour, to be honest. Imagine the fuss if someone did realise there were toothpick-wielding pixies at war with salamander-riding imps at the bottom of the garden?

But as unobtrusive as Callum is, he does lack my talent for subtlety and small spaces. Which means I get to do the dirty work to get him in places while he sits out here and smokes a cigarette. And yeah, I could tell he'd been smoking in the car while I was risking my tail in the clinic. Ugh. I peered out at the day again, hoping the rain had cleared up in the last minute or so. Nope. If anything, it seemed to have got heavier.

Well, no use complaining. Now or never and all that.

I jumped over him and ran for the gate, slipping through the bars and running up the crushed gravel drive, smelling expensive cars and pocket dogs. It wasn't far to the house, but my fur felt sticky and unpleasant by the time I got there, and I stopped in the shelter of the porch to shake myself dry before I investigated further.

The intercom panels indicated that Walker was in a third-floor apartment, which was promising. People like leaving bathroom windows open when they think no one can reach them. I slipped back out into the rain and found a windowsill that gave me an easy jump onto the roof of the porch. I scrambled up its slope to the ridge, and stood there getting steadily wetter for a few moments, weighing up my options. There weren't many. It was ivy or nothing.

Ivy isn't strong. I mean, I'm not a big cat. I'd refer to myself as svelte, although Callum has been known to call me scrawny. It comes in handy, though. I have a lot of floof that makes me look bigger than I am, and it means I can fit through gaps smaller than you'd expect. It still doesn't make me an ideal candidate for ivy-climbing, though. *Nothing* makes you an ideal candidate for that.

I bolted up the wall as fast as I could, leaves tearing loose in my wake, scratching wildly at the brickwork when the roots gave way under my paws. I rested on windowsills on the first floor, then the second, taking my time on that one. There was a nice little overhang that kept the worst of the rain off me there, and I could see that the ivy was getting thinner. Just because we get nine lives doesn't mean I'm in a rush to waste any more of them. The wind was sneakier up here too, ruffling my wet fur and making me shiver. I leaned out and peered up the wall, spying a window sitting ajar on its latch. No telling if it was actually Walker's or not, of course, but one could only hope.

I gathered my hindquarters under me and launched myself up the wall. No pause, no hesitation, go, and go, and keep going, don't give physics a chance to catch up to you. I ran out of ivy and skittered onto bare brick, then flung myself at the window. I hooked my paws over the sill, and for one moment was sliding backward as my claws found no purchase on the slick paint, my hind legs pedalling frantically at the wall. I took a final convulsive leap, found some tiny imperfection I could get one front claw into, and muscled myself snarling upward, cursing Callum and the job and dentists with aspirations to posh-ness. Then I was in, ears back and heart pounding, finding myself perched on top of a toilet cistern. I spat a few more choice curses – it's a great stress-reliever – then jumped down, nosed my way around the door, and headed off to find the intercom.

ONCE I'M IN SOMEWHERE, the rest is easy sneeze-y garden peas-y, or whatever. You know, as long as there aren't any unexpected dogs, but I can usually sniff them out before I'm even in. Well except for that once, with that monster of a poodle which was so drenched in *eau-de*-fancy-dog-groomer that I just about stood on the mutt before I realised it was there. I'm pretty certain I set a new speed record getting out of that one.

But the way it usually goes is that even if Callum can't see me, he gives me ten minutes then hits the buzzer for the apartment we're after. That's long enough for me to get in, short enough that if something's gone wrong he's a distraction at just the right moment. Usually. This time he'd watched me scale the wall like a sodden black spider, and the intercom phone was buzzing by the time I got into the open plan living/dining/kitchen etc. etc. There was no whiff of other pets in here – not surprisingly. Walker didn't strike me as the animal-lover type. I jumped to the kitchen counter, stood on my hind legs to press the talk button on the intercom, and said, "You rang?"

"Deep Cleaners," Callum said, in case anyone was listening in. "You booked us for an assessment at twelve?"

"Come on in," I said. "Make sure you wipe your feet." I pawed the little gate key button, ignoring his snort, then settled to cleaning a little of the excess rain off until the intercom went again for the main door. I repeated the whole performance, then investigated the door itself. Callum's pretty adept at locks, but it's not the ideal thing to be messing around with in the middle of the day. Luckily these ones weren't too complicated. One of those twisty types with handy grooves in the knob that took half a dozen jump and holds to roll it open, then the main latch that Walker hadn't even bothered with. Careless, especially when you're harbouring priceless books. Better for us, though – Callum just turned the handle from the outside and let himself in, a canvas tool bag in one hand.

"Hey," he said.

"Hey," I replied.

"Found anything?"

"Oddly enough, I've been a little busy to look."

He pushed the door shut behind him and strolled over to the kitchen, depositing the bag on the counter. "Really? And here I thought we were in a hurry."

"I didn't want to deprive you of the fun stuff." I stalked into the lounge part of the big room, leaving small wet paw prints behind me. "Besides, scaling three stories of sheer, dripping wet brick to get you inside requires a mite of recovery time."

"So you repeatedly tell me." He wandered after me, passed me a couple of Dreamies, then stared around the room. "Should be easy enough to find."

"You'd think so." The man had no books. None. There weren't even shelves. Just an obnoxiously large TV and some pretty poorly done paintings of the sort that probably cost a mint. No trinket-y things, no keepsakes, no photos, no magazines, no newspapers. The only reading material was a pile of post next to the stove. "Do you reckon he's illiterate?" I asked Callum.

He snorted. "Nah. Maybe he only reads ebooks or something." But he sounded dubious, and started pulling cushions off the sofa, fitting them back carefully after checking behind them. I squeezed underneath, looking for tears or zips in the base that might indicate he'd hidden the book inside the lining, but there was nothing.

"Bedroom?" Callum suggested, when I re-emerged with a very small cobweb on my whiskers. This place wasn't even properly untidy.

I followed him. "Maybe he sold it. Or chucked it. Doesn't seem much like he'd want to hold onto a book, even for spite."

"*Hmm.*" The bedroom did have shelves, but they were in the wardrobe and full of shoes and belts and ties and so on. Callum rooted through the dresser drawers and checked under the mattress, and I took a stroll under the bed itself, finding nothing more interesting than a novelty cuff link and a condom wrapper. The place didn't feel like somewhere you lived. It was a place moved into, then moved out of. It had had no time to collect the detritus of life, and didn't even feel as if it wanted to.

"Nothing," Callum said, and rubbed the back of his neck. "Maybe he is keeping it at the office."

"Kitchen?" I suggested. "Maybe it's a cookbook."

"I'm sure he stole his ex's family heirloom cookbook."

"Hey, when a breakup goes bad, it goes bad."

He raised his eyebrows but didn't say anything. We both knew I was right.

THE KITCHEN CUPBOARDS were clean and poorly stocked. A stack of takeout menus in the drawer most people use for cooking utensils suggested he didn't need to keep it stocked. There were a couple of cheap pans, some decent glasses and some okay plates. I think our little office is better set up. It definitely feels more like a home.

Callum checked the cupboards, the drawers, even the enormous silver fridge and freezer, but no book, and we both stood there frowning at the frozen meals for one and microwave soups as if they could tell us where the thing was.

"It could still be in the office," he suggested to me again. "We could go back tonight and check it out."

I sat down and scratched my chin. "I suppose." Even if it was there, I bet there'd be alarms. Always the problem with offices. "He's going to be really careful now, though."

"Oh? So you did tip him off?"

"You said it yourself. He'll be nervous. Just because."

"Uh-huh," Callum said. "You sure that's all?"

I wrinkled my nose at him. "What else would it be? And, you know, maybe he even keeps it on him."

"Possible," Callum agreed. "Anyway, we should get out of here in case he comes home for lunch. Or figures there was something weird about the cat that broke into his office *and talked.*"

"How—" I stopped, glaring at him as he grinned at me.

"You can't help yourself, Gobs. You're well-named. You really are a gobby cat." He closed the freezer.

I sniffed. I wasn't rising to that. Anyway, Walker had been too worried about his precious drill to really appreciate that I'd talked. I hoped. I peered into the drawer at the takeout menus. It was a hell of a lot tidier in here than it was at his office. And there just weren't that many hiding places. No loft. No cellar. No floorboards to prise up – it was all expensive wooden laminate. I wasn't sure he *would* keep it on him – he'd accused me of being sent by his ex, so he obviously thought she *would* send someone. Odds were it'd be someone big enough to remove the book by force, which, actually, made it a bit weird she *hadn't* done that. But anyway. If you were that worried you mightn't leave it in a safe in the office your ex would likely know about, either. My gaze drifted over the kitchen. The fridge and freezer would be damaging for a book, and we'd checked them anyway. The microwave would be used for his frozen dinners and soups. The oven … The oven. There hadn't been any frozen pizzas, oven chips, none of that stuff.

"G, let's go," Callum said.

"The oven doesn't work," I said. "Look, nothing on the display. No clock, nothing."

He grabbed the oven door and pulled it open. No book, just clean walls and the faint smell of cleaning products.

"Drawer," I said, and he pulled out the drawer below the door to reveal a stack of unused pans. He rattled through them, and there it was, something chunky and vaguely book-shaped bundled in a supermarket carrier bag, and the hair on my back shot to attention, damp or not. "Don't—" I started, but Callum had already opened the bag and pulled out the box. He looked half repulsed, half-fascinated as he stared at the ancient wood, worn almost black by the passage of many lives and many hands.

"I better just check …" he said, his voice faint and strained, and opened the lid, releasing a whiff of something rotten and muscular and *alive*. I caught a glimpse of dark, slick leather pressing out from under the lid, and felt its urgency. Felt its *need*.

"Don't touch it!" I snarled, and jumped from the counter to the floor. I snagged Callum's jeans in my claws, catching the skin underneath and making him flinch. "Shut it, *shut it!*"

He tore his gaze from the book and stared at me.

"Get the box shut and wrap it up quick!" I hissed.

"G, what the hell?"

I could smell it, smell the sickly stench of it, sweet and stomach-churning and hideous and so, so powerful, and I knew exactly why she'd told us not to take it out of the box. She should have warned us. Properly warned us, not cryptic orders with no meaning in them. Although I suppose she thought G & C London were just any old PI agency. The risk, though … if I hadn't been here, Callum would never have known, he'd have touched it, just checking, just doing his job, and then …

"G, what's going on?" He hadn't shut the box, but he hadn't touched the book, either.

I eyed him and said, "What's going on is you can be damn glad you have a cat for a partner. And I know why she was wearing so much perfume. That book is bad, bad magic. I'll explain when we're out. Just wrap it up and let's get out of here." He looked at me for a long moment, and I added, "Like you said, I may have kind of raised Walker's suspicions. He'll be back to check on it."

Callum gave me a dubious look, then nodded, closed the box carefully and re-wrapped it in the carrier bag before slipping it into his tool bag, covering it with a socket set and a couple of grubby rags. Then we let ourselves out the door and left, my tail still doing its best impression of a feather duster.

Gods-dammit. All I had wanted this time around was a quiet life. Make enough money to eat salmon a few times a week, have a warm bed to sleep in and a human to open the odd packet of Dreamies. This book – this was *not* what I signed up for.

6

THE BOOK

WE MET AN ELDERLY WOMAN ON THE STAIRS, BUT CALLUM just smiled at her, called her ma'am, and offered to help her carry her bags to her door. He was good at that. He had the sort of dimples and smile that certain women and men like, and as big as he was, he came over as harmless to the ones the dimples didn't work on. He was a handy-man, fixing a leaky tap, or cleaning windows, or installing a new TV, and completely forgettable. His new friend gave him a chocolate from a selection box and we left. She never even noticed me.

We marched to the gate together, the rain heavy enough now that I squeezed my ears flat to my head and looked woeful. Callum glanced at me, sighed, and picked me up in his free hand, holding me against his chest and leaning forward slightly so I got a little shelter from the downpour. He'd left his coat in the car. Not many handymen turn up in hand-me-down trench coats. I peered at the bag in his other hand, baring my teeth at it. I could still smell that damn book.

At the car he set me down while he got it unlocked, then started to put the bag on the passenger seat.

"No!" I screeched. "In the back! Put it in the back!"

"Okay, okay. Jeez." He leaned into the back seat.

"No, you turnip! The *back!* The *back!*"

He stared at me. I probably looked a little unkempt, fur standing in all directions as alarm fought against the wet, my teeth bared and my eyes wide. Hey, it's not my fault that cats aren't at their best when damp.

"The boot," he said, rain dripping off his nose.

"Yes! The *back*."

"Right." He straightened up and plodded to the back of the car while the rain got heavier still.

I shivered, resisting the urge to tell him to close the damn door, then yelled, "Don't touch it! Callum! Callum! Callum! Don't touch it! *Callum!*"

He slammed the boot rather harder than necessary and stomped back to the driver's door, nodding at an old man with a green polka-dot umbrella who had stopped to stare at me as if unsure what he was seeing. I glared back at him.

"Weird, isn't it?" Callum said to the old man. "Almost sounds like he's talking."

"Ye-es …" the old man said uncertainly, and the spindly chihuahua-type thing he was dragging around with him yapped at me. I spat back with all the dignity I could muster, and Callum nodded.

"Nice." He climbed in, pushing me off the driver's seat and shaking his sodden jeans out. "Real nice, Gobs." He nodded to the old man again and shut the door.

WE WERE SILENT FOR A MOMENT, waiting for the old man to stop staring and totter on. Eventually he did, half-dragged by the tiny dog. It had a coat that matched his umbrella, and its legs and belly were caked in mud. No sense of decorum, dogs. Callum did the knob-pulling and pedal-pressing act again, then got the car going, the heater wheezing lukewarm air over us.

"Talk," he said. "What the hell was all that?"

I set to cleaning myself, worrying scraps of brickwork out from between my toes. "Later. When we get back." It felt like the damn book was leaning over our shoulders, and I could imagine it pressed against the back seats, throbbing like a boil infected with things you didn't even want to think about. I didn't want to talk about it here. Not when the thing felt like it was *listening.*

"No," Callum said. "And don't talk while you're doing that. I can't understand you with a tongue full of fur. Plus, it's gross."

"*You're* gross." I sat back and looked at him, my tail thumping the seat. "You want to know why I took a perfectly reasonable exception to sharing a seat with that thing?"

"I want to know why you freaked out."

"I did *not* freak out," I snapped, and went back to my toes. My tail was sodden, but it wouldn't stop thumping enough for me to grab it, so it was going to have to wait.

"Fine. You didn't freak out. But why don't you like it, and what is it?"

"Same answer to both. Can we *go?*"

"No, G. Tell me what the hell's going on."

I glared at him, and he just looked back at me with his eyebrows raised expectantly and rain dripping from his messy hair. He was ridiculously patient. It was one of his worst qualities, in my mind. He'd just sit here and refuse to leave until I talked, and I wasn't about to walk home in what was apparently the Yorkshire monsoon season. I sighed, and sat up. "Fine. You know there's more in heaven and earth, Harold, etc. etc., right?"

Callum rubbed his forehead and reached into the back to get his cigarettes from his coat. I didn't stop him. "Horatio."

"Who?"

"*There are more things in heaven and earth, Horatio, than are dreamt of in your philosophy.*"

"Who calls their kid Horatio? That's harsh."

He sighed, rather more heavily than necessary in my opinion. "Whatever. Look, I know there are talking cats, which is plenty."

I scratched my ear. "What else do you remember about … then?" *Then*, when I'd been a kitten. Old enough to remember the creatures of the Inbetween that had ended my last life. Young enough to think I could take my chances slipping back in there when the other option was hanging around to be thrown about like a hacky-sack by a bunch of idiot humans, all giggling like it was the most hilarious thing they'd ever seen. Kitten bones are soft, but they do break. Eventually. And I hadn't thought the beasts would still be waiting for me. I hadn't even *imagined* that when they had a scent, they could leave the Inbetween.

Callum looked at his cigarettes, then put them down

again. "I was pretty messed up, G. I'm not even sure what I saw."

So messed up he'd fallen over twice all on his own while the kitty-kickers laughed hysterically, but he'd also punched out two of them (including the one that had left the scar on my side, a shiny cigarette-sized disc where the fur never grew), and slammed a third into a wall so hard I'd heard his arm break. I'm not sure Callum would have managed against the last two, but by that time the beast had been tearing its way out of the Inbetween after me, and while the torturers might not have exactly seen it, they'd known something was wrong. Felt it, maybe, the way the dimensions tore around it, or heard its toneless shrieking in their bones, no thought to it, just endless, raging hunger. They'd fled, and Callum had stomped on the tentacles (or tendrils or limbs or feelers or whatever the hell those bits of the Inbetween beast were) hard enough to spit blood that froze in the air like dark diamonds as it dropped me. Then he'd picked me up and legged it, running into a wall and falling over a kerb on the way out, but it was still a damn good rescue.

And as messed up as he'd been, he'd been able to find me some food and someone to patch me up, and hadn't seemed at all surprised by the fact that I was cursing my attackers, the beast, and the Watch (who had nothing to do with the kitty-torturers but everything to do with why the bloody beasts of the Inbetween had my scent) in very fluent and very inappropriate English. On such things are partnerships built.

"You remember the beast?" I asked him now.

He wiped his mouth. "Kind of. I saw all sorts of weird stuff. No idea how much was real."

"That was."

"Fair enough." He picked up the cigarettes again, shaking one out. "I'm not going outside in this."

"Those things'll kill you."

"So will the book, apparently. Or the beast. Can you get back on subject?"

"Okay. So, beasts aren't all there are."

"I know," he said. "We had that case with the gnomes."

Ugh, the gnomes. All living in the cellar of the pub and drinking so much beer the landlady had hired us to find out who was stealing from her. I'd wanted to pin it on the cook who stepped on my tail once, but Callum wouldn't let me. He said I couldn't be sure it wasn't an accident, but I was sure. I threw up a hairball in the greasy hack's shoe, and we'd solved the beer problem by switching the gnomes to the cooking sherry, which *had* got the cook fired. Karma.

"Yeah, gnomes," I said. "And there's the Watch, who keep the magical world and the human world apart—"

"Cats, right?" he said, lighting the cigarette and blowing smoke out the window he'd rolled down just slightly. I coughed, but it was more for effect than anything else. The fumes from the leaky exhaust would probably get us before his smoke did.

"Cats," I agreed. "And we've talked about avoiding certain bridges due to trolls, and the prevalence of hobgoblins at nightclubs."

He nodded. "Which explains a lot, really."

"So, in addition to the various magical Folk, who're

really just Folk humans don't notice, there are kinds – people – who are more powerful. A *lot* more. Some of them were even considered gods at various times, but these things go in and out of fashion, so who knows these days. And some of these kinds have books of power, invested with their magic. You can only hold so much magic in you before it splits you apart at the seams, so they sink the excess into these books. They're almost creatures in their own right, the books. There's so much power in them."

"And that's what that book is?" Callum asked. His voice was quiet, and I couldn't tell what he was thinking. Smoke coiled from his cigarette and crept out the window as if it didn't want to be here.

"It smelt like it. It *felt* like it."

"So Ms Jones is one of these … what? A god? A witch?"

I shrugged. Language can be pretty limited to describe such things. "They're called witches sometimes, but it's really just what men have always called women with power. It doesn't mean much. Sorcerer is probably a more polite term when talking to someone that can likely chuck you through a hole in reality."

He seemed to remember his cigarette, and took a drag on it with the sort of enthusiasm a drowning man has for good clean air. "What the hell. No wonder she wants it back so much."

"Yeah. To steal one you've got to be desperate to destroy the owner's power – to destroy *them*. But if you touch the book, you're bound to it. It'll give you every-thing you desire, but unless you know how to control it, sooner or later it'll eat you alive. If you *can* control it, you'll have more power than you know what to do with. You can remake the world in your image, but the cost will be huge – that's why so many sorcerers used to be into sacrifices and so on. And if you can't control it, it'll ride you like a demon until it's done with you, eaten you up from the inside, then it'll return to its original owner. That's if they don't find you first and take you apart themselves."

"Fun," Callum said.

"Yeah. And the books can't be destroyed, whether you've touched them or not. They're eternal, at least in this dimension. If you take one, you have to be able to bend it to your will, break the original holder's bond, use it to break *them* before they can break you. Otherwise you're going to be one soggy moggy."

He looked at his half-finished cigarette, stuck the end out in the rain until it went out, then shoved it in a take-away cup that was wedged between the seats. "You're saying Walker stole it, and Ms Jones was actually being really nice by asking us to get it back, rather than letting the book do its thing, or going after it herself?"

"Maybe she really loved him." I thought about it. "Or he's a lot scarier than he seems."

There was a pause, then Callum said. "Are you sure she's not a witch?"

"Call her that if you want. But she's really some ancient, potentially multidimensional being. No wonder she was wearing so much perfume. If I'd sniffed her out, we'd never have taken this case."

"She has a magic book that can steal your soul. Witch seems apt."

"Eh." I shrugged, and looked out the windscreen. "I'd stick with sorcerer unless you want to be changed into a parsnip. And we need to charge more for jobs like this."

"She's already paying us well above the odds. And I'm definitely not renegotiating with a multidimensional sorcerer. Or god."

"*Potentially* multidimensional."

"Oh, well. That's fine, then." He ground the car into gear and got the windscreen wipers working. "Anyway, we're not holding the book to ransom, Gobs. Don't you remember what happened with the dog case, when you decided to sneak out an email asking for more money? And that one had nothing to do with sorcerers and magical books."

I did remember. But, to be fair, the guy had presented us with a very simple case of a missing dog. He hadn't said *anything* about the dog in question being a champion rottweiler, or the surprisingly seedy underworld of dog breeders. There was still a bald patch on my tail from that one, and we *had* deserved more money. Although, admittedly, the email hadn't worked as well as I had expected. I hadn't anticipated in it resulting in me spending an hour of my Sunday trapped in the tiny bathroom with Callum while the dogs tore up the office. I probably could have worded it better.

I glanced into the back, as if I could see the book pulsating away in the boot, malevolent and semi-sentient. I could definitely smell it, a sick-sweet stench creeping through the car even over the reek of the exhaust fumes and the lingering whiff of cigarette smoke.

"Why do you think she came to us?" I asked.

Callum shrugged. "Same as anyone else. We're cheap."

"She didn't need cheap."

We were both silent for a while. We had never intended to take on any Folk work, but the local rats had introduced me to a sewer dragon who'd lost her hoard, and suspected leprechauns (she'd been right, too. Bloody green vermin), and then *she'd* put us in touch with a water sprite who was having a turf war with a bunch of amphibious pixies (pah). So it had just sort of happened.

And remember the Watch I mentioned, how they keep the world of Folk and humans apart? Yeah, well, one of the things they *definitely* frown on is cats or any other Folk chatting to humans, other than a select handful approved by them to be harmless (hence, cat ladies). Humans who see too much get their memories wiped through some pretty advanced magical suggestion techniques. Folk, who should know better, get dealt with. If there was word getting out that there was a certain PI firm that dealt in both Folk and human problems, the Watch would be sniffing around before long. And I would be in more trouble than a ferret in a pixie storm. Again. I didn't fancy ending another life in the Inbetween. I was going to run out of lives well before time at this rate. And dying *hurts*.

We paused at a stop sign, and Callum reached over to scratch the top of my head and give my back a quick stroke with one long-fingered hand. I gave him a startled look and shook myself off in proper *I did not approve this* manner.

"It'll be cool, G," he said. "We'll get the book back to

Ms Jones, get the payment, and lay low for a bit. We could even find some place new on that money."

"Of course," I said. "It's not like I'm worried or anything."

We drove home through the unceasing rain with just the hiss of the tyres and the groan of the windscreen wipers for company, while the book in the boot waited and brooded and pulsed, and I thought I could feel it calling out to Walker, calling out to the man who'd stolen it. Calling out to the man it wanted to devour.

I couldn't wait to be shot of the damn thing.

7

NOTHING TO IT

I SPENT THE ENTIRE DRIVE HOME EITHER PEERING OUT AT the street with my paws on the dashboard or window, or prowling into the back seat to check the road behind us.

"Gobs, stop it, can't you?" Callum said. "You're making me jumpy."

"*I'm* making you jumpy? What about the nasty bloody book in the boot?"

"Yeah, but the book's not wandering around the car hissing at traffic lights. And people are giving us weird looks."

"Oh, well. *Weird looks.* We can't have that." I sat back down, tail twitching. "You're not taking this seriously."

"I am," he said. "But the only thing we can do is get the book back to Ms Jones. Let her deal with it. And you're worrying about nothing, anyway. Even if Walker's already discovered the book's gone, he's not going to have any idea who took it."

"I think he got a pretty good look at us at the clinic." I was having some misgivings about our approach so far. It *had* made sense to make sure he was actually at work, and not somewhere curled around the book like a pale, balding dragon with bad teeth, but maybe trying to search the exam room while he was actually in it had been one of my less clever ideas.

Not that it was a *bad* idea, exactly, as cats always have their reasons, but right now I wasn't sure I had any good ones to offer up. And then I'd had to go and talk, which was a good distraction technique for the average human (between the screaming and trying to pretend they hadn't heard anything there was generally plenty of time for a getaway), but less beneficial when dealing with someone who knew about magic.

Yeah. Things had not exactly gone as well as they could have with this entire case, right from when Ms Jones walked in our door. I should have been warier. I'd *known* the scent was covering something. No one took a swim in a perfume bottle for no reason. I should have realised something was up, should have known no one offers a couple of back street investigators that amount of money for an ordinary book. But we'd needed the cash. We still needed the cash.

"So he saw a guy and a black cat. Doesn't mean a lot, G," Callum said, with that infuriating calm that meant he really had no grasp of the situation at all. "Even if he guesses Ms Jones sent us, he's got no way of knowing who we are or how to find us."

"I suppose." I stood up again, peering out the back. "Was that car behind us before?"

"What one?"

"That one. Kind of chunky. I think it's black. Or maybe blue. Green? Dark, anyway."

Callum nodded. "I imagine there has been a car fitting that description behind us at some point."

I gave him my best haughty look and gave up. He was right. I'd never spot Walker if he was behind us. And sure, the book'd be driving him mad, and he probably did go home every chance he got to pet its pages or whatever weirdness passed as worship for him, so the odds were good he already knew it was gone. But that didn't mean he'd be some sort of homing pigeon for it. And while we were excellent investigators, our reputation had hardly spread enough that he'd have heard of us. We were probably safe. All we had to do was keep the book secure until Ms Jones came calling.

Nothing to it.

OUR SPOT in the alley was taken, and we had to park two streets over, hurrying back over the soaking pavements while Callum cradled the tool bag and its nasty cargo gingerly under his coat, trying not to let it get too wet. I shouted at him from the shelter of a rotting sandwich board to make sure the tool bag was zipped, and that there were no holes in the carrier bag, and to try to only touch the handles, and not to look at the book, or preferably even think about it, and he hissed at me to shut up before anyone overheard. I forget sometimes. And if there was ever a situation designed to make you forget certain aspects of discretion, this was it.

We pushed through the main door of the building (the lock had never worked, and half the time it just hung open), and hurried up the musty, dimly lit stairs to the second floor. My tail was struggling to bristle, damp as it was, and Callum seemed to have finally caught my sense of urgency. We peered out into our hall cautiously, seeing nothing but stained carpet and patchy lighting.

"Anything?" Callum asked me.

I prowled out carefully, whiskers bristling, but I couldn't sense anything amiss. A whiff of boiled meat from the old guy two doors down, and candle wax from Mrs Smith. She must've had clients today. She always covers up the IKEA cabinets with tie-dyed throws and lights purple candles all about the place when she's doing her tarot thing. All rubbish, of course, and I'm pretty sure she knows it too, but I'm not one to shed on anyone's business.

"I think we're good," I said.

Callum didn't answer, just took the tool bag out from under his jacket and held it at arm's length like a dead thing as we hurried to our door. He fumbled with the keys while I gazed around anxiously, half expecting Walker to emerge from somewhere, roaring in fury and waving dental picks around. Then the lock turned and we were in, smelling the faint, familiar staleness of too many books and not enough heating. Callum slammed the door behind us, locked it again, then went straight to the filing cabinet. He took the box gingerly out of the tool bag, holding it as carefully as a newborn alligator, and dropped it in the bottom drawer, then locked the drawer. It wasn't exactly a wall safe, but as it was the only thing in the place that did lock it was going to have to do. Only then did he straighten up and push his hair out of his face.

"Phew," I said.

"Yeah," he agreed, and wiped rain off his forehead. "Could you hear it?"

"Hear it? No, nothing like that. I mean, I can still smell the damn thing, even in there, but it's not exactly yodelling at me."

"I thought I could hear it. It was …" He looked around for a moment, as if confused. "Maybe I imagined it."

"Probably not," I said. "Books of power can be persuasive. Cats are kind of immune to that sort of thing, though. It's all based on impossible desires and wants, and we're pretty good at getting what we want anyway."

"Lucky you," Callum said, peeling his coat off and going to hang it in the tiny bathroom. "Right now I wish I still drank."

"Yeah. Because reduced impulse control and impaired thinking mix so well with magic books trying to eat your soul."

"It does shut the voices up, though," he said, sitting down on the edge of the desk to pull his boots off. His socks were sopping, and he frowned at them. "I think I need new boots."

I looked at my own very wet paws and said, "Failing that, can we turn the heating on?"

YOU KNOW those days when there's a storm coming, only you can't see it yet? Like the sky's all blue, but your stomach keeps turning in on itself, and your skin itches, and your fur bristles at nothing? And every click of a pen or closing of a door sounds like a scream, until you're so exhausted you can't *wait* for that first crash of thunder?

Or maybe you don't know. Humans are so weirdly unperceptive at times. But, whatever, the rest of the day was like that. I tried to sleep, and Callum tried to read, and both of us kept getting up and going to the window, or checking the filing cabinet was still locked, or (in Callum's case) opening the door and peering out into the hall. Callum dropped a mug and it broke, spilling tea everywhere, and I fell off the windowsill, thinking it was someone smashing the door down, and we both shouted for a bit then pointedly ignored each other for a couple of hours.

Finally Callum got up. "I'm going for a walk," he said. "I can't stand this. I swear I can still hear the bloody thing whispering away in there."

I gave the filing cabinet a dubious look. "Hope she calls tomorrow."

"Me too." He gave the drawer a good shake, making sure it was locked, then looked at me. "Coming?"

"I don't know. Do you think it's safe to just leave it here?"

"I'm not sure," Callum admitted. "But I can't keep listening to it. It keeps telling me that if I just take one little look it'll stop. No more whispers. Just one look. Then it'll be quiet. Everything'll be peaceful. I'll have all the peace and quiet in the world. In the *universe*. But I just need to take it out and have one quick look."

I considered the fact that a magical book which was

meant to offer the user their heart's desire was just offering him quiet. People are strange, in both good and bad ways. "What if Walker turns up?"

"He won't," Callum said. "I told you, he has no idea who we are. He's not going to find this place."

I wished I had his confidence. But I was also fed up of feeling like – as the saying goes – a cat in a room full of rock guitars. Or was that rock gardens? Either way, I was edgy as anything. "Alright," I said. "Can't hurt for an hour or so."

"Exactly," Callum said, and led the way out, making sure both locks were on before we left.

―――

THE RAIN HAD EASED to a drizzle that wasn't so bad, and we wandered down to the Turkish place a few streets over with the broken neon signs outside and warm, crowded rooms inside. We sat in a corner booth where I could be on the seat without being too obvious, since restaurants get a bit weird about it sometimes, smelling the rich scents of sweet tea and hookah smoke and roasting meat. Callum ordered too many little plates of veggie dips and fried cheese pastries and bread and what have you, and after a whispered argument got me some octopus salad. It was loaded up with vinegar and onion and was completely hideous, so I ate his cheese pastry and meatballs instead while he gave me a *told you so* look. Well, I didn't know. Why would anyone ruin perfectly good fish with all that rubbish?

But it was good to not be sitting in the office with the

book lurking in a drawer like a particularly deadly and charming cobra, promising salvation and destruction in the same breath, and we probably dawdled longer than we really needed to. It wasn't like we had any other jobs on. And, you know, there's something to be said about the concept of scarcity. If someone came to book us, it was as well that they thought we spent all our time out on cases rather than hanging about inside waiting for the next job to fall in our laps. See? Always looking at the big picture, me.

So it was getting on by the time we headed back, our late lunch/early dinner having run into the autumn dusk. We walked without talking, Callum with his hands in the pockets of his long coat and his head down, watching the pavement while I padded next to him on silent feet, my tail up and my eyes on the shadows. People barely glanced at us. Just another badly adjusted human hanging with the animals, I suppose. Humans have very strict margins of what's acceptable and what's odd, I've discovered. And then there's a whole yawning gap between odd but good and just odd. We hung pretty close to the edge on that one.

"Want some custard?" Callum asked me, pausing outside the 24-hour corner store that wasn't actually open 24 hours.

"Don't think you can bribe me into letting you smoke inside," I said.

"Wouldn't dream of it," he said, and I trailed after him into the shop while he took his time buying a can of custard and some cigarettes and more chocolate biscuits. He exchanged a few words with the woman behind the counter, who stared at him as if suspecting him of nefarious intentions and answered in monosyllables, then we were out on the pavement again, the street to our building yawning to one side of the shop.

I could feel Callum's reluctance, heavy and unhappy, and wished again that the creature calling herself Ms Jones had left a way to contact her. I still didn't understand why she hadn't just taken the book back herself. She must be desperate for it, for that part of her out in the world and lost. Whether she had harboured enough affection for Walker to be worried about hurting him in a confrontation, or whether she just didn't want to get her hands dirty, it was strange. And dangerous, with the book in there calling for someone else to touch it, someone to answer its siren song and be enslaved to it. Looking for someone to drain and destroy until it could be held by its mistress again.

I understood Callum's reluctance. He knew about things that devoured you, even if his experience was more chemical than magical. It didn't make it easier to ignore the voices.

We trudged back in silence.

WE WERE out of the stairwell and into the second-floor hall before I smelt it.

Peppermint mouthwash.

I stopped short, almost tripping Callum.

"What the hell, G," he started, and I cut him off.

"He's here!"

"What? Oh, *bollocks.*" Because he'd just spotted the light seeping from under our door into the dim hallway.

"We can't let him get it! We can't!" Not just because that was our pay cheque right down the drain, but because who knew what the hell he'd do to us if he'd learnt to harness even a breath of the book's power. He could turn us inside out, throw us into the Inbetween, turn us into cockroaches. Well, maybe not the last one. Metamorphosis was pretty advanced magic. But the first two were bad enough.

"Right, well—" A crash from behind our door swallowed Callum's words and he cursed, lunging forward and throwing the door open, running into the room and yelling something about the police being on the way and various other vaguely legal-sounding threats.

"Callum!" I shouted. "Don't get too near it! Don't touch it!" The last thing we needed was a wrestling match over a book of power. There was no way that could ever end well. In fact, it'd probably end with someone turned into a newt, and I didn't intend that someone to be me. I ran after him, straight into an astonishing amount of devastation for such a small room.

The crash had been the desk being thrown over. The filing cabinet was on its side, spewing papers and torn files and my souvenirs everywhere, and the armchair was upside down against a wall, missing all its cushions. Books had been flung all about the place, the chairs from the desk were tangled together in the corner, loose pages and bits of notes and pens were still tumbling across the floor, and Walker was in the middle of it all, clutching our cricket bat. His thinning hair was sticking up at wild angles, and he was wearing the sort of tracksuit and trainer ensemble people wear when they have no intention of actually doing any exercise.

"*Where is it?*" he shrieked, waving the bat at us. "*Where is my book?*"

"Put that down and we'll talk about it," Callum said, hands spread in front of him in his *easy now* pose. I don't know why he bothers. It's worked exactly zero times. Maybe he's going for twentieth time lucky, or something.

Walker smashed the bat down on the windowsill and the glass shattered, raining shards all over the tatty floor. Fantastic. "*Give me my book!*"

"I don't know what you're talking about," Callum said, his voice even, and I glanced at the filing cabinet. Walker had apparently been at it with the cricket bat, because the bottom drawer had burst open and the base had sheared away from the sides. And the book was nowhere to be seen.

So that was awesome.

8

HAZARD OF THE JOB

"I KNOW YOU HAVE IT!" WALKER BELLOWED. "I KNOW IT'S here somewhere! Give it to me!"

"We don't have it," Callum said, and I took a moment to scout out the filing cabinet, nosing through the drifts of case notes. There was no whiff of ancient, muscular power. And that constant, prickling unease was gone, too. Which was a relief, but it was replaced by the rather more visceral unease of wondering who the hell had the book and what Ms Jones was going to do to us when she found out we'd lost the damn thing.

"Hairballs," I said conversationally.

Callum scowled at me, and Walker yelled, "My ex sent you, didn't she? *Didn't she?*"

"Look, we don't have any book," Callum said, and nodded around the devastated office. "I think you can kind of see that."

We all looked at the office. There were a *lot* of books on the floor, but pretty clearly none of them worth more than the ten pence Callum had probably paid for them, if that.

Walker stumbled over the debris to wave our cricket bat in Callum's face. It seemed kind of rude. He could at least have brought his own. "It's here somewhere. I stuck a tracker on it, because I guessed she'd send someone after it."

Callum glanced at me, and I shrugged. It was a bit hard to spot a tracker when you were trying to stay as far from the book as possible. "Really. So where is it, then?"

Walker kicked through the scattered paper and disembowelled books, finally exposing the discarded carrier bag and the dark wood box nestling in it, both hiding under a cushion. The box was embossed with stained runes and inlaid with yellowing bone, and as soon as Walker freed it from the bag I could smell the remnants of the book's magic, like soap scum in an empty bath. He picked the box up and pointed at a tiny black transmitter stuck to it like a tick. "You tell me."

Callum and I stared at the box. Had Ms Jones come by while we were out and helped herself? Why hadn't she taken the box as well? Was the transmitter too well stuck – and even if it was, why was someone like her worried about Walker knowing she'd taken her own book back, anyway? I padded a little closer, snuffling for evidence, but all I could smell was age and the greasy residue of old, dark magic layering the wood.

"*You*," Walker snarled, and grabbed me before I could react, seizing the loose skin at the back of my neck and hoisting me into the air with the whites of my eyes showing. I tried to hiss at him as my tail tucked helplessly up against my body. "I bet it was you that sneaked into my apartment, wasn't it? And you just about got me sued by bloody Abbott. Damn cats. I *hate* cats."

"Put him down," Callum said, his voice flat.

I tried to indicate to Walker that he really should listen to Callum, but I couldn't do anything except show my claws a little.

"Not until you give me my book," Walker said, and gave me a painful shake.

"We don't have it," Callum said. "Okay, we *did* have it. It was there when we left. But it's gone now. Maybe your ex took it back after all."

"She can't," he hissed. "She can't touch it. I made sure of it. I counter-cursed it."

Oh, Old Ones take humans and their greedy little hearts. Counter-cursed books of power? We *really* should have charged a whole lot more for this job.

"Then it looks like we got robbed," Callum said, shrugging. "Hazard of the job."

"*Hazard of the job?*" Walker shrieked. "That's my property! I *need* it!"

"Well, we do have every intention of finding it again," Callum said.

"*Now!* Find it *now!*" He shook me, which was about as unpleasant as you imagine.

"*Put the cat down.*" Callum's voice had gone from flat to hard. "Put him down and then we'll talk."

"No, *you* do what *I* say—"

"What on *earth* are you doing to poor Gobbelino?" someone shouted from the doorway, making us all jump. Well, Walker and Callum jumped. I widened my eyes slightly, and peered around as well as I could. Mrs Smith was standing on the threshold holding a stack of Tupperware, her wilderness of white hair up in some sort of strange waterfall arrangement. She glared at Walker with a quite surprising level of ferocity. "Put him down, you horrible man!"

"Who the hell—" Walker started, and his grip on my scruff slipped just enough that it went from painful and immobilising to just plain painful. I twisted hard, snagging his fancy sweatshirt sleeve and hauling myself around until I could wrap my legs around his forearm and apply teeth and claws with great enthusiasm. Walker shrieked and grabbed me with his free hand, trying to pull me off, but I had no intention of letting go before he did. Callum lunged forward, collecting a handful of the other man's hoody and hauling him onto his tiptoes.

"Let him go," Callum said, far too calmly in my opinion, considering the tooth doctor had been shaking me about like a kitten just a moment ago. Walker growled, a look on his face that suggested things weren't going so well in his bowel region. I bit him a little harder, wondering if I should beat a valiant retreat in the face of intestinal distress, but he was ignoring me. Mrs Smith was shouting about animal cruelty, and the dentist stopped trying to scrape me off his arm and waved his free hand about, still with that uncomfortable expression. I took a small break from chewing on his wrist and glanced around.

Things in the room were airborne. Books and files were drifting through the air like errant leaves, and the desk was lifting one foot then the other off the floor, like a bird on hot sand. Cushions from the armchair were puffing heavily about the place, and the battered client chair was aiming all four legs directly at us.

I spat out a mouthful of dentist and yelled, "*Duck!*"

Callum dropped Walker and hit the floor as the chair spun past us and smashed into the wall, then he grabbed for Walker's legs, trying to wrestle him to the ground while books flung themselves at his head and shoulders like aggressive, papery pigeons. Walker smashed the arm I was attached to down toward the chattering desk so hard that it was jump free or find out how good the vet was at splints. I let go and bounced away, spitting curses as Callum scrambled to his feet and grabbed the back of Walker's jacket, trying to trap his arms. The filing cabinet was headed for the two men, rolling across the floor like a rowdy, angular tumbleweed, and I launched myself back into the fray, bouncing off the desk and going for Walker's face as he flailed rather ineffectually at my partner. Hand to hand combat was evidently not his thing.

A mug caught me a good clip on the ribs before I could reach the two men, throwing me rather dramatically off course, and I looked up to see the filing cabinet slam into the back of Callum's legs, sending him crashing to his knees. Walker wrenched himself away and raised both arms in the theatrical manner of someone who's watched *The Lord of the Rings* too many times.

"*Give me my book!*" he roared, and every item in the room – the broken desk, the avalanche of paperbacks, the tattered files, a half-dead peace lily, the armchair and its pillows, the mugs – all rose to the ceiling and hovered threateningly over us. "Give it to me *now!*"

"We don't have it!" Callum yelled back, and Walker gave a scream of rage that I was pretty sure was going to do some permanent damage to his vocal chords. I bunched my legs to leap, thinking that, judging by the way things kept bumping into walls and each other and even him that he wasn't too in control here. If I could just bite him somewhere sensitive he'd probably drop the lot. He pointed at me, giving another inarticulate scream, and the peace lily bumped off my head hard enough to make me see flying fish as the desk went galloping at Callum. Walker roared triumphantly, and for a moment I thought we might actually be in trouble.

Then a Tupperware spun across the room and smacked the dentist squarely on the nose, disgorging lemon drizzle cake all over the floor.

"*Ow!*" he yelped, clutching his face with both hands, the furniture and sundry debris starting to rain down around us as his concentration broke. "Ow, what the *hell*—"

Callum scrambled forward and tackled Walker to the ground, forcing the dentist's arms up behind his back as he wriggled and complained, and I bounded toward them.

"How's he doing it?" Callum asked me. He was bleeding where something had nicked his ear. "How do we stop it?"

Walker was growling like a cornered dog, writhing around and trying to throw Callum off, but there wasn't much chance of that unless he started hefting desks about again. All around the room broken bits of furniture and torn pages were flopping in alarm, like chickens unsure which way to run.

"His hands," I said, remembering the wizard-esque (and totally unnecessary, if you know what you're doing) waving. "He was directing it. Check for something – a ring, some tattooed runes."

Callum trapped Walker's hands against his back and inspected them. No rings. No tattoos. He shoved the dentist's sleeve up and found one of those fitness watches on his wrist. We both looked at it.

"You think?" Callum said.

I snuffled at the watch. It smelt pretty gross and sweaty, and suggested the man overdosed on cologne pretty frequently, but there was something else there, too. I suppose it was no different than dosing jewellery with magic. Hell, for all I knew he could have a snapshot of some runes on the damn thing, trapping a little of the book's magic into portable format. Enchantment by Blue-tooth. "That's it," I said.

Callum grabbed the watch and pulled it off, the plastic band snapping easily, and Walker gave an indistinct screech of fury. The books stopped moving. The furniture subsided. And Woo-Woo upstairs pounded on the floor so loud I thought she was going to come through.

"Oh dear," Mrs Smith said, and surveyed the shattered room. "That was the last of the cake, too."

CALLUM HAULED Walker off the ground in much the same way the dentist had lifted me, one hand around the back of his neck. He was whining. Not as in complaining. As in the way a dog does, steady and unrelenting. It made me want to bite him again.

"Thank you, Mrs Smith," Callum said to our newest hero. "I'm sorry about your cake, though."

"That's alright, dear," she said, looking around dubiously. "I still have some shortbread. From a packet, though."

"I'm sure it'll be lovely."

We all stood there for a moment, no one saying anything. Walker tried out snivelling instead of whining, pushing ineffectually against Callum's grip, and I wondered if Mrs Smith had noticed the levitating furniture or me shouting, or if, like most humans, she just attributed it to someone else or her own imagination. Then she looked at Callum and said gravely, "I hope you and Gobbelino are both okay. Come over once you're done here and I'll heat some shepherd's pie up for you."

"Oh, we've already eaten," Callum said, giving Walker a shake to try and shut him up. He paused the snivels and went back to whining instead. "And this is going to take a bit of tidying up. Thanks so much anyway. You absolutely saved the day."

She gave a squeaky sort of giggle and waved at him. "Not at all. I'm sure I only got in the way of your investigations. As if I could help an officer of the law!"

"You really did," Callum said. "We were in trouble there."

Mrs Smith tucked a plaited lock of hair behind her ear and beamed at him. "Well, alright, dear. Just let me know if you need anything else." And she closed the door carefully, leaving us alone with the dentist.

We were silent for a moment, then Walker said, "I want my book." He sounded like a toddler begging for his blanky.

"Even if we had it, it's not your book," Callum said.

"It is!"

"It's not."

"Is. I took it. Broke the bond. It's mine." He nodded at me. "Ask the cat. He knows that's how it works."

I glared at him. My back hurt from him swinging me around, and my side hurt from the mug, and my head hurt from the peace lily, and I'd just noticed my microwave bed had split, little heatable beans spilling all over the place, which meant no cosy bed for me tonight. *Dentists.* "You expect us to think *you* broke the bond?" I snapped at him. "You're a nasty, talentless little earwig."

"It's *mine*," he insisted.

"Could he have broken it?" Callum asked me. "Does it work like that?"

"Sure. You can break the bond to the previous owner and bind the book to you. I mean, you'd have to seriously know what you're doing to manage it without it destroying your mind and going back to its original owner, but it's possible. Pretty high-level stuff, though, especially if you're taking it from a creature of power and not just another human." I surveyed the dentist, his hoody pulled up to expose pale, hairy belly and his thin hair sticking up in every direction. Set him against Ms Jones, reeking of power, and it seemed pretty doubtful.

Callum didn't look too convinced either. "How do we know?"

"We don't. And it doesn't matter. He's not our client."

"Yeah, but if the book actually belongs to him—"

"Yes!" Walker yelped. "It does. So you can't give it to *her*."

"He's not our client," I repeated.

"We're not in the business of stealing things, G. Returning them to their owners, okay, I can work with that, but if it's not hers anymore—"

"Dude. Does he *look* like the rightful owner of a book of power?"

"How do I know?" Callum asked. "Maybe that's just how it works."

I stared at my toes. "It's a boot point, anyway. The book's gone."

"Moot point," Callum said absently.

"Moot? What the hell does that mean?"

He ignored me, examining Walker as if he could divine the truth in his sweaty ears or something.

Walker glared at me, then tried to twist to look at Callum. "It's really gone? You weren't just saying that?"

"Really gone," Callum agreed.

"Oh no," Walker said. "Oh, that's really bad."

"Man's a genius," I said. But he wasn't wrong.

"You have to find it," he said. "I'll pay you twice what she offered you."

"Twice?" I said.

"Gobs," Callum said, frowning at me.

"What? You were the one saying he might be the rightful owner after all."

"I *am*," Walker insisted. "Yes, I stole it, but only because she was using it to keep me. Like I was a pet or something. I couldn't leave."

I gave him a doubtful look. But, you know. No accounting for taste.

"I studied, and I figured it out. I knew the only way I could escape was to break the bond. And it took ages, but I did it. So the book's *mine*, and she can't take it back herself because I counter-cursed it. But if she gets someone else to break the bond to me, the counter-curse is broken too, and she can take it back."

"Joy," I said, and looked at Callum. "You were bait."

"What?"

"She was on to us. She wanted you to grab the book, figuring Walker hadn't had it long enough for it to remain bonded to him if someone else took it. Or, if it was, that I'd help you break the bond when we realised the book was going to devour you otherwise. Then she could take it back off us easy as pudding."

"That's just like her," Walker said, shaking his head. "And then she'd probably have taken both of us as slaves." He craned over his shoulder to look at Callum. "You're not really her type, though."

"Ew," I said.

"Lucky escape," Walker said, and tried to pull away from Callum.

Callum let him go. "Suppose we believe you," he said. "What then?"

"You mentioned twice the pay," I said to Walker. "But at the time we set the original price we didn't realise we were dealing with a book of power. I think quadruple would reflect the seriousness of the situation better."

Callum frowned at me. "Gobs, don't you think the bigger question might be who the hell has the book now?"

"Well, yes. But are we being paid to care about that?"

"Yes. That is quite literally what *everyone* wants us to care about."

"You can't give her the book after what I've told you," Walker protested, trying to straighten his tracksuit. "She'll just trick someone else into using it so my bond with it'll be broken and she can take it back."

"We'll take the case," I announced. "Deposit of 25 percent, plus damages for the office. Payable in cash. Now."

"I don't have any money on me," Walker said. "Can't I do card?"

I looked around. "Does it look like it?"

"Oh." He tried a smile. "Sorry about that. But the book *is* my property. And you might have been trapped by it if it weren't for me."

"Sure, I'd have let that happen," I snapped.

Callum pinched the bridge of his nose. "We're still working for Ms—"

"Off you go," I said to Walker, before Callum could ruin everything. "Cashpoint at the shop on the corner. And get me some tuna while you're at it."

"Um. Okay." He looked at Callum. "Can I have my watch back?"

"No," we both said, and he looked crestfallen, but picked his way to the door and let himself out. Callum looked at me, then went to check he'd actually gone. Both locks were smashed, and the chairs were too broken to hold it closed, so he dragged the filing box in front of the door, then we both stared at the ruins of our home.

"I don't like this," Callum said.

"Nope," I agreed. "But, you know, we have to find the book one way or the other. We can decide who we give it to later."

Callum pinched the bridge of his nose. "You don't think that's a *little* risky, considering one's a multidimensional non-witch, and the other just blew our office apart?"

"Well, yeah," I admitted. "But we don't know who has it now. They might be even better. Or worse. Depends on your perspective."

Callum took his cigarettes out and said, "If you say *anything* about me smoking inside, I'm putting you out the window."

I let it go. One has to know what fights are worth it. Besides, with the broken window it felt like we were outside already.

9

FURTHER HAZARDS

WE SAT AMID THE DEBRIS FOR A WHILE, CALLUM SMOKING and me staring morosely at my devastated bed. Eventually Callum got up and set the desk upright, which at least gave him somewhere to pile all the broken-backed books. The floor was a wilderness of shattered mugs and glass from the smashed window and destroyed fluorescent light tubes (we were down to one now, casting uneasy shadows everywhere), and there were drifts of paper like snowbanks all over the place. The filing cabinet was bent on one side, and the drawers wouldn't shut anymore, and the armchair had unfolded itself into its bed form and wouldn't go back. The pillows and bedding that lived in the filing cabinet were lying in a puddle of rain that had seeped in the window, and one of the pillows had been disembowelled, leaking cheap stuffing sadly. The less said about the two chairs from the desk, the better – they hadn't been in the best of health to start with.

All three cupboards in the kitchenette had come open, and the door had been torn off one. Everything had emptied itself into the sink and onto the floor, and nothing breakable had survived the exodus unscathed, although one of the mugs was whole other than having lost its handle, so Callum fished the kettle out from under an old copy of the local paper and made tea. I sometimes think that the capacity of humans to cope with disaster is directly proportional to the availability of tea. That, or whisky. It depends on the individual.

"You want some of that custard?" he asked, splashing water into the mug.

"Nah," I said. "The whole place stinks of magic, and it's making my mouth go funny."

"Fair enough." He opened the chocolate digestives and set them on the desk, then went back to picking up books. There were quite a few loose covers and pages drifting around the place, and he looked at them woefully, as if a friend had been injured.

BY THE TIME Walker got back, Callum had blocked the broken window with the shattered chair seats, which didn't do much for our view but did keep the damp night out. He was trying to bash the filing cabinet back into shape with a chair leg, but every thump got us an answering pound on the floor upstairs, so he wasn't getting too far.

"Um. Hi," Walker said, peering around the unlocked door. "Can I come in?"

"Did you bring the cash?" I asked.

"Some," he said, and I gave him a withering look that

was probably somewhat wasted, considering the fact things were shadowy in here for me, let alone for human eyes. "The cashpoint at the shop was broken and there were all these kids hanging out around the one down the street, so I had to just get cash back over the counter." He waved a can at me. "I got tuna, though."

I squinted at it. "Better be in spring water."

"Um." He squinted at the label as Callum gave up on bashing the filing cabinet and dragged it away from the door so Walker could get through. "Oil, I think? Sunflower?"

"Delightful."

"Sorry." He wandered in and watched Callum push the filing cabinet back into place, then looked around. The books were off the floor and everything else had been swept into one corner, awaiting either the bin or some daylight to sort it out. "Hey, it looks much better!"

We both stared at him, then Callum said, "Do you want a cup of tea?"

"Don't you have anything stronger?"

Cheeky git. Trashes our home then expects us to supply him with booze? I'd have told him what he could do with his drink, but Callum just nodded and said, "Most everything's broken. You'll have to use the pen holder."

Walker looked dubiously from the bottle of whisky Callum fished out the kitchenette to the square, clear plastic container with ink stains in the corners, then shrugged and sat himself on the edge of the desk to open the bottle. The desk leaned slightly, creaking in alarm. "All tastes the same, right?"

"Sure," Callum said, and dropped into the armchair.

He hadn't been able to get it to fold back upright into a chair again, and neither would it go entirely flat into a bed, so he just perched on it sideways with his hands between his knees, looking tired and not very comfortable. "So Gobbelino tells me that, as the rightful owner, you should be able to summon the book to you, or at least track it." He glanced at the box sitting on top of the desk. "Magically, not using GPS."

"Well, see, yes, but no."

"Edifying," I said, jumping onto the desk so I could see them both better.

"I mean, yes, I *should* be able to, but I haven't had it that long, and I, um, haven't learnt that bit yet."

"You haven't learnt it?" Callum asked, picking up the biscuits and offering one to Walker. He waved it away, slurping whisky.

"No, well, you know, I was kind of desperate to get away, so I just focused on how to break the bond with the previous owner and how to bind it to me. Then I was working on attracting fortune, you know?"

"You didn't think she'd steal it back?" I asked. "Kind of seems making a really secure bond and keeping the damn thing safe should have been priority number one."

"Well, yes, but I had a new apartment, and the rent was due on the practice, and I *was* learning how to defend myself, and—"

"Genius," I said. "And how was that attracting fortune working out for you? Looked like you were really smashing it in the tooth business."

Walker made some vague noise of outrage and waved at me, his face pink. "Hey—"

"Shut up, Gobs," Callum said. "Look, Mr Walker, I'm still not convinced you're the rightful owner—"

"I *am*. If I wasn't, she'd have summoned the book back in the first *day*."

Callum looked at me, and I shrugged. "Fair point, actually."

"And she hasn't come to take it back herself?"

"No. One of the first things I did was put protective charms on the practice and my apartment, so she couldn't come by personally. I figured she'd get someone else to do it, but I didn't actually think you'd find it. I had hiding runes all over the place." He sounded put out, and I snorted.

"Dude, you have a *lot* to learn. Runes work great for your average human, who doesn't see Folk or the hidden world. They make them look straight past anything the runes are protecting. But for anyone who sees properly, especially anyone looking for what you're trying to hide – even Callum can see through that rubbish."

"I didn't even notice there were any," Callum said.

"I didn't say you were the most perceptive creature around," I said, although, to be honest, I hadn't noticed them either. Look, I'd had more important things on my mind, okay? Like not falling off walls, mostly.

"Well, whatever," Walker said, topping up the pen holder with more whisky. "I need that book back. And my watch. If she comes for me now, I've no defence against her whatsoever."

"It's not like we can just nip out and grab the book from lost property," I said. "I mean, we have to find it first, and then if someone else has claimed it we're going to have to break *their* bond before you can claim it again."

"Well, no one can have claimed it yet," Walker said. "I'd know." There was a pause while we looked at him, then he said doubtfully, "Wouldn't I?"

"You're the super-magician-dentist," I said. "You tell us."

"I don't know," he admitted. "I was going to learn all this, but I was busy, you know?"

"We need to find the book before anything else," Callum said. He was looking into space, frowning slightly. "We'll figure out the rest after."

"I'll work with you," Walker said. "I can break the bond if someone else *has* claimed it. I know that bit. You just find it, and I'll break the bond. Teamwork, you know?"

I scratched my ear. "Well, glad to hear you know s*omething*. Quadruple pay we agreed, didn't we?"

"No, Gobbelino," Callum said. "We took payment from Ms Jones already. We don't just drop out on a client." He was still staring into space, and I wondered if the filing cabinet had hit him in the head or something.

"Situations change," I told him, and he scowled at me. "She's not here, is she?" I pointed out. "And can we really let this poor man go back to being her slave? What sort of life would that be for anyone?"

"No, exactly," Walker said. "And she'll try to trap you, too!"

Callum gave me a sideways look that I couldn't quite read. Quite possibly it said he knew I was trying to appeal to his better nature, and that I should stop it. I gave him my best big-eyed look in return, and he shook his head.

"Let's just try to figure out where the damn book's gone, shall we?"

"Yes! Yes, I've got some ideas—" Walker stopped as Callum held a hand up.

"Not you."

"But I can help! I told you! And I have the deposit on me!"

"How much?" I asked. "And don't forget we charge for expenses, too."

"Oh, well. I could only get fifty quid on cash back."

"*Fifty quid?* What do you think we live on, carpet fluff and dirty air?"

"Shut up, Gobs," Callum said again, pushing himself out of the armchair. "Keep the money, Mr Walker. We'll be in touch."

"Hey, hang on," I protested. "What about damages? It might replace the mugs, at least. And what about my bed?"

"No," Callum said, and took the pen holder off Walker. "Off you go."

"I really think we should discuss this more," Walker protested, sliding off the edge of the desk while it groaned and wobbled unhappily. "I can get you more money tomorrow. I'll bring it over first thing. All of it, if you want."

"Go home," Callum said, fishing Walker's watch out of his own pocket and passing it over. "There you go. You can keep it. You'll be all safe now."

"Well, not *really*—"

"Bye." Callum opened the door and ushered the older man out. "If you figure out how to track the book, then come talk to us."

"But—"

Callum shut the door in his face and pulled the filing cabinet in front of it again.

I arched my whiskers at him. "That was a bit hasty."

Callum shook his head. "I don't think so, G." He walked to where the broken chairs were wedged into the window frame, and pointed. "We have to honour our original contract. What sort of business are we running if we don't do that?"

I squinted at him. "Well, yeah, but when situations change—"

"No." He pointed at the chairs again, and I stared at him. He pointed again, waggling his finger like I'd pooped on the carpet (as if). I got up and jumped onto the desk, wondering what the hell he was playing at as I padded over to peer at the chairs. That filing cabinet really did hit him pretty hard.

I didn't see them until I was right on the edge of the desk, peering through the thin light at the splintery wood holding back the night. I have no idea how Callum spotted them from right across the dim-lit room, especially with human eyes. They were small, subtle, done with the skill of long, long practise. I couldn't smell them over the reek of spent magic in the room, not even when I was looking right at them, and I was almost certain that even without the covering scent of the missing book and Walker's sideshow magic they'd have been unnoticeable unless I had my nose right on them. Clever. And I should have known. Our lovely Ms Jones had left listening runes scorched into the underside of the chair where she'd sat the day before, eavesdropping on everything that had happened. I licked my chops and sat down, tail twitching.

"You're right," I said aloud. "I get ahead of myself sometimes. And I doubt he could pay us enough anyway."

"Exactly," Callum said, and pulled the chair bases out of the window. "I'm going to take some stuff down to the bins. Coming?"

"Sure," I said, and we made such a production of leaving the room that I'm certain she would have known we'd spotted the runes if she'd been listening.

But we were too late to cover up the missing book. That horse had well and truly kicked the bucket.

CALLUM CARTED the shattered chairs with their spying runes down to the big communal bins in the alley and dumped them in, neither of us speaking. Then we retreated back upstairs, shivering in the damp draft coming through the window. Callum had pulled a couple of boxes that didn't stink too much out of the recycling bin, and he shoved those against the broken glass where the chairs had been, fixing them in place with the gaffer tape we used to stick bits of the car back on when they fell off. That done, we inspected the room for more runes.

We went over the whole place twice, swapping over and double-checking each other's areas to make sure neither of us missed anything, but there was nothing. Not that Callum could see or I could smell, anyway. We looked everywhere we thought she could possibly have touched, and more besides, but there wasn't a whiff. So maybe that was it. Just a couple of little precautionary runes, and maybe she hadn't even been listening in when it mattered. Or, who knew? Maybe she was, maybe she'd even been listening when our thief stopped by, and knew the book had been taken before we did. If her little spy runes had let her eavesdrop on the theft, maybe she'd decide to just go after the thief and never even come here.

We could be lucky, right?

Callum finished clearing the debris off the floor while I helpfully pointed out where there were still bits of broken glass and shattered mugs and crumpled paper and light tube shards that he'd missed. He grumbled a lot, but what does he expect – I'm a *cat*. I can't do his job for him.

Eventually the room looked something like it used to, even if the last fluorescent tube was flickering rather unhappily, suggesting it wasn't long for this world, and we had to open the bathroom door to help light the place. Callum covered the unfolded armchair with the torn duvet, which was less damp than the sheets, and set the undamaged pillow in place. We sat side by side on the makeshift, not-quite-flat bed, him with another tea in the handle-less mug and me with some custard in a serving spoon, since all the plates were broken.

"So. Odds are she knows we've lost the book," Callum said.

"It's pretty likely," I agreed.

"And that we were talking to Walker about giving the book to him when we did find it."

"Quite possibly."

"Should we leave town?"

"Maybe."

"Would it help?"

"Unlikely."

"Reassuring." He took a sip of tea, and was about to say more when the door blew open, sending the filing cabinet tumbling across the floor to collide with the desk. The cardboard in the window shot outward, carrying the last of the glass with it, and the neatly stacked books on the desk exploded across the room in a confetti of torn pages. Both the last fluorescent and the bare bathroom bulb shattered with a scream, plunging the room into a darkness relieved only by the light coming in from outside, and there wasn't a lot of that, given that one of the more popular local pastimes was smashing streetlights.

The kitchenette cupboards flew open again, and a second door fell off as the few remaining contents threw themselves across the room with even more enthusiasm than before. I ducked as our last pillow flew over my head, then took shelter under Callum's arm while the blanket thrashed about like a living thing. The desk and the filing cabinet did a complicated little dance, then screamed across the floor until they fetched up against the wall, and as the air filled with gyres of torn paper and devastated books someone stepped into the room, the faint light of the hallway casting their shadow long and deep ahead of them.

"Goddamn," Callum said in an aggrieved sort of voice.

"Hairballs," I said.

10

NO SUCH THING AS COINCIDENCE

Ms Jones stalked into the room. There was no perfume today, and the stink of power clung to her like a wet dog of the Baskerville variety, all dark and toothy and hairy, and with a hint of rolling in goblin poop. She'd discarded her pony set outfit in favour of skinny jeans and daisy-print Doc Martens, and a patchwork jacket that looked older than me. She looked less proper, more dangerous, and as if she had every intention of putting those boots to good use. I tucked my tail in a little closer.

"You lost it," she said to us, her voice alarmingly calm.

"Yes," Callum said, because there wasn't much point in denying it.

"This really shouldn't have been that complicated. I honestly thought you two could handle it. Get the book and keep it safe until I came to get it. That was all. Simple, really."

"But that wasn't quite all," I said, making sure my tail didn't get away on me. "I mean, it's not actually yours anymore, is it?"

"Details," she said.

"We're not thieves for hire," Callum put in, which was all very nice and *ethical* but kind of missed the point. You know, the one where a fricking sorcerer was standing in our devastated room being displeased with us. No one needs a sorcerer displeased with them. Especially not one who can make daisy-print Docs scary.

Ms Jones obviously thought he wasn't quite getting it, too, because she said, "Someone *is* a thief. More than one someone, if you count the fact my ex-husband also stole it. I want my book back. I hired you to get it. I still expect you to do so."

"We're going to be on it first thing tomorrow," I told her.

"I feel so much better," she said. "What's your lead?"

"Well, you were the one spying on our office," I said. "Did you hear anything?"

She scowled at me. "That's it? *I'm* your lead?"

"It's worth asking," I said.

She seemed to consider something (I fervently hoped it wasn't anything to do with turning me into a hamster), then shook her head. "No. I heard the door open, and a bit of movement, then it closed again. I thought you'd come back for something. What the hell were you doing leaving it unattended, anyway?"

"We do have to eat," I said, and Callum poked me. "What? We do!"

"We'll find it," he said. "Do you know what time it was when you heard them in the office?"

"Not exactly," she said, folding her arms. "Not long

after you went out, I think. I'm not doing your job for you, you know."

Callum and I looked at each other.

"Someone followed us," he offered.

"Not necessarily," I said. "You said the thing was whispering to you. Maybe someone just heard it through the door and came looking."

"Could be. Someone in the building, then."

"Although, depends how loud it is. The downstairs door doesn't lock, after all."

"So, it could be anyone, then," Jones said. "You're telling me anyone could have it. Jesus, Morrigan, and all the rest." She shook her head again. "And you came recommended."

"Who by?" I asked.

"That's not important," Callum said. "We'll sort this."

"You'd better," Jones said. "You think having your office trashed is bad? You should see what I can do when I'm actually upset."

We stared at her, and I said, "Actually, your ex beat you to it in the trashing-the-office respect. But thanks for really finishing the job."

She scowled at us, a hard figure sketched in greys and shadow in the dim room. "*Do not* give that idiot the book. No matter what he offers you. He may call himself the rightful owner, but he can't handle it. You know that, cat. Books of power take years of training before you can even touch one. A couple of weeks of YouTube tutorials isn't going to cut it."

"But if he's now the rightful owner, and he's cursed the

book so you can't take it back—" Callum started, and she waved her hand impatiently.

"You will act as my intermediary. I'll tell you how to break Walker's bond, then you hand the book straight to me, before it can bond to you. Easy."

"Our price definitely just went up," I said. "You *really* should have told us about this. We're not your little sorcery shrimp."

"Pawns," Callum said automatically.

"Which is the same as a shrimp, right?"

Jones stared at me. "Your price will be what I say it is. Or I can tell the Watch you're meddling in the affairs of Folk and humans. They don't take kindly to that sort of thing." She thought about it. "Or I'll cut out the middle-cat and just throw you into a different dimension myself. I can, you know."

I bared my teeth at her, the hair on my tail pouffing out furiously, and Callum put a hand on my back. "That won't be necessary," he said. "We'll get you the book."

"You better," she said, then turned and strode out, leaving us staring at the newly ruined ruins of our ruined office.

"I'm getting really sick of people breaking our stuff," I said.

"I'm getting really sick of having to tidy it up," Callum said, and went to wedge the door shut again.

I DID NOT SLEEP WELL. My microwave bed was beyond salvation, so we were both squeezed on the armchair-bed together, and Callum kept tossing and turning, and I could hear every shouting human in the alley outside through the broken window, and the rain coming in stank of rats and mildew. Not that I have anything against rats, as you know, but I don't need to be able to smell them all night. And cats need their sleep. Anything less than sixteen hours does not make for a happy Gobbelino.

I gave up at around four a.m. and went stalking about the room, digging through the piles of papers and muttering to myself, trying to catch a whiff of who our intruder had been. Our *thief.*

"Gobs," Callum said, and I peered over the edge of the filing cabinet at him. Even with my night eyes, I could only just see him sitting up on the little bed, his hands clutching his head like it was about to explode. "What the hell are you doing?"

"Trying to figure out who robbed us."

"Can you do it more quietly?"

"Oh, well, *excuse* me. Here I am, slaving away while you doze on all comfy-like and catch up on your beauty sleep, and do I get a thank you? No—" I was cut off by him swearing rather more loudly than was necessary and wrapping the blankets around his head as he lay back down. Fine. He'd be singing a different tune when I went to him and told him I knew how to find the book. Which I would. Somehow. There *had* to be a scent, and I was going to find it.

By six, the room was so cold I could see my own breath, and all I could smell was cold still air and old grimy dampness. I crept in next to Callum, complaining loudly until he relinquished a shred of blanket, then we both lay there shivering and pretending to sleep until we realised it wasn't going to get any warmer.

"This sucks," I told him.

"I know," he said. "Did you find anything?"

"No. All the magic flying about the place really screwed the scents up. There's nothing."

"Great." He poked his nose out of the blankets and huffed at the cold room, his breath hanging in the air like a wispy dragon. "I've got to patch that window today."

"Reckon the cafe'll be open?"

He peered at his watch. "Yeah."

"Then let's go. You can fix the window later. Right now I want bacon. And sausages. And fish."

"You're a really expensive cat, you know?"

"I'm worth it," I replied smugly, and wriggled into the warm spot he left when he ran to the bathroom to splash water on his face, pulling his coat on as he went.

THE CAFE WAS WARM, the windows damp and hazed with condensation, and it smelt of decades' worth of cooking grease and old coffee and the ghosts of toasted teacakes, all piled up like sedimentary layers of history. It was glorious. We claimed a spot as close to the radiator as we could get and sat there shivering. Callum even let me sit on his lap, and I could feel the chill of his legs through his jeans.

"Are you two alright?" the waitress with the oil burns asked, sliding a pot of tea onto the table. She was called Petra, which I thought was a nice sort of name. It sounded like she might be the descendant of some European oligarch, fallen on hard times but still walking the world with her own sense of grace. It suited her. "Looks like you had a rough night."

"You could say that," Callum said, putting both hands around the cheap metal teapot then yelping and letting it go again. "Ow."

"Yeah, watch that. Boiling water and all." She wandered off, and Callum patted the pot rather more carefully.

"Smooth," I said.

"I wasn't trying to be smooth."

"Well, you couldn't have done a worse job at it if you had been."

"Shut up. There's too many people in here for you to be chattering." His voice was barely more than a whisper, and, given the clientele at that hour, no one was going to look twice at someone talking to themselves. There was a youngish man in the window singing Christmas carols to his bacon butty, and a woman in the corner feeding crumbs to a taxidermied sparrow that she appeared to have glued to her shoulder. No one was going to be calling the police over a man talking to a cat.

"Yeah, I'm really concerned," I told him, but subsided when Petra came back with a full English for Callum and a plate of bacon and sausage for me.

"Should he be eating this?" she asked Callum. "I mean, it's not really cat food."

"He's a glutton," Callum said. "He wanted kippers as well, but I said no. They make his breath stink."

"Okay," she said, with a slightly less bright smile than

usual, and left us to it, although not without a couple of backward glances over her shoulder.

"Me talking is not an issue," I told him. "Those sorts of comments, however, are how you become the weird guy in the corner."

"I became that the day you turned up," he said, and attacked his eggs.

———

BY THE TIME WE LEFT, finally feeling rather less like death lightly chilled now our bellies were full and our limbs thawed, the sun had come out and was beating down in a most unseasonable way. It painted the grungy buildings gold and cut through the grime on the windows, and turned the exhaust from cars and vents into the sort of luminous mists poets go soppy for.

Callum lifted his face to it, eyes closed. "That's nice."

"Yeah, well. Don't get used to it," I mumbled around the sausage I was carrying. I was keeping to the sunny section of the pavement, soaking the heat into my dark fur. It felt like a bone-deep hug. "We'll probably have hail by the afternoon, knowing our luck. I'm going to nosey around. Talk to a few people. See if anyone noticed anything. You going to fix up the office?"

"Yes, sir," Callum said, touching his fingers to his forehead, and I gave him a sour look. Silly lettuce. He just grinned back and wandered off toward the bins, no doubt in search of more cardboard. Well, there wasn't much point replacing the glass – or anything else – until people stopped coming in and breaking things.

I took a different route around the building, padding down the mucky passageway with my head low and my eyes narrow in the sun. There was a grate back here that didn't fit quite flush to the ground, and it left a nice little gap for small, slick creatures to come and go as they pleased. I sat and waited, enjoying the warmth of the morning after the awful chill of the night, and presently a small nose poked out of the shadows. It snuffled a couple of times, whiskers twitching, then was joined by two bright eyes and a sleek, dark brown body, then finally a hairless tail. I tried not to look at the tail. There's something weird about a creature with a naked tail.

"The lovely Susan," I said.

"Gobbelino," she replied, cleaning her whiskers and peering around. "Nice day for it. Feels like summer."

"Climate change." I pushed the sausage over to her with one paw. I'd been pretty hungry, but there's only so much one cat can eat. Besides, bribes are handy.

She sniffed the sausage. "Not bad."

"Local cafe's finest."

"Yeah, that's not saying much, though, is it?" But she dragged the sausage to the grate and pushed it into the darkness beneath, where it would no doubt be distributed to hungry mouths.

"I'll try and be more upmarket next time."

"A little variety wouldn't hurt, too. All that fried food's bad for you."

I looked down at myself. "I'm positively svelte."

"Your arteries are probably shutting down as we speak."

"Well, as lovely as it is to come here and have my lifestyle choices *and* gifts insulted, I did want to know if you noticed anything odd last night."

"You mean other than the fights in your office? Two, if I'm not mistaken?"

I sighed. "Yeah, other than those."

She shrugged. "Nope. Guy that smelt of toothpaste went in and out a couple of times, and a woman who scared Nessie so much she hasn't left the nest since, but that's it. And I imagine you know about them – we could hear the shouting from down here."

"No one else at all? Before toothpaste guy, especially?"

"No one."

Well, that was weird. The rats saw everything, and they talked about everything. Whatever one of them saw, the others would know about within twenty minutes or so. They were the true information network, and if you wanted to know what went on in other buildings, you just had to ask. You got a lot for the price of the odd sausage, and a little respect. I never understood why some cats – and humans – were so down on rats. They were good friends to have.

"And you didn't smell anything weird?" I asked. Maybe Jones *had* been able to summon the book, and was just pretending she couldn't. Although I couldn't actually think of a single reason why she'd want to do that, or get us involved if she had done it. But, sorcerers, you know. Weirder than humans.

"Not last night," Susan said. "Well, other than the stuff in your office. What in the realms are you mixed up in, G?"

"I'm actually not entirely sure anymore," I admitted.

"You should get un-mixed up, then," she said. "There's some nasty old power rolling around. Particularly with the woman who scared Nessie."

"I know," I said. "I'm trying."

We sat there for a moment in the warm sun, Susan's whiskers ever-twitching, her eyes shifting from the tarmac of the alley to the walls to the sky, missing nothing. It was less nervousness than perfect awareness, and I admired her for it. It looked too exhausting for my taste, though. I just relied on my kitty reflexes to get me out of trouble when needed.

Then something occurred to me.

"You said not last night?"

"Yes."

"What about this morning?" That's a problem with rats. They can be very compartmentalised, and not prone to elaboration unless invited.

She looked at me with bright eyes. "Can't you feel it?"

I shifted. "Well, the sun's nice—"

"No. Come on. All these meals on tap are killing your instincts."

Well, that was just rude. I lifted my face to the sun, closing my eyes, ignoring the small secret scent of the rats and the big swelling stink of cars and heating and bins and the general, heavy press of humanity in a city, and let my whiskers tremble at the small shifts of the air.

At first there was nothing, and for a moment I thought she was just being rat-paranoid, because it wasn't like the rotting throb of the book or the muscular stench of Ms Jones, or even the pattering stink of Walker. This was something else.

This was something that wound and wove its way around the streets and alleys, that pressed into the brick of the buildings and plucked at the windows and teased the weeds that forced themselves into life in unexpected places. It was *everywhere.* It was like waking up to find that the sky was just one shade of blue different. It changes everything, but you don't even notice it until someone points it out to you. Then it's all you *can* notice, because the world is suddenly not what it should be anymore. Unfamiliar. Maybe dangerous.

Probably dangerous.

"What the hell is that?" I said.

Susan shrugged. "It's new. And I don't like it."

I didn't like it either. Not least because I don't believe in coincidences.

"Hairballs," I said.

11

POPCORN & AQUARIUMS

I left Susan eyeing up a tomato she'd found under the bin – she offered me some, but as I pointed out, I'm not a rabbit. Or a rat. Cats need meat, even if it is of the greasy spoon variety. Instead, I padded down the street toward the corner shop, my ears up and my senses stretching. I wanted to see how far this strange new scent spread.

I walked straight past the shop. I mean, yes, I was a little caught up in my own thoughts (I had just remembered the sad demise of my heatable bed), but, still. Callum and I have walked to that shop more times than I care to think since we took over the office. We're not exactly big supermarket people. We rarely have the funds for a big weekly shop, for a start, plus supermarkets tend to be weird about letting animals in. Which, you know, is ridiculous, since they herd people about like cattle and offer up multi-buys like they want everyone to be the fatted hog. And no self-respecting animal would scrap the way shoppers do over reduced-price pork pies. But, anyway. The corner shop suits us just fine. Milk, tea, some sardines for me and some toast and beans for Callum. What more could we need?

The point is, I could have sleepwalked to that shop. But I swear by the hairs on my chinny-chin-chin that my whiskers didn't even twitch as I wandered past it. It wasn't until I got to the next corner that I stopped and looked around, blinking at the golden light and realising where I was. The neon signs on the adult shop across the road fought against the sunlight, and I squinted at them. It was too far off for me to read them, but the colours seemed different. Less violent pinks, more the smooth yellow of old lamps and firesides. I turned around, looking back the way I'd come, suddenly aware that I hadn't been side-stepping discarded crisp packets and dropped coffee cups, and that I hadn't had to skirt even a single broken bottle.

The pub on the corner with the barred windows wasn't leaking its familiar stink of stale beer and vomit all over the stained pavement. Instead there was a faint whiff of the movies drifting out – popcorn and sweets and anticipation. It wasn't open yet – even around here pubs didn't open that early – but I couldn't imagine that anything short of a biblical flood and maybe a cleansing by fire could have lifted the stench of fury and despair and old, spilt fluids from that place. However. Popcorn it was.

I padded slowly back up the street toward our shop, using my eyes this time rather than just my nose. I wouldn't go so far as to call this the main road of our neighbourhood, because there's nothing like a heart to the place or anything, but it was where the newsagent with its tatty collection of magazines and extensive selection of knock-off spirits was, as well as the greengrocer that sold a few unhappy apples and a lot of phone cards, and the damp-smelling chemist and the betting shops, the adult shop and the chippy.

That sense of things having *changed*, of some new scent that I couldn't quite put my nose on, was all but dripping from the walls. It was everywhere. The green-grocer was standing outside her shop staring at the boxes of apples, which shone like they'd just been dropped by the serpent and smelt so good I even reconsidered my firm stance against fruit. She lifted a box and found a tray of grapes underneath, fat and red and glossy, and there was a tray of pomegranates next to that, as well as a box of fat purple fruit that smelt of honey.

"What the hell?" she said, and popped a grape in her mouth. I heard it crunch, saw her lips twitch into a smile. "What …" She took another grape and turned to look at her shop. Potted ferns framed the rolling doors, and the torn lino floor looked polished clean. Shiny multi-coloured peppers were stacked in pyramids next to a display of dried fruit like rough-cut jewels, and the whole place smelt of vanilla and cinnamon. "Muuuum!" she yelled, and headed for the back of the shop.

I didn't think Mum was going to be able to cast much light on things. I helped myself to a grape, just out of curiosity, and came to the conclusion that while cats are definitely not fruitarians, it wasn't the worst thing I'd ever tasted. I trotted on.

IT WAS the same all along the block. I went all the way back to our shop on the corner, and it looked like a gourmet deli in Rome or Paris, or as if that was where it wanted to be. Legs of cured ham hung from the ceiling, and the counter that yesterday had been cluttered with jars of cheap wrapped sweets had turned into a display case stuffed with fragrant cheeses and open vats of dips and marinated tomatoes and olives of varying sizes and hues. The ancient man who owned the place was standing in the middle of the shop with a cigarette in his left hand and a baguette in his right, alternating drags on the one and bites of the other. His fluffy hair was even fluffier than normal, and his glasses were askew.

I decided he looked like he might throw things, so I didn't go in. Instead, I went back past the greengrocer and stopped to look at the betting shop next door. The couple who ran it were standing outside staring at the pictures of winsome (and, take it from me, totally unrealistic) kittens in cute bows that had replaced the posters of horses thundering down the home straight.

"You think it was them across the road?" the skinny one said, jerking a thumb at their competitors (it never fails to astonish me just how many betting shops and off licenses can survive in one tiny area. It makes no sense, except that humans are creatures of habit, and they'll always have a favourite. As well as the funds for both dreams and the forgetting of them).

"I dunno," the other said. "But I like the gingery one. Look at his cute little nose!"

"Well, yeah," the first said. "It's not sending exactly the right message, though, is it?"

I padded on. The orthopaedic supports and haemor-rhoid creams in the display window of the chemist were gone, and there were fish in their place. Live fish, like an aquarium. It hadn't suddenly been transformed into a fishmonger or anything. I peered through the glass and a small porcupine fish goggled back at me, then ducked behind a bubbling pirate's chest. Further in, something large and muscular drifted over the flooded aisles, and a small school of silvery fish darted away in alarm. I wasn't quite sure how the water wasn't leaking out the door, but some things just have to be accepted. However it was working, the staff were going to have fun when they arrived.

I loped across a side street to check the next block along. Here, the strange, not-bad-but-not-*right* scent was fainter. There was a crop of buttercups growing in a drain, but they looked diffident and out of place, arriving too soon for the party. There were three empty cans of extra-strong lager rolling in the doorway of the shop that sold second-hand electronics, and a one-footed pigeon pecking at cigarette butts. Ugly, yes. But also *normal*. Real life had reasserted itself.

I veered across the main road, spitting at a cyclist who shouted at me and watching him wobble dangerously for a moment until he recovered and peddled on. Honestly, humans. Two legs are unstable enough. Two wheels is just being silly. He righted himself just as he reached our block, the one with kittens in the betting shop and the underwater world in the chemist, and I squinted after him. There are times when having cats' eyes is awesome – at night or in low light there's not much that can touch us – but other times it pretty much sucks.

Like now. I thought – *thought* – that there was a *ripple*, a shift in the air as Mr Cyclist moved into our block. It wasn't anything really noticeable, and I certainly hadn't seen or felt anything when I'd crossed the street, but it was enough that it drew your attention to the fact that our block was *brighter*. Cleaner. The sun was stronger. The buildings looked less grimy. There wasn't a clear-cut line, like light and shade, which was why it was hard to tell unless you were watching someone pass through it. But once you saw it, you couldn't unsee it. Just like the odd, new scent.

I kept going.

IT WAS JUST OUR BLOCK. I circled the whole thing twice, and our building was at the epicentre of it, the weird changes and improvements washing away from it like the vibrations of an earthquake, fading the further they went. Our greasy cafe was just outside its influence, I was pleased to note, and Petra was leaning against the wall outside, drinking a large mug of tea and staring at a tree on our side of the road with a puzzled look on her face. I didn't blame her. The tree was covered in the sort of pink wash of blossoms you normally only see in photos of Japanese springtime, and it was almost November in Yorkshire. She looked at me as I padded past, and said, "Hey, kitty."

I stopped and looked at her.

"Where's your human?"

Well, she knew how things worked, anyway. I wandered over to her and let her scritch my ears. She smelt of toast and bacon and warmth.

"Something weird's going on, isn't it?"

I looked up at her and gave my best aren't-I-cute mewl.

She sighed. "Fine. Don't tell me, then. Cats." She straightened up, giving the tree a last dubious glance before she went back inside. There was a chorus of birds singing in the tree like extras in a princess cartoon, and I glared at them. Cats indeed. We needed to get this figured out before the Watch came sniffing around. If they got a whiff of magical doings and started looking into it properly it wouldn't be long before it all came back on us. And then the dentist with bad teeth and the sorcerer with a bad temper were going to be the least of our problems.

The Watch are what you might call meticulous. And they don't believe that dying cleans the slate. The crimes of one life are carried with you for all nine, which is really pretty draconian. Just like their punishments.

Gods-dammit. What had happened to a nice "who's cheating on who" case? Was it really so much to ask?

I'D PROBABLY HAVE WALKED past our building just as I'd walked past the corner shop earlier if I hadn't become attuned to the weird changes around the place. As it was, I stood on the pavement just staring for a few moments before I ventured up the stairs. I mean, we only left for breakfast a couple of hours ago, right? Less than that, probably. And the door had been hanging ajar and broken, with a poster for a comedy club and some rather suggestive phone numbers slapped on it, while the two steps up to it had been chipped and stained and the whole area had reeked of dumped rubbish and human urine. I mean, seriously. You complain about cats marking their territory. We don't *pee* on things.

Anyhow. The door was now whole, bright red, and had a real, honest-to-the-gods brass knocker in the shape of a lion's head in the middle of it. How the hell that was supposed to work when there were like twenty-something apartments inside, I don't know. There were stained glass panels in an arch above it, and two fancy lanterns hanging from brackets on the wall. Curvy shrubs perched in stone planters (without a single cigarette butt in them) on the steps, and the whole place smelt of furniture polish and ice cream. It was gorgeous. And, honestly? I didn't want to go in.

You see, in my experience there are two possibilities when something's just screaming out, *come in, come in!* One is that it's a trap, and the other is that it's not talking to you. And considering the fact that the doormat was made of that rough hessian that is just *perfect* for sharpening claws, I was pretty certain it was a trap in some form or another.

Maybe the book hadn't actually gone anywhere. Books of power can get a little … idiosyncratic. Sentient might be pushing it, but it also might be almost accurate. Maybe the thing had concealed itself, deciding it didn't want anything more to do with Walker, who, it had to be admitted, was aiming pretty low in his goals. Maybe it was under the floorboards of our apartment, quietly reworking our world into something we'd never want to walk away from, whispering to Callum about how perfect things could be. How everything could be quiet and calm, how he could read his books and sit in stillness, how he could sleep without nightmares and not check over his shoulder when the night drew in.

Above all, it would whisper of how the voices in his head could be silenced. Whispering and whispering until he couldn't resist it, or couldn't stand listening to it anymore. Whispering until he put his hands on it and held it close and was swallowed by it. And Callum might be a great lump of a human, and be annoyingly *ethical*, but he did have that magic in him. That quiet, deep magic that peopled his dreams and gave the world different lights, old magic leftover from old times, passed down to him in his blood. Most humans have a touch, but he had far more than most, even if he wasn't aware of it. He would never have been so easy with me, would never have been able to save me from the beast that chased me out of the Inbetween, if he didn't have it. And books of power *love* that. It gives them a foothold in the soul.

I'd left him alone far too long. Maybe it was *him*. Maybe he was even now sitting cross-legged on the floor of the apartment, cradling the book and smoothing its greasy pages while change washed over the world and he remade it into some weird cotton-candy reality. Next thing we knew there'd be communal gardens and open-air libraries on every intersection and firemen would be saving kittens in the trees, and young men would be helping old ladies across the road rather than being beaten up by them for looking a little too interested in their shopping bags.

Hey, old ladies living in our neighbourhood are not to be messed with.

I glared at the shiny new door, the fur on my spine standing to attention, and growled at the back of my throat. There was nothing for it. I had to go in.

I stalked up to the door, then stared at it. There was no handle, just that ridiculous knocker. Helpful. I pawed at the wood hopefully, but it just remained red, closed, and obstinate.

"Great," I growled. "That's a real improvement right there, isn't it?"

The door didn't reply, so I spat at it and slipped back down the stairs. There was an unhealthy – well, *previously* unhealthy-looking tree on the pavement under our window, the scabby dirt around it usually littered with dog poo and beer cans, which probably explained its ill health. Now, however, it was surrounded by wildflowers and the roaring hum of happy little bees. I snarled at them and flung myself at the trunk, running straight up from branch to branch with my ears back and my eyes wide, peering out through the tree's unexpectedly dense leaves at the wall of the building. Truthfully, I was grateful for the sudden health of everything, as a few hours ago I'm pretty sure the whole lot would have shattered under even my elegant weight before I got halfway up. As it was, the branches dipped and swayed with graceful strength, and before things got too hairy I was almost level with our window.

I shuffled out as far as I dared, clinging to as many fragile branches – hell, twigs – as I could at the same time, everything bouncing and shifting under me and shedding leaves like a green snowstorm. Then, with a quick prayer that the gods of gravity were looking the other way, I flung myself at the wall. I screeched down it briefly with all my claws bared, hooked next door's windowsill, scrambled up, scooted along it and flung myself from there to our window, where I pressed myself against the glass and mewled pitifully.

Wait.

The glass?

12

OLD-FASHIONED DETECTIVE WORK

CALLUM SLID THE WINDOW UP – IT RAN SMOOTHLY, without squalling or jamming or spitting chipped paint everywhere, which was just *weird* – letting out a flood of warm air and a whiff of cookies.

"Hey," he said. "What're you doing out there?"

I glared at him. "I couldn't get in downstairs, thanks to the new door, so I had to climb."

"New door, huh? That wasn't there when I came in." But he didn't sound surprised. I suppose you don't, when you've come up to fix the window with cardboard and found it not only looks like it's never been so much as cracked, it's now double-glazed.

I eyed him suspiciously, but he didn't seem to be hiding the book under his T-shirt, or to have been interrupted in the middle of remaking the world in some rose-tinted image. "What've you been up to, then?"

"Um. Waiting for you?" He sounded slightly shifty, and I peered past him into the room.

When I'd last seen it, it had been covered in torn books

and broken furniture and dismantled files, thanks to Ms Jones finishing the job her ex had started. Now it was immaculate. But not just that …

I jumped to the floor, the wooden floorboards slick and polished under my paws where there had been chipped, shabby laminate this morning. There was a thick, deep red rug in front of the heavy wooden desk that was similar to our original only in the fact that you called them both desks. This one looked like even magic couldn't flip it over, and it had a deep shine that suggested it probably cost more than a new car. And that was without the flashy computer on top of it that Callum had apparently been playing games on. I arched my whiskers at him, and he shrugged.

"I was waiting for you. What was I going to do, not touch any of it?"

"You didn't do this?" I rounded the desk, sniffing for magic, but there was only that same scent that seemed to be underpinning the whole day, twining its way through all the changes. No stronger, no different. Just a low-level wrongness, a tickle at the back of the mind.

"No. How could I—" He broke off, and glared at me. "Jesus Christ, Gobs, no. Of course I didn't take the book. How could I? You were with me the whole time until it vanished!"

I investigated the big leather desk chair he'd been sitting in, which looked quite comfy for a snooze and smelt of posh men's clubs. Two smaller but no less appealing chairs faced it across the desk. "Magic tends to find a way. And I was thinking about it. It might be looking for someone else. Books of power can be sneaky.

It could have *wanted* to be found by someone other than Walker, someone it could use more. Someone with deeper reserves of magic, who it wouldn't hollow out in a heartbeat."

"Well, it wasn't me." He sat down in the big chair and picked up a mug of tea. "And what do you mean, someone it could use more?"

"Books of power can get kind of … wilful. It'd explain why Walker was able to steal it from Jones when he's obviously a hack. It *wanted* to be stolen. Jones probably had it on a short leash, barely using its power. A book that old gets greedy, hungry. It wants to be used, because the more the owner uses it, the more the owner *wants*, the more it grows. Hey, *nice!*" I'd just discovered that the wooden flooring had heating under it, making my paws toasty as I padded to another big rug set in front of a sofa and an armchair, both facing a small fireplace with a TV mounted over it. I jumped onto the sofa and stared at a set of cupboards on the wall behind it. "Wait …"

"It grew," Callum said. "The apartment's almost twice the size it was. As far as I can tell, there's a queen-sized bed that folds out of those cupboards. There's a power shower in the bathroom, *and* a corner tub with jacuzzi jets." He raised his mug. "And there's a tea pot and loose-leaf tea."

"It was like this when you got back?"

"Sort of. I think things keep changing when my back's turned. Like the desk was here, but the sofa wasn't. I went into the bathroom, and when I came back it had appeared."

I jumped back to the floor, savouring the heavy pile of

the rug and working my claws into it. "You're sure you didn't touch the book? Even by accident? I mean, this is like, *nice*." I was sure there was a better word for it, but *nice* kind of wrapped it all up.

"Sure," he said, and I believed him. It's not the sort of thing he'd lie about. In fact, Callum didn't lie about much. Ethics again.

"It's still here somewhere," I said. "It has to be. This … home improvement thing is spreading, but the centre is here."

"It's outside too?" he asked.

"Take a look out the window," I said. He did, leaning out into the weirdly warm air and peering up and down the alley.

"Our car's still there," he said after a moment. "I can just see it. But there's a pancake shop where that dodgy chop-shop garage was, and I think I just saw a red squirrel in the tree."

"Damn," I said. "Maybe we'll get a new car later, if it spreads some more. Or we should move it closer."

He pushed himself back into the room and slid the window shut. "This isn't right, G. Something's gone really screwy."

"I know," I said. "But can't we just enjoy it for five minutes? I mean, look at this rug. Look!" I flopped to my belly and wriggled over onto my back, stretching. "It's *glorious*."

Callum laughed, but he had that serious look on too. Well, fine for him. *He'd* been in here enjoying it while I was out gathering information. That hardly seemed fair.

"This can't be right, though, can it? I mean, there's got to be a cost to this."

"Yeah," I said, still on my back. "It'll cost whoever's doing it."

"We need to find them, then," he said. "This is a lot of magic. It's going to mess them up, right?"

I sighed, and rolled back onto my front. "Right. So I suppose we just wander around asking who's trying to make the world a better place, then tell them they can't?"

"I suppose so," he said, and he sounded almost as disappointed as I felt.

Now, the thing to remember about magic, as I mentioned before, is that there are rules. It doesn't come out of nothing. The book would be quietly devouring whoever was using it, especially as they probably didn't even realise what was going on and so had no way to guard against it or control it. Probably they'd heard the book calling out to them, same as Callum had, and all they'd thought was how pretty it was and how much they wanted to protect it. And then it had got to prodding them, finding out their heart's desires, because that's how magical objects work – they use your desires against you. You can have *this*, and all you have to do is bleed a little here, or lose a little of yourself there, or sacrifice a goat or your firstborn or whatever.

Each gift gets a little bigger, and the payment gets bigger still, until the magic has consumed you, and then it starts calling out to someone else. It doesn't necessarily happen straight away, especially if the user isn't really doing much controlling of things, which was probably the case here, given the shopfront aquariums and restocked greengrocers. Control – *resistance* – costs a lot more than just riding the wave of the book as it siphons magic from wherever it finds it. It'll still catch up with you, because everyone's magic is finite, but it'll take longer.

The exception is people who know how to counter the book and protect themselves, both guarding and tapping into their own magic, because we've all got a bit. Cats more than humans, of course, but even that grumpy old man who shouts at the kids on their bikes and the dogs on the street and everyone else he comes across is a little bit magic. He doesn't know it, though, and that sense of something being lost that he never knew he had is at least part of what makes him so grumpy. If you know how to tap into your own magic you can use it both to protect yourself and to wield magical objects. It's risky, though. You have to know what you're doing, else while you think you're in control, your magic object will be turning your own power against you. Sorcerers – the old ones, like Jones – have traded their humanity for magic for so long they're basically nothing *but* magic. But even for them, books of power can be a challenge. It can pull more and more from them, until the balance shifts.

Long story short – the book likely had hold of someone who didn't know how to control it, because a) there aren't many people who do; and b) no one with an ounce of magical control was going to try and turn the world into a picture book. The cost of even changing a few streets would be astronomical, and if they were doing it consciously it wouldn't have surprised me if they weren't much more than a hollowed-out shell already. But it was likely it was all rising from their subconscious, spilling over from a desire to just have a nicer front room or whatever. And we had to try to help them, as it was *kind* of our fault, plus either Walker or Jones were going to skin us if we didn't get hold of the damn thing.

So we started off as all good detectives do – going door to door. Which, by the way, is mind-numbing, but it wasn't like Callum could do it on his own. With his puny human nose he'd never sniff out the book.

We started next door, with the old guy who always looked like he hadn't bought any new clothes in about eighty years, and had slept in them in the meantime. He opened the door a crack and peered at us, letting out a whiff of pipe tobacco and roast dinners. Which was a change from the usual dirty laundry smell.

"Yes?" he said.

"We're from next door," Callum started.

"I'm not buying anything," he said, and I tried to sneak through the gap in the door, but he pushed it almost closed. "Keep your monster out! He'll kill my birds!"

"Sorry, he's just nosey," Callum said, and I sat back, glaring at the old man with my tail whipping. Now he'd mentioned it, I could smell birdseed and hear musical squawks from behind him. "We just wondered – have you noticed anything unusual today, by any chance?"

The old man squeezed the door closed until we could just see one eye and a ferociously bushy eyebrow. "No. Go away."

I looked at his purple velvet slippers and the sharp

crease in his cream and navy pinstripe pyjama bottoms. He was standing on carpet so thick it came halfway to his bony ankles, and he had a silk dressing gown on over his outfit. Things were obviously going well, but that didn't mean the book was there. I mean, look at our apartment. And I couldn't smell anything strange. I wandered off down the hall, and Callum looked at me, then nodded at the bird-man and said, "Alright. Sorry to disturb you."

We didn't have any more luck at the other doors on our floor, either. One, the guy threw open and just about dragged Callum in, revealing a cavernous room that should have taken up the space of about three good-sized apartments, all polished wood floors and swings hanging from two-story rafters, and a lot of activity going on involving said swings, trampolines, people in elaborate costumes, and others in not many clothes at all.

Callum stared about in astonishment while I sniffed around and had my ears scritched by at least four naked people, then he politely declined an invitation to take his coat (or more) off and we left. Further on, at the door belonging to Boiled Cabbage Lady, I could see nothing but pink velvet cushions, sparkly angel figurines, satin upholstery, and white Persian cats in smoking jackets and lace, all of whom stared at me in mute hostility. Purebreds, man. How can anyone look so sniffy when someone's sticking doll's clothes on them? Anyhow, there was definitely no book in there. No cat in the world would be sitting around with bows in their hair while that was in the room. Not even Persians.

Mrs Smith was out, which was disappointing. Things being as they were, I'd been anticipating some filet mignon or something. I wasn't quite sure what filet mignon was, but it sounded like the sort of thing posh cats eat, and it seemed a shame to pass up the opportunity to try it. Or maybe lobster. Lobster would be good.

We tried upstairs instead, where Woo-Woo doctor gave me a vegan cat treat that I promptly *hurk*-ed all over her bamboo flooring, and we had to listen to tinkly chime music while she splashed us with essential oils to clear our auras. I actually have no idea if anything had changed in her room. It looked the size it should have and she was wearing the same floaty white trousers and shirt she always did. Maybe there was something to be said for all the woo, if her ideal version of the world was no different to her usual one.

All in all, it was a wash. Not everyone answered the doors, but I sniffed around the door frames where I could, and there was no stink of old magic. There was nice lighting in the halls, and the carpets were clean and smelt of sunshine, and no one had peed in the stairwells. But no book, although it had to be here. It *had* to, the way all that magic was washing out everywhere.

"I think it was Woo-Woo doctor," I told Callum, as we let ourselves back into our apartment. We'd acquired a big coffee table in front of the sofa while we'd been out, and the space to fit it in.

"I thought you didn't smell anything," he said.

"Yeah, but all those oils and rubbish could have thrown me off. And she's all peace and light. All *nice*. It fits."

"*Hmm*." Callum opened the fridge, which had grown into a big stainless thing with a water tap on the outside. "You want some fresh mackerel? There's some in here."

"If you cook it first. I'm not a savage."

He shrugged, and found a frying pan in a cupboard. "Sushi's good for you."

"I think you mean sashimi, and no. You eat raw fish if you want. I want some butter on mine."

He set the pan on the four-burner gas stove to heat, and we both stared at it. It had been a one-ring hotplate that morning, lying on the floor with its control popped off. It was disturbingly easy to get used to this new and improved life. Coming home for lunch and actually having something to cook. Not shivering in the draught from the single-pane window. All the lights working. The fridge not wheezing in the corner while it produced pretty much exactly half the coolness the draught did.

"We need to fix this," I said, as firmly as I could.

Callum nodded, unwrapping the fish. It smelt firm and salty, fresh enough you almost worried it was going to make a break for it. "It can't go on," he said, rather unconvincingly, and took an avocado and a fat tomato out of the fridge. There was a bread bin on the counter and he opened the top, fishing out a loaf that looked appetising even to me.

"We'll investigate after lunch," I said, licking my chops as the smell of frying fish drifted to me.

"Can't work on an empty stomach," Callum agreed, tearing an end off the bread.

There was a scratch at the door. We looked at each other, puzzled, and I wondered if one of those Persians had been less put off by a bit of street cat than they'd acted. I sauntered behind Callum as he opened the door, angling myself so the scar on my shoulder showed, and displaying my tail to its best advantage. I have a *great* tail, despite the current bald patch.

Then I leaped back with a yelp and shot for the window as a calico cat with mismatched eyes met my gaze, her white paws pressed neatly together in front of her.

"Shut the door!" I yowled. "Shut it, shut it!"

Callum was already doing it, but calico was too fast. She was on her feet and through the gap even as he slammed it, barely saving her tail and giving him a glare that made him take a step back. I leaped onto the windowsill, pressing my back to the glass, and yelled, "You'll never take me alive!"

She sauntered across the room, those cool eyes never leaving me and her tail twitching slightly as she came.

"*Callum!*" I wailed.

"Um. Okay." He took a step toward the intruder, and she stopped dead, looking up at him.

"*Excuse* me," she said, her voice a velvet rasp. "You weren't going to *touch* me, were you?"

"Um," he said again.

"Good." She swung her gaze back to me. "The Watch, Gobbelino. We wait, and we hold."

BIG OLD MAGIC

LET'S JUST GET THIS STRAIGHT, OKAY? I *DID NOT* FAINT. I kind of slipped, because I was right on the edge of the windowsill, and the damn Watch cat was right in front of me, and Callum wasn't doing anything except standing there looking gormless, and okay, I knew she couldn't grab me and shift out of there, because I had shift-blocking runes all over the building for just that sort of eventuality, but *she was there*, which meant the Watch was onto us. So I lost concentration and slipped. And maybe I even bumped my head on the window. And my head was still tender from the peace lily attack, so, you know. It's possible, okay?

Okay.

Anyway. I splatted ungracefully to the floor but scrambled up again almost immediately. Calico was just sitting there looking like she was about to start laughing any moment, and Callum looked like he might either laugh or hit the cat upside the head with the fancy vase that had appeared on the coffee table, but hadn't decided which yet.

"Alright, Gobbelino?" the cat asked.

"Not very," I snapped. "What're you doing here? I paid. You took my life, remember? I know the record stays, but I *paid*."

She tipped her head just slightly, as if looking up at a memory. "Before my time on the Watch. I did hear about it, though. Harsh justice. Too much so, one might say."

Well, I wasn't going to be sucked in by that sort of fake camaraderie. I shook myself out, trying to get my fur to lie flat. "Yeah. It was harsh. And it's done."

"I'm not here about that," she said, then sniffed. "Is something burning?"

"Aw, bollocks—" Callum ran into the kitchenette – although I suppose we could call it a kitchen now, as there was actually counter space and a wooden island on wheels with a couple of bar stools that had popped up from somewhere, as well as an actual oven and the fridge – and grabbed the pan off the stove. "It's okay," he called. "Blackened mackerel, you could call it."

"How fancy," the strange cat said.

"You want some?" Callum asked her, and I gave him a glare that I hope said in no uncertain terms that I was vomiting my next hairball into his coat pockets.

"If it's going," she said, and ambled across to the desk, jumping on top of it and surveying the room. "Nice place."

"It's not bad," I said.

She favoured me with a thoughtful look. "Bit unusual around here."

Feeling somewhat at a height disadvantage, I jumped

onto the desk as well, keeping a decent distance between us. "Well, yeah. Improvements have been made."

Callum put a plate in front of each of us, and we looked at our fish, then I said, "Wait, *she* gets the head?"

"She's a guest," he said, coming back with his own plate laden with a rough sandwich. "Anyway, is the head really better? Eyes and stuff? Ugh."

"You can have the head if you want," our guest said. "I'm not fussed."

"No, it's *fine*." I prodded the bony tail with one paw. "You didn't just pop by for a lunch date, anyway."

"No," she agreed, and looked at Callum, settled into the big desk chair with a mouthful of sandwich, then back at me. "You really should be more discreet, Gobbelino. The Watch has changed over the past five years, but there are still those who'd sanction you severely for consorting with a human, and—"

"Whoa," Callum said around some avocado. "*Consorting?*"

"She just means hanging out with," I said. Watch cats. So pompous.

The cat huffed laughter and took a bite of mackerel. "*Mmm.* Blackened," she said, and arched her whiskers at me.

I swallowed my own laugh, and said, "So you're going to come in here and insult my human's cooking, now?" I mean, what did I have to lose, right? No point pussy-footing around her.

She snorted, and licked a scale off her chops. "Hope you didn't adopt him for his cooking skills."

"I'm sitting right here," Callum said. "And you can have

it raw if you want, but fussy here reckons that's only for savages."

"No, I always liked the taste of charcoal," she said, and took another bite while I pretended I was choking on a bone rather than laughing.

Okay, so she wasn't terrifying. She was, in fact, sort of okay. But she was Watch, and they *were* terrifying. And I couldn't eat with her crouched there next to me like her buddies hadn't just thrown me to the beasts of the Inbetween way back when. "So what d'you want?" I asked.

She regarded me with those odd-coloured eyes, one pale blue and the other pale green, both luminous and far, far too perceptive. She was mostly white, patched with tabby and ginger like they'd run out of the original material, and she smelt of Watch. Smelt of the depthless void of the Inbetween, and the dusty magic of safe houses and Watch bases and old, old secrets, never to be told.

"I'm not here as an enemy," she said. "Or even as Watch, exactly. I told you, things have changed. The Watch leader has changed. And sometimes things don't have to happen in an official capacity."

"So you're not about to drag me out of here for consorting with a human?"

She glanced at Callum, who frowned and said, "I really don't like that phrasing."

She snorted again. "Apologies. And no, I don't care. Consort away. There are worse things than having a few humans who know there's more to the world than just the stuff they care about. That they have to share with other kinds. I think we could do with more humans knowing that, to be honest."

"So …?" I asked, still not quite trusting her. I mean, she was *here*. That was bad to start with.

"So this whole place has exploded with magic, and here you two sit in the middle of it." She glanced at Callum. "You don't seem like a magician."

"I know a couple of card tricks," he said.

"He doesn't," I said. "He always gets them wrong."

"Just because I don't practise enough. I'm pretty good with coins, though."

"Middling," I said.

She shook her head. "That's not magic. You said it – tricks. This, what's happening here, is magic. This is big old magic that's going to get noticed. Some of it has already been noticed, in fact, but I happened to be in the area so said I'd deal with it."

"Said to who?" I asked.

"The Watch members who'd be charging in here looking for a culprit if I hadn't come instead. Who *will* be looking for a culprit if you don't get this tidied up *toute de suite*."

She pronounced the words with a proper accent, not a boring *toot sweet* like most people did, and I have to say – for a Watch cat, she was more than okay. She was kind of awesome.

"How do you even know that what's going on has anything to do with us?" Callum asked. "I mean, there's a whole building worth of people here."

"None of them are private investigators of both Folk and human business," the cat said, and this time I actually did choke on a bone.

There was much hacking and coughing, and I played it

up for a bit because, Old Ones take them, as awesome as our visitor appeared to be, that meant the Watch *knew*. They *knew* about us, about me, and how the hell I wasn't already strung up with my toes in the Inbetween I didn't know.

Callum put a glass of water in front of me – no, I don't use a *bowl*, come on – then said, "Look, um … what's your name?"

"Claudia," she said. "May your coat be warm and your hair shed pleasantly."

"Um. Yes. Thank you?" He considered it for a moment, then added, "Pleased to meet you. Look, Claudia, before Gobs has a heart attack—"

"Gobs?" she said, arching her whiskers. Great.

"Gobbelino. Before Gobbelino has a heart attack, can you please just tell us what you're doing here? You said something about it not being in an official capacity?"

"It's not," she said, and looked from one of us to the other. "Call it advance warning, though. The Watch is calmer these days, less militant. The new leader saw too many cases like yours, and is more interested in coexistence than wiping out any instance of contact between Folk and humans. She doesn't want the Watch to be feared. She wants it to help Folk live better, not create more rifts. And, like I said – it's not the worst thing for there to be some contact between kinds. Shake humans out of their myopia a bit, maybe. She shares that view."

"It's a novel approach," I said, and she gave me an amused look.

"Don't think everyone feels that way. A lot of cats would prefer to be just as hard-line as we used to be.

Hence some things going through rather less official channels. A few of us have a certain leeway to keep things quiet, to deal with disturbances without making a fuss if there's nothing malicious about them. But in some cases we can only be so lenient. For instance, when whole city blocks are being transformed. That's not exactly keeping a low profile."

"Really not our fault," I said. "We were hired under false pretences."

Claudia nodded. "I didn't imagine it was deliberate. Sorry, Gobs, but it's pretty clear you're not exactly a great magician yourself."

"Gobbelino," I said, and bared my teeth at Callum, who ignored me. "And I could be if I wanted. You know, if I trained up."

She just looked at me.

"Okay, so I'm not. But we know what's causing it."

"Then fix it," she said, getting up. "Thanks for the lunch. Just be aware this is attracting attention. I'll hold off any further investigation for a day. I can't do any longer – whatever this is, like I say, it's big magic. Things'll start getting wonky, and the last thing we need is a bloody great reality gap in the middle of Leeds." She jumped to the windowsill, then looked at Callum and said, "Be a good human and open it, yes?"

"Sorry, sure." He almost dropped his plate he got up so fast, then hurried to the window and opened it for her.

"Cheers," she said, and leaped out, her body long and luminous in the sun in the moment before it vanished, winking out of existence in mid-air as she stepped smoothly into the Inbetween and through to wherever she went after that, leaving the air empty again and the room silent. Callum stared at the tree for a breath, then shut the window and sat back down, picking his plate up.

"There seem to be fairies in the tree," he told me.

"Can't be," I said. "They're too big for trees. And you said faeries with an e, right?"

"Why?"

"They know if you say it wrong. Always say it with an e. Stroppy eggs, faeries."

Callum took a bite of sandwich. "Alright. So what would be small, blue, and sunbathing on the leaves?"

"Imps," I said. "Don't feed them. You'll never get rid of them."

"Alright," he said again, and went to put the kettle on.

I'D LOST MY APPETITE. I poked the fish with a paw moodily, then gave up and jumped off the desk, stalking a rough circuit of our new, bigger apartment. The Watch were onto me. Well, Claudia was onto me, in her *unofficial channels*, but I wasn't silly enough to think she was the only one. And new and improved Watch or not, that was still a little too close for comfort to a bunch of self-righteous felines dragging me off for a trial that was all show and no justice at all.

Although, *technically* I had been guilty. But, you know. I was young. Only on my second life. And technically we're all guilty of something, right? Cats should really buy into second chances more. Or fourth and fifth.

"Callum," I started, as he came back into the room with

a biscuit tin and another cup of tea. The man probably had more tea in his bloodstream than plaster. Parasols. Platypus? Blood stuff, anyway.

"Look," he said. "The biscuits are so posh they come in a tin."

"That's great, but—"

"And the tea has little flowers in it."

I glared at him, and he shrugged. "What? We've got a day of it left, at most. We may as well enjoy it while we can."

"Yeah, well, I'd like to continue to enjoy my hide while I can." I'd made my mind up. There was no point messing around, not with the Watch and scatty characters like Walker and Jones involved. Although, to be fair, Jones was more terrifying than scatty. But the whole situation was getting out of hand. "We need to head out. Be nice if the car was upgraded, but if not let's just get as far as we can before it dies on us."

Callum sipped tea and examined his posh biscuit. "To where, G?"

"Anywhere. Spain. Majorca, maybe. Somewhere with nice weather."

"We don't speak Spanish."

"We'll learn."

Callum dunked his biscuit and said, "And when they catch up again? The Watch, or Ms Jones, or even Walker?"

"We'll keep a lower profile this time. Only regular human cases. We stay well clear of Folk. They won't even get a whiff of us."

He looked at me for a long, thin moment, then said, "I know you had a bad time with the Watch before—"

"They killed me."

"I know, I know. But mightn't this be a good opportunity to clear the slate? To be done with worrying about them all the time? Claudia seemed to indicate that things were changing. If we get this situation with the book sorted, maybe it'll actually get you in good with them."

"It won't. And it won't clear the slate, not with everyone. She said it herself, not everyone agrees with this new chippy hippy leader. And now they know where we are and what we're doing." I looked around the apartment. "Pack up. We need to go."

"We're going to have Walker, Jones, *and* the Watch after us by this time tomorrow, if not before."

"Well, good luck to them," I spat. "We'll just have to move faster than they do."

Callum put his mug down and folded his fingers together on the desk, for all the world like a professor about to lecture me on ethics and morality or some such pointless rubbish. "You can't keep running away, G."

"I can and I will. You weren't there, Callum. What you saved me from in this life, when I was a kitten – that was bad. I would've been done for if you hadn't come along. I owe you that. But, before then … in my life before, when I died last time, I was in there with them. With the beasts, like that one you saw. In the dark, in the Inbetween. And it's not just dark. It's … it's more than that. It's so dark it hurts, like your very sight's been hollowed out and crushed, and you can't even remember what sight *was*. And it's hungry, and it fills every broken part of you, parts you didn't even know were broken, and uses them to shatter the rest, and floods your soul until you think you're drowning, and it's full of monsters. And they're not cute picture book monsters. They're big and starving and faster than thought, and they eat your fear as well as your soul, but they send you insane with the agony of it first."

I was struggling to breathe, the fancy new apartment suddenly too small, the air too thin, too full of unfamiliar scents. My paws ached, and when I looked down I saw my claws digging into the rich grain of our new floorboards. "That's where the cats of the Watch put me, Callum. They carried me in there and passed me from one of them to the other, so they could keep leaving and were barely in there at all, so the beasts never caught their scent, but I was *always* there, and they did it until the monsters had torn me to shreds, and had my scent so strongly that they'll be on me in an instant if I ever go back, and then they'll do it all again." I swallowed hard, the burned fish tasting bitter and poisonous at the back of my throat. "So forgive me if I don't trust even the charming Claudia. I don't want to take that chance."

Callum stared down at his tea and the tiny flowers floating on the milky surface, and for a few breaths the apartment was silent, the sun painting gold across the heavy grain of the desk. Then he looked up and said, "D'you want to bring the rest of that mackerel? And I think there's some shrimp, too."

"I'm fine with sardines, to be honest," I said.

"Well, they're easier to pack," he replied, and got up to start opening cupboards.

14

HIT THE ROAD, PAT

So you probably think I'm a coward, and a complete mercenary, running as soon as the Watch are so much as mentioned. And I'm not going to argue. You'd be a coward too, if you'd been there in the dark with me.

It's silent, you know, not just an absence of sound, but a silence so vast it's like there can never be another noise in the whole world, in the whole *universe,* and you can yowl your head off and there's not even a whisper. You could drown in that silence, be swallowed and suffocated by it.

But *they* make a noise. Their teeth. The passage of them through the dark, through the void that's not as empty as you wish it was.

Yeah, they make a noise. Not in your ears. I think it's somewhere in the primal part of you, that part that never stops screaming again, no matter how many lives you get. I'll still hear that noise and still be screaming in my bones when I'm ending life nine.

It's bloody hard to get your sixteen hours sleep after that.

So you can call me a coward. I'll take that. And, I mean, I've been called a lot worse. You should try being cursed out by dryads. Now, *they* can turn an insult.

And the bit about being a mercenary? Not even worth arguing. Not only is it an excellent attribute in a PI, I'm a cat. You know how it works. Give me a few biscuits and a scratch under the chin and I'll give you at least a few head-bumps. Well, until the biscuits run out. You have to earn anything more than that.

But I was glad Callum was coming. I mean, I could still have gone, could have jumped a truck or a bus – there's always somewhere to hide – but it's a whole lot more comfy to ride in the front seat and get to have a say on what music gets played. And less scrounging in bins and fighting over scraps with unfamiliar toms involved. I wasn't even sure how to swear in Spanish yet, which was going to put me at a serious disadvantage.

It took us about ten minutes to be ready to flee the country, which still felt like forever. Callum has a passport because I made him get one pretty early on, when it became clear he might be my ticket out. I got one at the same time, although the whole business of having a microchip injected in me almost put me off. *It doesn't hurt them*, the vet had said confidently, while shoving something the size of a LEGO brick into my shoulder, *sans* anaesthetic. It took all my self-control not to jump him and shove one into his silly neck, see how he liked it, but this was what one dealt with when one couldn't shift.

Passports and microchips. More things the Watch is to blame for.

Anyhow, have passport, will travel. Always have an escape plan. Callum packed our papers, the remains of Ms Jones' deposit, some fancy tea, his posh biscuits, and some extra clothes in a backpack. All of this was accompanied by him complaining that the apartment had terrible taste in clothing, and that he couldn't find any of his own stuff, and that all there was in the cupboards were skinny jeans that barely reached his ankles and body hugging, V-neck shirts that made him want to suck his tummy in (and which made him look like a scruffy, overgrown ten-year-old, all gangly limbs and knobbly elbows). The problems of not having fur. But eventually he grabbed his coat and switched off the computer, and then we were gone. Hit the road, Pat.

We clattered down the stairs and headed out the new front door, looking about warily as we went. I couldn't see any cats lurking in the shadows, but there was a shiny red postbox on the pavement that declared it was cleared four times a day, and a wooden cart full of fruit and vegetables all nestled in straw sitting on the road out front with an honesty box perched amid the courgettes. Neither of them could have been there long, considering the postbox was un-graffitied and the honesty box was still there.

Callum stared at it, and said, "Is this really so bad?"

"It is for whoever's doing it."

"This shouldn't be bad," he said, almost to himself. "It's making everything *nice.*"

"Nice has a price," I said, and looked at him expectantly, but he ignored my excellent rhyming skills.

"What if there wasn't a price? What if the book *wants* to do this? To make things nice?"

"It does want to do it. It wants to do it because the person it has hold of just wants to live in a *nice* place, where everyone's *nice* to each other and everything's *nice* and pretty."

"That's not such a bad thing to want."

"No, it's not, but the book will be getting stronger all the time. And it'll be telling whoever's got it that there's more they can do. That, never mind the street, they can make the whole town nicer. The whole country. Hell, the world. No more wars, no starvation, no discrimination."

"That sounds pretty good," Callum said.

"Sure. But it's not possible. People aren't nice. Humans aren't. Folk aren't. We do what we can, we're nice when it suits us, but we're just not built to be nice to each other all the time. Everything devolves to not-niceness."

"Cynic."

"Realist. And it means that the magic needed to sustain this sort of change can't last. Even if the person wishing for this is just riding it, not really doing it consciously, it'll start to take more and more effort to keep things going. And things will slip, and they'll notice none of it is quite as nice as it was, or they'll just want more, consciously or not. The book will be feeding off that, so they'll start to get more and more drained, and things will slow. Then they'll start really *trying*, wanting more and more and reaching out to get it."

"That sounds bad."

"It's only the beginning. One of two things will happen next. If they've got a lot of magic in them, as soon as their guard slips the book will take control, draw on the magic like a vampire until it stops warping reality and starts tearing it apart, at which point things get *really* messy, and stopping the person may not even be enough to stop the world breaking down. But that's unlikely – most people don't have that much magic. In that case the book will suck them dry, take everything they are, and the whole nice thing will just collapse in on itself. Then the book will nom on their soul, and it'll be even stronger when the next person picks it up and starts remaking the world as *they* want it."

"But why can't it stay a little bit nice?" Callum asked, dropping fifty pence into the honesty box and selecting a perfectly curved, almost luminous peach. "I mean, it wouldn't hurt to have a little more niceness in the world, even if it was just one street."

"Because balance, you pine nut. If this goes on for long enough, even if it doesn't spread, a botanical garden somewhere will wither and rot into a swamp of, I don't know, used tissues and cigarette butts, or a row of quaint little shops will be infested with telemarketers and handbag dogs in tutus, or a bunch of charity workers and nurses will turn into bankers and politicians. There's nice in the world, and not-nice. Balance. Can't have one without the other. Now can we just go?"

"Fine," Callum said. "But if we're leaving all this nice-ness behind, I want a decent apartment overlooking a beach. *La playa.*"

"Genius," I said. "We're going to be absolutely fine in Spain with your grasp of the language."

"*Sí*," he replied, grinning, and I wished I could roll my eyes. You'd be surprised how often cats wish that. But that wish remained ungranted, so instead I trotted down the block, leading the way to where we'd left the car. With any luck, the book's magic might have spread enough to heal up the terminal oil leak that meant the car marked its territory like a greasy dog at every stop. Callum followed me, long coat still flapping around his legs in spite of the afternoon sun. That coat hadn't been improved by all the niceness drifting about the place. Maybe he'd lose the thing once we got to warmer weather.

One could only hope.

TWO STREETS over turned out to be too far away for any improvement other than the fact that none of our windows had been smashed or wheels stolen, but that was a pretty rare occurrence anyway. As I said, we keep a rough car. The wheels aren't worth stealing and there's probably not a lot of satisfaction to be had in smashing the windows in when it would just kind of make the whole car's aesthetic a bit more cohesive. Callum unlocked the door and let me in, then finally peeled the horrible jacket off and threw it in the back with the bag. He'd caved and put one of the skinny black V-necks on, but was still wearing his tatty old jeans, held up with a belt he'd had to make new holes in. He shuffled behind the wheel, pumped pedals, pulled levers, and turned the key.

Nothing.

He tried again, and I growled at the back of my throat. Not even a dying click.

"Might just be a connection," he said.

"Well, go look," I snapped, and ran over him to jump onto the street as soon as he opened the door.

"Watch it," he told me, but he sounded more resigned than angry. And sure, it was only a matter of time before the car died, but *now?* Now seemed weird. Coincidences, see. Not really a thing.

I paced around on the pavement while he got the bonnet open, then jumped up next to him and stared at the mystifying collection of hoses and wires and plastic bits that made the car go.

"Well?" I demanded. "Can you see what it is?"

"I'm not a mechanic," he said, wriggling various things and peering into the gunky recesses of the engine. There was oil splattered everywhere, and it stank of dead dinosaurs and something burning.

"What're you *doing*, then?" I demanded, bumping his arm with my head. "Let me see."

"Why? What do you know about cars?"

"As much as you, by the sounds of things." I tried to push past him again and almost fell into the engine. Okay, so I was getting a bit overexcited. But we had to go. I felt like there were cats massing behind windows, watching and waiting. And more than cats, too.

"Gobs, bloody hell—"

"Hello, dears," a bright voice called out. "Car trouble?"

165

Callum jumped, knocking the support away and releasing the bonnet, which promptly fell down and smacked his nose, making him yelp and stagger back. I screeched as the thing crashed toward me, and took a flying leap onto the road as Callum lunged back to grab it, trapping his fingers underneath as it latched again. He jerked them out with a howl, swearing enthusiastically.

"Oh *dear*," Mrs Smith said, hurrying toward us. She was towing one of those shopping bags on wheels ladies of a certain age so often seem to favour when they don't drive, and her hair was twisted up in a complication of scarves. "Are you alright? I'm so sorry – I didn't mean to scare you."

"Fine," Callum said indistinctly. He was sucking his fingers, his eyes squeezed shut.

"Are you sure? That looked terribly painful."

"*Mm*," he said.

"Come in with me," she said, hooking an arm through his. "You need to put some ice on that."

He took his fingers out of his mouth long enough to say, "I'll be fine, Mrs Smith, thanks," then put them back again. He was sweating and looked rather pale and queasy.

"Nonsense," she said. "You can't drive like that anyway. Come along. You too, Gobbelino," she added, favouring me with a sunny smile. "I just bought some Jersey cream as a little treat. Do you think you'd like some of that?"

I looked from her to Callum, then at the car.

"We're really in kind of a rush," Callum said, trying to resist as she pulled him down the road with her. "And the car's not locked."

"Oh, well. That's no good. You lock the car then come with me."

He looked at his fingers woefully. He still had the clammy pallor of someone who was about to lose their avocado and tomato sandwich all over the road at any moment, but that served him right for eating all those vegetables. Enough to make anyone sick, that was. I ran to the car and jumped in, looking back at him expectantly. The longer we stayed around the building, the more likely we were to be caught. He nodded, and put his good hand on Mrs Smith's shoulder, managing a smile and giving her the dimples.

"I'm so sorry, Mrs Smith, but we really have to go. It's this case we're on. It's really important."

"But you should see a doctor about your hand. That looked terribly painful."

"It was," he said with feeling. "But I'm sure it's just bruised. As long as the car will start, we really need to go."

She smiled then, and patted his cheek. "I do love how you treat Gobbelino as your equal. The world would be a much nicer place if more people were so considerate of others, animals or not."

He smiled at her. "He doesn't give me a choice in the matter, Mrs Smith."

I snorted, but she was laughing and didn't hear me. "Alright, then, dear. I'll just wait and be sure it starts."

"Okay," he said, and hurried back to the car while she smiled and waved her fingers at me. I blinked at her. I mean, I'd have waved back, but that was kind of a dead giveaway that I wasn't just some poor dumb animal Callum was being so sweet to.

Callum shut the door, looked at me, and mumbled, "Let's hope it was just a loose wire."

I just looked at him, and he nodded, did the lever and pedal thing again, shut his eyes, and turned the key.

There was a startled cough, a roar, then the engine clattered into life, all asthmatic and sneezy but *working.* I swallowed a cheer while Callum raised both hands, fists clenched in victory. Mrs Smith clapped happily, and after a few nasty grinding noises Callum got the ancient car in gear.

We pulled away from the kerb with a belch of exhaust fumes and coughed down the alley, leaving Mrs Smith waving her hands in front of her face, nose wrinkled. We were off. We were going to be okay. I closed my eyes and said a quiet but fervent prayer to any small gods who were hanging around and looking after the doings of cats and PIs, then tried to find a comfy spot on the seat to settle myself into. There actually seemed to be less springs digging into me than usual, and the split vinyl was less pinch-y than I was accustomed to. It must be the relief, I decided. Everything was just going to get better and better as we left the city in our rear-view mirror and headed south.

"How far to the ferry?" I asked Callum as he pulled onto the next road. "Or do we take the Eurotunnel? Will the car make it? What do we do if it doesn't? Train? I don't like buses, but I'm not sure about flying, either. I—"

"Gobs, shut up," he said, turning into a side street and parking up behind a Transit van that looked even more rickety than our car. We were well out of the influence of the book here, and there were three patchy pigeons fighting over a pie crust in the middle of the street, where they'd pulled it out of the drifts of crisp packets and discarded cans. The sun hadn't bothered to accompany us, leaving the day grey and vaguely clammy.

"What're we doing?" I demanded. "Why've we stopped?"

He covered his face with both hands, and for a moment I thought he was trying not to shout at me. His injured fingers looked red and painful. Then he slid his hands down, wiped his mouth and leaned his forearms on the wheel. "I didn't fix the car."

"Well, you obviously did," I said. "Loose connection, right?"

"No," he said. "Everything was on tight. I did nothing."

"Well, it's an old car," I said, perfectly aware there was a rhinoceros in the room but really, really trying not to look at it, because if I did I was going to have to do something about it. And we'd already decided on the best course of action, dammit. We'd *decided*. "It's like your computer, right? It works better when you hit it."

He just looked at me.

I looked at my feet, and noticed the torn vinyl had a soft glow to it, warm and supple. It looked almost leather-like, and there was an air freshener plugged into the vent, wafting roses softly over us. "Hairballs," I said. "Hairballs, and … and wet dogs and muddy feet." Then I added a bunch of human swearwords, because they're just better.

Because I could run when it was just a hypothetical someone who had the book. Someone faceless and nameless, some poor sod who'd just walked past the door at the wrong moment, some thief who'd brought this all on themselves. Some hypothetical person who just wanted the world to be nice, who wanted nice things in the shops and pretty trees outside, and stairwells that didn't stink of pee and sidewalks that weren't covered in dog poo, and kittens instead of gambling problems.

I could run when it was just anyone thinking they could make the world a better place by wishing it, like a kid with a fairy clock.

I couldn't run when it was the one person who put niceness into the world already.

I couldn't run when it was Mrs Smith.

15

JUST NICE

WE DROVE BACK AROUND THE BLOCK, PARKED UP, AND SAT there watching swallows nesting in the eaves of our building, because it suddenly had eaves. And swallows. I'm pretty sure the pigeons and sparrows would have bullied them out of town just yesterday.

"Hairballs," I said again.

"Yep," Callum said. "But it solves a lot, you know? I mean, it's Mrs Smith. We'll just explain the situation to her, and she'll give the book back."

I looked at him. "If it was that easy, she wouldn't have taken the book in the first place. I mean, when has she ever let herself into our apartment before? Or taken anything that doesn't belong to her?"

Callum scratched a hand through his hair, making it stand up in weird directions. "Well, okay, but I'm sure once we *talk* to her—"

"Book of power, Callum. And it's been splashing that power *everywhere*. Mrs Smith may not be feeling quite herself."

He sighed, drumming his fingers on the wheel, then said, "Well, it's still the best way to start, right?"

I personally thought the best way to start involved a covert night raid and no confrontation, but this was Mrs Smith. As far as humans go, she was pretty good. She brought us sardines and pasta bakes when things were tight, and had even been known to lie to the odd large and irate visitor about where we lived. So, okay. I got where he was coming from. We owed it to her. "Alright," I said. "But if the book's really got its teeth into her, this isn't going to go easy."

He nodded, and opened the door. "Let's just try."

WE APPROACHED the building like it might drop its shiny facade at any moment and lunge at us with rotting brick teeth, but it just sat there looking innocuous and impossibly clean. Ivy had sprung up from somewhere and wound its way up the walls, giving it a touch of country house charm that sat rather uncomfortably among the tatty streets. Or almost tatty streets. Things were getting tidier all the time, rubbish-strewn gutters turning to grassy edging and flower beds, and trees sprouting up along the pavement to lend the place a little life. I was willing to bet that by tonight there'd be lanterns in them, or fairy lights strung from one side of the alley to the other, and pretty painted shutters on the windows. Which was all an improvement on filthy glass and boards, but if an accordion player popped up I was going to bite someone.

"Why's no one saying anything?" Callum asked, watching a woman open a window on the third floor and lean out, smiling up at the afternoon sun. "They must see it, right?"

"Would you be objecting that things had got a little nicer if you didn't know the truth behind it?"

"Yeah, but … it's *so* different to yesterday. It's barely the same place, and that doesn't just *happen.* Surely people must realise something's up."

"Humans are masters of self-deception," I said. "Especially when it comes to comfort. They'll be saying everything looks so much better in the sun, or isn't it nice how the council have finally cleaned up a bit. Because the alternative is admitting there's magic going down, and no one's going to say that. They'd probably consider aliens, but not magic."

"What about the suddenly much nicer apartments?"

I snorted. "Yeah, *no one's* going to be talking about those. All they need is the landlady getting a whiff of how much more she can charge."

"Eh. True enough." Callum shifted his grip on the backpack. "Well, let's go ruin everyone's day."

"And save the world," I added.

"Dramatics, Gobs," he said, opening the door.

"Hey, a book of power is on the loose, and it's only a matter of time before it starts getting out of hand. It's not exactly small carrots."

"Potatoes. Small potatoes."

"Whatever. They're all root vegetables." I followed him into the foyer, where the grubby lino floor had turned to polished marble and the previously painted walls now had some rather intricate wild animal wallpaper going on, and we headed for the stairs. I wasn't looking forward to this any more than he was. Not least because I doubted Mrs Smith was going to just hand the book over, and as mercenary as I may be, I still had no desire to bite a really very nice old lady. Especially when she'd just offered me Jersey cream.

The stairwell was softly lit, and some sort of mural featuring cherubs and harps and fluffy pink clouds had apparently been hand-painted on the walls. Somewhere tinkly music was playing. It was creepy, and I didn't actually think it was much improvement on the half-lit, dingy space it had been before. Although my paws no longer stuck to the treads, so that was nice. We peeked out the door on the second floor and found the hallway carpet had taken on rich red hues and become even deeper and softer than earlier, and the doors all had brass nameplates on them. There were potted ferns in the corners and orchids on a spindly-legged side table, and the music up here was more like pan flutes or something. I hoped that didn't mean there were going to be fauns. I could do without fauns.

"This is getting a bit excessive," Callum said, looking at the carpet as if he was worried about walking on it.

"Yeah. Let's get it sorted before you wake up with a crewcut," I told him. He grabbed his hair with one hand to make sure it was still what he called *tousled* and what I called *Mum never taught you to groom yourself*, then we marched to Mrs Smith's door.

Callum took a deep breath, then knocked neatly. There was silence for a moment, and we waited.

It seemed to take a long time, and Callum had lifted his hand to knock again when we heard the roll of the latch, and a moment later Mrs Smith was beaming up at us. She was wearing some sort of silky pink loungewear, the sort that look like pyjamas, but which no one actually sleeps in. Her hair was pinned up in a froth of silver curls and ringlets, festooned with butterflies that, on closer inspection, appeared to be alive.

"Callum!" she cried. "And Gobbelino! Oh, how *wonderful*." And she truly sounded as if we'd made her day just by turning up. It was how she always sounded when she saw us, and it made my tail droop a little. "Do come in. I was just going to have a little cocktail." She giggled. "I mean, it *is* the weekend."

It was? Who knew.

"It is," Callum agreed, following her in. "Mrs Smith— oh."

Oh, because her drab little foyer, which had always been clean but was as small and cold and tatty as everything else in this building, was now all warm wood floors with bright, funky rugs. It opened onto an enormous lounge full of exotic potted plants and peppered with low, colourful sofas piled with cushions and throws. Floor to ceiling windows lined the wall, and looked out over what appeared to be a jungle of some sort. There was a bright blue parrot sitting in the doorway bobbing his head in time to some pop music, and some sort of boar with a lot of bristles and big curly tusks tottered up to us with a tray on his back. Mrs Smith took two glasses of bright pink frozen stuff off the tray, handing one to Callum, then took a carrot out of her pocket and gave it to the boar. He wandered off, munching happily, and I noticed there was an alligator asleep on one of the sofas. Or it might have been a crocodile. I wasn't about to ask it.

"Wow," Callum said, looking at a snake wound around the rafters. The fact that the apartment had rafters really wasn't that odd, considering everything else.

"Isn't it wonderful?" Mrs Smith said happily, and slurped her drink. "I always wanted to live in a tree house. And Barry – that's the warthog – is an excellent bartender. This drink is all natural!"

Ah. Warthog, not boar. I should have paid more attention to those BBC documentaries Callum liked so much. Although I was fairly certain none of them featured bartending warthogs, whether they were called Barry or not.

"Come sit down, come sit down." Mrs Smith grabbed Callum's hand and towed him to a glass-topped cane table sitting next to a mini waterfall, pushing herself up into one of the chairs and swinging her feet. I followed them, squinting at the koi in the pond beneath the waterfall. "Are you hungry? I have some lovely pasties I just baked."

"No thanks," Callum said, and a lizard twice my size shoved its head out of the undergrowth, lifted its frills and hissed at me. I jumped onto Callum's lap and hissed back at it from relative safety. He didn't push me down for a change, just set the drink aside and said, "Mrs Smith—"

"Yours isn't alcoholic, dear. You can drink it."

He gave it a dubious look. "Thank you. Mrs Smith—"

"Are you *sure* you aren't hungry? What about you, Gobbelino?" She leaned forward to give me a chin rub and I let her, taking the opportunity to snuffle her fingers.

Magic clung to them, dark and greasy and hungry. It was hard to tell over the stench of birds and animals and weird plants – as I watched, one snapped a small gliding squirrel out of the air, imprisoning it in the green vase of its stem – but the book was here. The magic was heavier the deeper into the room we were. You could feel it like a slick of humidity on your ears and whiskers, a thickening of the air that made it harder to breathe. Although that could also be fact that we seemed to be in a rainforest. But rainforests don't make your tail bristle. I don't think, anyway, my experience with them being limited to the botanical gardens.

I looked up at Callum, tipping my head just slightly in confirmation. He sighed.

"No, thank you, Mrs Smith. We're fine. But I need to ask you something."

"Of course," she said, smiling brightly. The drink had tinged her teeth faintly pink, which was alarming.

"You know all the fuss in our apartment last night?"

"Oh, yes. Dreadful. What a horrible man that was! Was he a client?"

"Sort of." Callum took a deep breath. "He was looking for a book we put in the filing cabinet. And the problem is, we can't find it. And we really need to get it back to its owner. You haven't seen it, have you, Mrs Smith?"

I've got to hand it to him. He's better at these sorts of things than me. I'd have just told her to hand the book back and to stop meddling in things she doesn't understand, but his way was better. *Nicer.* Assuming it worked, of course.

Mrs Smith looked at her drink, using the straw to mix

it carefully. There was a little paper umbrella stuck in it too, and a bunch of fruit decorating the side. "I wasn't going to keep it," she said. "I went over to see if you wanted some dinner, and the door was open, and the bottom drawer of the filing cabinet was out, and the box was just lying there. It looked terribly expensive, and I thought it was very risky to leave it there, when anyone could just walk in and take it."

"That was very good of you," Callum said. "We'd be in a lot of trouble if we'd lost it."

I hooked my claws into his T-shirt and tugged. The alligator or the crocodile or whatever had woken up and slipped off the sofa, and it was looking at us with a rather unpleasant intensity. I figured I was about snack-size for it. Callum ignored me.

"It's all safe," Mrs Smith said, nodding firmly. "All tucked away safe as can be."

"Wonderful," Callum said. "We'll need to take it back to our client now."

Mrs Smith made a *hmm* noise, swinging her legs in the chair like a five-year-old as she sipped her drink. "The thing is," she said thoughtfully, and I shifted my attention to the warthog. It had got rid of the tray and was circling toward us from the other side of the room. "The thing is," she repeated, "I really rather like it. It's proving very *useful*."

"But it's not yours," Callum said. "It belongs to someone else."

Mrs Smith nodded. The snake was winding its way along the rafters toward the table, and the parrot had been joined by a bunch of beaked and clawed buddies. I tugged Callum's shirt a little more anxiously. There were far too many things in here that looked like they might not be cat people.

"I do understand that the book *did* belong to someone else," Mrs Smith said, "but considering I stopped it being stolen by, oh, any number of awful people, I think I have a right to keep it. Finders keepers, as the saying goes."

Callum sighed, and this time when I pulled his shirt he finally glanced down at me. I jerked my head at the advancing critters, and he blinked at them, then looked back at Mrs Smith. "You need to understand, it's no ordinary book," he said.

"Of course it's not, dear. Which was why it was *so* important the wrong sort of people didn't get hold of it. And you just left it there! Drawer wide open, and the door not even shut properly." She tutted sadly. "Very careless. No, it needs to be kept safe."

The door *and* the drawer were open? Sentient was starting to sound like the right label for the damn thing.

"It needs to go back to its rightful owner," Callum said, and jerked away from the table as a really far-too-large spider jumped onto it. I shot onto Callum's shoulder, my tail bushed out. The damn arachnid was almost as big as me. I preferred the botanical garden version of rainforests, to be honest.

"Oh, don't be afraid of her," Mrs Smith said, smiling at the spider. "She mostly eats birds."

Well, that was reassuring.

Callum got up, clutching the backpack in front of him and shuffling away from a phalanx of meerkats that had appeared at his feet. I don't know what they thought they could do, but they were all baring their teeth at us. "Mrs Smith. That book is not safe to use," Callum said. "Please."

Mrs Smith looked at her hands as if she was considering it. The critters waited. Finally she looked up and said, "With anything, it all depends what you do with it. Think of what some people would do if they were granted the ability to change things." She waved around. "I just want things to be nice. Is that so bad?"

"No," Callum said, and he crouched in front of her, which brought me on eye-level with a distinctly grumpy-looking goat. We glared at each other. Callum took Mrs Smith's hands in his and said, "But things like this don't come free. The book is giving you the world you want, but it's going to twist it. It's going to change you, hurt you, even. You need to give it back."

She returned his gaze levelly for a long moment, while the alligator crept closer and the snake swung from the rafters above us, then she patted his cheek gently and said, "I think you should go now, dear."

"Mrs Smith," Callum tried again, and a murmur ran through the room. The alligator opened its massive jaws and hissed. The spider reared up on its hind legs, of which it had far more than it needed. The goat stamped its feet and narrowed its yellow eyes. The parrots shook their wings out and ruffled their feathers and postured like prizefighters. And the meerkats just stood there looking meerkat-ish.

Mrs Smith got up, straightening her loungewear. "I'll take very good care of the book," she said. "I'm going to take very good care of *everything*. Especially you two. You'll see. Life is going to be just lovely now. No more nasty clients or horrible cases. I'll look after you." And she ushered us to the door, the host of birds and animals crowding in on us from all sides so that Callum *had* to move. It was that or have a warthog stand on your foot. Or an alligator. I scanned the room from Callum's shoulder as we retreated, trying to figure out where the damn book was. But it could have been anywhere. Magic swamped the place, heavy and stinking, and there was no telltale mirage-shimmer of the source anywhere. Not that I could see through the vines and trees and pampas grass, anyway.

Callum paused at the door, turning on the threshold to look at Mrs Smith. She stood there smiling, with the warthog on one side and the goat on the other, and the snake looking over her shoulder. "Please, Mrs Smith," he said. "It really isn't safe to use. It's dangerous. It won't let you stay you."

She smiled. "I've been me for seventy-five years. Maybe it's time to be someone different."

Then she closed the door and left us staring at the dark wood, while I wondered if it was too late to head for Spain after all. At least there wouldn't be giant, bird-eating spiders to contend with.

16

OUTSOURCING

WE WENT BACK TO OUR APARTMENT, FINDING THAT IT NOW had a bedroom, and bookshelves had filled the wall where the cupboards for the bed had been before. There was also a rather inviting and luxurious cat bed with a heating pad plugged into the wall. I sighed. It was so much easier to find your motivation when magical things just tried to kill you.

Callum dropped the backpack to the floor and said, "So what do we do now?"

"We could still run," I suggested, more for appearances than anything else. Even for me, it'd be pretty unfair to leave Mrs Smith in the middle of the whole mess, despite the fact that she did seem to be enjoying herself rather a lot.

Callum rubbed his face with both hands. "We can't, G. We brought that book in here. We put her in the damn thing's path."

"I know," I said, and tested out the cat bed. The heating pad was already on, and the cushion was just the right balance of supportive and squishy. "We're going to have to steal it back."

"That should be easy, given the wild boar and giant spider and so on."

"Warthog. And what choice do we have? She's not just going to give it back, is she?"

"Maybe I could try again."

I made another petition to the cat gods for roll-able eyes. "She's not going to budge, Callum. The book's got its claws in her, good and proper. So it's steal it back or nothing."

"Great," he said, and wandered into the kitchen. "How much insect spray do we have?"

"I'm more worried about the alligator."

THERE WAS no point crashing in there and trying to toss the place, not with half the London zoo in residence. At the very least, I was at high risk of catching fleas, or something more tropical and scary, and it felt fairly likely that at least one of us would end up bitten – or eaten. Plus, all that aside, there was no way we were going to have a physical confrontation with our elderly neighbour. We were PIs, not monsters.

No, we needed to be sneaky, and we needed to know exactly where the book was before we went off doing said sneaking. Reconnaissance was required, and while I couldn't do it (I can't shift, remember, so how was I going to get in? Besides, that spider had creeped me out), I knew just the person for the job.

I trotted back down the stairs with Callum in tow to act as doorman, since the stairwell doors also stayed firmly shut these days, rather than resting on their broken latches. I was starting to disapprove of these improvements. Outside, the afternoon sunshine was still far too warm for a November day in northern England, and I led the way around the corner of the building to the rats' grate. I set down a rather fragrant wedge of Camembert, licked the scraps off my chops, and sat myself at the edge of the grate to wait.

It didn't take long – that cheese had a whiff and a half on it. I'd barely had time to really soak the sun up in my shoulders before a familiar nose edged into view, followed by Susan's quick eyes and twitching ears.

"Twice in one day," she said. "People will talk."

"Let them," I said. "If they can't understand love, worse luck to them."

She snorted, and inspected the cheese. "Well, not exactly stepping up in the health stakes, but this is *nice*, Gobbelino. You doing alright out of all this transformation stuff?"

"Yes and no," I said. "I kind of need to transform everything back."

"I figured someone would have to," she said. "Not that the wool beds and dry tunnels are anything to complain about, but there's magic stink everywhere. It's not right."

"Yeah, it's all getting a bit out of hand," I said. "So will you help?"

"Depends." She pushed the cheese into the grate behind her, where eager paws tidied it away. I arched my whiskers at her. "Oh, that's just for coming out to talk to you. It doesn't mean I'm going to *do* anything."

"And here I thought you were my heart, my soul—"

"Shut up, Gobbelino."

"Fair enough. Look, there's a book of power behind all this. We know what apartment it's in, just not exactly where. And the apartments have got a bit … sprawl-y, so searching the whole thing is out. Any chance of some scouting?"

Susan cleaned her whiskers thoughtfully. "A book of power? That's some nasty stuff, G. We're not touching the thing."

"Wouldn't expect you to."

"Any particular hazards to watch out for? The place isn't going to be laced with rat traps, is it?"

I thought of the snake hanging from the rafters and the alligator dozing on its sofa. "No traps, no. Maybe a few, um, hostile residents."

She looked at me silently.

"Okay, fine, there may be a couple of animals in the apartment already. But you can circumvent that, right? In the walls, sneaking around, being all ratty and elusive? Isn't that kind of your *modus operandi?*"

"I have no idea why I help you at all sometimes."

"Sausages. Also I beat the crap out of any other cat that comes about the place thinking they're going to throw their weight around."

"Eh. You do have your uses." She considered it for a moment longer, then said, "Fine. I'll grab a couple of the girls and we'll take a look. But the *slightest* sign that someone wants to eat us, or anyone starts turning into a pumpkin, we're out."

"Horse," Callum said. He was leaning against the wall of the building, giving us our space and smoking a cigarette, his face turned up to the sun. "And it was mice, actually, that changed into horses. The pumpkin turned into a coach."

We both looked at him for a moment, then I turned back to Susan and said, "Deal. You're the love of my life, you know that?"

"You're a teapot," she said, and with that rather enigmatic insult vanished into the grate.

I ambled back to Callum. "Helpful."

"They were horses."

"Whatever." I examined him. "Got some spare pockets?"

He looked down at himself. The heat rose from the pavement in a pleasantly unfamiliar shimmer, baking my belly. He didn't have his coat on. "Not really."

"You'll just have to carry them, then. And put that thing out. You can't be breathing cigarette breath all over them."

He frowned at me, but stubbed the cigarette out and wandered over to flick the butt in the bin. A moment later Susan resurfaced from the grate, followed by two sleek young rats with glossy fur and big ears.

"Esther and Abigail," she said. "If they can't get in somewhere, there's no getting in."

"Hey," I said to them, and they nodded back at me. Abigail had a scar running over her nose of the sort young rats get when they push rat traps a bit too far. Not that it ever stops them. "Human here is Callum. He'll give you a lift."

The two younger rats huddled behind Susan as Callum crouched down, all elbows and knees. "Hi," he said quietly, and offered them a hand. There was a long pause, then Susan stepped forward and climbed aboard, grabbing his thumb in her pink paws to steady herself. The other two followed, not looking particularly happy about it, and Callum stood up carefully, cradling them against his chest. "All set?"

No one said anything, so I just led the way back to the front door, hoping the two young rats were as good as Susan said they were. Otherwise I was going to have some rodent deaths on my conscience as well as the corruption of a very nice seventy-five-year-old.

Callum was opening the front door when someone said, "Hey," from behind us.

He almost dropped his keys, recovered himself, and looked over his shoulder at the young waitress from the cafe. "Um, hi," he said. "Ah, Petra."

She bent over to rub her fingers at me, the way humans do, but I wasn't in the mood. I ignored her and looked up at Callum impatiently.

"I was looking at the trees," she said, straightening up. "It's like it's spring or something. Only better." She shook her head. "It's sort of weird. I mean, I haven't been here long, but it doesn't usually do this, does it?"

"Um. Yeah," Callum said, still turned toward the door, keeping the rats hidden from her. "I mean, no. Very unseasonable. The sun, I mean. And the trees."

I squinted at my paws and wondered how someone could read so much and yet be so bad at words.

She nodded as if he'd been completely coherent. "And there's a fruit cart there. That's new, right?"

"Brand new," he agreed.

"Yeah." She looked at him for a moment longer, then at me. "So, you live here?"

"We … I really need to go," Callum said. "Work."

"Oh. Sure." She looked a little disappointed, and, you know, I'd usually be all for Callum hanging out with a nice human, but there's a time and a place. Neither of which are while smuggling rats into an enchanted building in search of a stolen book of power so a little old lady doesn't tear reality apart in her quest for niceness. "Maybe we could get a drink sometime?"

"I don't drink," Callum said, and I shook my head slightly.

"Right," she said. "Sure. Sorry." She took a step back. "Didn't mean to bother you."

"No, I'm sorry." He turned away from the door, lifting his free hand apologetically. "It's just we're on this really stressful case right now, and—"

"Are those rats?" she asked, staring at Susan and the two younger rodents, crowded together in the cradle of his hand. "Why do you have rats?"

He looked down at them. "I … raise them."

"You raise rats."

"Yes. Fascinating creatures. Really very intelligent."

She looked from the rats to me, then back at him. "Why aren't they in a cage?"

"I also train them," he said, nodding firmly. "Circus rats."

"*Circus* rats?"

"And movies. Movie rats."

Okay, this was going downhill fast. I stood on my hind legs and clawed at his jeans, *mraow*-ing, and Callum gave me an alarmed look. There was sweat on his forehead.

"I need to go," he said. "They've had enough outside time for today. They need a nap. And rewards. Snacks, really. And I need to feed Gobbelino, because I don't want him getting too hungry around them."

Esther looked like she was about to make a break for it, and Susan nipped her ear.

"Sure," Petra said. "Sure, that makes sense." She raised a hand in a half-hearted sort of wave. "See you around, then."

"Yes. Yes, that sounds good," Callum said, and stood there while she walked away, glancing back once with a puzzled look on her face. Callum waved at her, then opened the door and we piled into the cool, waxy interior.

"Dude," Abigail said. "That was the *worst*."

"Don't you start," Callum said.

CALLUM SET the rats down in our apartment, and they wasted exactly zero time in scooting across the floor, tiny feet swift and silent. They gathered at the door, conferred briefly with twitching noses, then split up, investigating the cupboards. A moment later they were gone. Callum stared at the walls and said, "Now what?"

"Now we wait and see what they bring back," I said.

"I hope they're going to be alright."

"I hope we can go back to the cafe," I said, mostly because I didn't want to think about where we'd just sent the rats. I should've been more specific in my warnings, but we needed the help. I couldn't risk Susan saying no. I just hoped the snake was asleep.

"We can go back to the cafe," Callum said, opening the window to let in the warm, sweet-scented breeze. We'd acquired a window box, flowers of some sort basking in the heat. "I wasn't *that* weird."

I stared at him until he said, "Well, I wasn't banned-from-the-premises weird. You want some custard?"

"Sure," I said, and we sat in our new sofa with our shiny new crockery, him drinking tea and me lapping at some premium custard with flecks of actual vanilla bean that looked like dirt in it, waiting for the rats to come back and tell us what we had to do next.

We didn't have that long to wait. They were *fast*. I mean, even if we hadn't been warding off alligators and so on, turning over the whole of Mrs Smith's jungle apartment would've taken us ages. There's an astonishing amount of nooks and crannies even in a non-magical apartment, and, as I'd told Susan, things had got sprawl-y.

That worried me, too. You can't go messing with dimensions for too long before they start tearing. As it was, Callum was only on his second cup of tea and I'd barely finished my custard when there was scratching behind the cupboards and the three little critters came pitter-pattering across the floor toward us. Callum put his book down and sat up properly, and I examined them. No one seemed to be bleeding, and all limbs were still attached, so that was promising.

Susan scrambled up onto the coffee table and glared at me. "You might have mentioned the snake."

"I did say there were animals," I protested, rather weakly.

"Which I took to mean dogs. Other cats. Hamsters. Maybe a ferret, at worst. Not a snake, and three burrowing owls, and some weird plants that tried to eat Esther."

Esther did, indeed, look a little damp and dishevelled.

"We had to just about gnaw its roots through before it gave her back," Abigail said. "You suck."

"I'm sorry," I said, and Callum looked at me.

"You seriously didn't tell them?"

"Well …"

"You do suck." He got up and went into the kitchen. "Grapes? Cheese? Some fancy dried sausage thing? Gobbelino's custard?"

"Yes," Susan said. "Especially the custard." She went back to glaring at me until Callum put the food on the table and sat down again. Then she helped herself to a grape and said, "Despite some really very hazardous conditions, however, we did find the book."

"You did?" We both leaned forward.

"Yeah. She keeps it in that shopping trolley thing, all wrapped up in a raincoat or something. She had it out while we were there, and was sitting there singing to it, lullabies or some such. Things kept growing out of nothing and vanishing again while she was doing it – plants and butterflies and so on."

"That doesn't sound good," Callum said.

Susan shoved half a grape into a cheek pouch, giving her a lopsided look. "She was stroking it, too, like it was a pet. Then the owls jumped off a lamp and onto our rafter, and the snake came at us from the other side, and Esther fell into the plant, and it all got a bit hectic. But I saw her put the book back in the trolley."

Callum and I looked at each other. Which likely meant she was keeping it with her. She'd had the damn thing on her when she'd seen us at the car. So there was no point waiting until she went out. We were going to have to go in and take it from her.

"Ugh," I said.

"Yep," Callum said.

"Do you have chutney?" Abigail asked. "This cheese needs a little something."

CALLUM CARRIED the rats back downstairs, along with an enormous bunch of grapes, a loaf of bread, and the rest of the sausage. Susan stopped before she climbed onto his hand and looked at me.

"It's dangerous in there," she said. "The animals and the plants aren't just *there*. They're guards. They'll stop you getting to the book if they can."

"Alright," I said. "So going in isn't really an option. Maybe we can try and grab the trolley while she's out with it."

"That'll go well," Callum said. "Mugging a nice old lady on the street."

"Whatever you do, hurry up," Susan said. "It's all still nice around here, but in there things are starting to fray. You can feel it. The carpets are beginning to take on strange angles – one minute flat, then sideways, then nothing that makes sense. There are holes in the chairs that go on forever. And there's something living in the bathroom that's all legs and suckers."

"Octopus?" I suggested, a little weakly. "She does seem to have a soft spot for wildlife."

"There were dimensions oozing out under the door," Susan said. "Not sure what sort of octopus that is."

"Fantastic," Callum said, and Susan climbed onto his hand. He carried the rats out the door and I stayed where I was, staring at the afternoon as it pulled on into dusk, and thinking that if things were already starting to fray, Claudia had it wrong.

A day was more time than we had left before the book tore the world apart.

17

A SNAKE IN YOUR POCKET

CALLUM DROPPED INTO THE LUXURIOUSLY BIG CHAIR behind the desk, shaking a cigarette out of the packet.

"What do we do, G?"

"I don't know," I admitted. "We have to get that book off her somehow. And quickly."

He rolled the chair closer to the open window, so the smoke drifted out into the orange sky. "She's not going to go out again tonight. Either we have to go in, or we wait until tomorrow and hope we get a chance then."

"Tomorrow might be too late," I said. The walls of our apartment kept changing. One moment they were sleek, modern white, the next all embossed gilt wallpaper, and currently we seemed to be in a log cabin, complete with a rather put-out-looking deer's head. I hoped it didn't stay on that one. And I'd just seen a flight of cockatoos go past the window.

"What's happening?" Callum asked. "Why's it going all weird?"

"Because the bigger on the inside apartments and the full fridge weren't weird enough for you?"

He just stared at me, eyebrows raised.

"Fine. You know how I said if someone has magic in them, the book has more to work with? Mrs Smith's obviously got more to her than just tarot cards. The book's got a taste, and now she's lost control of it – if she ever had any control to start with. It's doing its own thing, building on every flight of fancy it catches off her, feeding on her to power it. She probably doesn't even realise. She just thinks she's finally been given the power to make things *nice*. And the more of her magic the book uses, the stronger and hungrier it gets."

"So anything she thinks of …?"

"It does."

"Awesome," he said, glancing uneasily out the window. I didn't blame him. The cockatoos were squalling like pterodactyls, and I wasn't sure if that was the sort of sound they were meant to make or not. Either way, I didn't like it. "We need to try and get in there, then."

"It's too dangerous," I said, examining a paw. Then I looked up at him. "Ask her to dinner."

"Dinner?"

"Yeah. That gets her out of the apartment. She'll take the book with her. It's still going to be tricky to get hold of it, but we'll have a better chance when there isn't a bloody anaconda hanging over her shoulder."

He tapped the fingers of his free hand against his thumb, one then the other, his eyes on the ceiling. There was a chandelier made of antlers up there, all pale and gleaming as the light faded and afternoon dusk started to creep in. Seriously. What is it with humans and decorating with the bones of dead things? Yet you whinge if we bring you a dead bird. Although, the reaction is the main reason we give them to you, if I'm honest.

"And then what?" Callum asked. "We get her away from the building and just try to snatch the damn thing?"

"Any better ideas?"

He dropped his cigarette butt into the bottom of his mug (*ew*), and got up. "Nope. None at all."

I SUGGESTED he should make himself presentable – the man has no sense of style – but he just ran his hands back over his hair, declared he hated all the clothes in the apartment, and pulled his horrible wet dog jacket back on.

"Are you just taking her down the chippy, then?" I asked him.

"Maybe the Indian," he said.

"I'm pretty sure they have a dress code," I said. "You might be safer with the chippy."

He ignored me, shoved his wallet in his pocket and said, "Coming?"

We padded over the thick hall carpet, and he knocked on Mrs Smith's door. It seemed to take her even longer to answer this time, and when she did it was with a blast of thick, humid air, heavy with the scents of unfamiliar flowers and rich warm earth and dangerous things. Somewhere, there was the trumpeting of elephants.

"Callum!" she said, smiling up at him brightly. "And Gobbelino. How *are* you?"

Just as if we hadn't only seen her a couple of hours ago and told her a book was trying to eat her soul.

"Good, thanks, Mrs Smith," Callum said. "Just heading out for some tea. Fancy joining us?"

She placed one hand on the little round of her stomach, considering. The pink loungewear had been replaced by some sort of safari get-up, all khaki and buckles and multipurpose pockets. I was half-surprised she wasn't wearing a pith helmet, although that probably would've messed with the intricate white loops and coils of her hair. "I am a mite peckish," she said. "Just one moment while I get my bag."

"Take your time," Callum said, and we stayed there while a large horned toad flopped past the door, and something screamed in the depths of the apartment, and a horde of butterflies swooped through the foyer.

"Dude, I am *not* going in there alone if she doesn't bring it," I whispered.

"That's fair," he whispered back. "I don't want to go in there either."

Mrs Smith tottered into view, ducking under a couple of vines and skirting a large fern that trembled threateningly, then spat a glut of pollen into the air. It caught a passing rabbit in the eye, and the rabbit squawked and fled, but not before the pollen had turned it iridescent purple.

"So lovely of you to think of me," she said. "I don't care what they say about young people these days, you're perfectly lovely."

Callum gave her a half-hearted sort of smile and

stepped back to let her through the door. "It's my pleasure."

Mrs Smith pulled the door shut behind her and jiggled the handle to make sure it was locked – although I think anyone who broke in would be regretting it pretty quick. She didn't have her shopping trolley in tow, but she did have an enormous pink handbag with bright green tassels clutched under her arm. I wound myself around her legs and let her scritch my ears, seeing if I could get a whiff of the bag. Then I gave Callum a quick, tiny nod. It was in there. I didn't even need to catch the scent of it. Just being near it made the hair on my spine hike upward.

We walked to the stairwell together, just a nice old lady and the two ruffians who were about to mug her.

Yeah. This is what I always wanted to do with my life.

I REALLY SHOULD HAVE TALKED the plan over with Callum a bit better. Well, we should have taken the time to muddle out a plan that consisted of more than just, "Let's invite Mrs Smith to dinner."

Because he waited exactly as long as it took us to reach the end of the block, with the last of the sunlight following us like a puddle of lost puppies, then said, "You need to give me the book, Mrs Smith."

She stopped short and glared up at him, clutching the bag to her. "*Excuse* me?"

"The book. You can't keep it." He waved back at our building, all done out in soft lamps and fairy lights, and the way the warmth slowly gave way to dinginess as the rest of the world encroached. The influence of the magic didn't seem to have spread all that much, just intensified at its centre, although Mrs Smith walked in her own pool of warmth and light, glowing gently against the grey walls of the alley.

"You asked me out under false pretences," she said, frowning at him. "I thought we were friends."

"We are," Callum said. "That's why I'm asking you to give the book back. It's not safe for you to have it."

"Oh, and I suppose you'll be fine, will you? Because you're young? And a *man?*"

"I don't want it for myself," he said. "I just want it to go back to its owner. Someone who knows how to handle it."

"I know how to handle it." She took a step away from him, and pointed at the building. "Look at all I've done already!"

"But it's not sustainable," Callum said. "It really isn't. It's going to *hurt* you. You need to let me help."

"Help me do what? Go back to living in a poky little studio in a bad part of town, with windows that leak and heating that only works in the summer? Go back to scrounging around for enough money to keep the lights on, and still find a way to keep feeding *you?*"

Callum stopped short, and I could see colour flaring in his cheeks. "Mrs Smith—"

"You and your damn cat," she said, scowling at me. Harsh. "I've looked after *both* of you, because who else was going to, and now something's finally coming back to me, something's finally going my way, you're going to try and take it away from me? No! I won't have it!"

"Mrs Smith—"

"No! I've done everything for everyone else all my life! This is *mine!*"

Alright, enough was enough. Callum wasn't going to talk her out of it, and I really didn't like the dig about a damn cat. It was time she listened to reason, and, after all, she was fine with magical books and jungle apartments. A talking cat wasn't exactly a stretch.

"Mrs Smith," I said, "while we appreciate—"

I didn't get any further, because she shrieked, took a swing at me with the bag which made me squawk and duck, then took off back toward the building at a truly startling pace for someone of her rickety build.

Callum swore and bolted after her, and I followed, wondering what the hell it was with humans and selective acceptance of reality. Seriously. An alligator on the sofa is just fine, but a cat has a word with you and you freak out? Humans.

"Mrs Smith!" Callum called, in that sort of wanting-to-be-heard-but-trying-not-to-shout tone. "Mrs Smith, please—" He caught her shoulder as gently as he could, and she screamed like an air raid siren, spinning around to clock him one with the pink bag. He yelped, raising an arm to fend her off, and she hit him again then legged it for the door. I raced in front of her, hoping she wasn't going to break her hip if she tripped, but she managed to leap over me, saying some very insulting things about my ancestry as she went.

"*Mrs Smith!*" Callum half-shouted, lunging after her and grabbing for the bag. He caught the straps and jerked her to a halt. "You *have* to give me the book!"

She screamed, something horribly inarticulate and

panicked, animal-like in its loss, and tried to claw the bag back off him. He held steady, dropping his voice, his free hand held out to her as he tried to do the soothing thing. I was about to tell him to just deck her and take the book, as unpleasant as that was, because she wasn't going to give the thing up willingly, when someone shouted, "What the *hell* are you doing?"

"He's mugging me!" Mrs Smith shrieked. "Thief!"

"I'm not," Callum protested.

"It sure *looks* like you are," the new voice said, and now I recognised it. Petra was standing on the other side of the street clutching the lead of a three-legged dog, which *whuff*-ed curiously at us. She looked furious. "You let her go!"

"You don't understand," Callum started.

"You heard her! Let me *go*," Mrs Smith hissed at him.

"Let her go now! Or I'll call the cops, and in the meantime I'll come over there and … and set Cyril on you," Petra said, waving threateningly with the dog's lead. The dog looked startled. "Bloody hell. And I thought you were one of the good ones."

"Aw," Callum said, managing to sound both flattered and disappointed all at once.

Mrs Smith tugged at her bag. "Let go."

"I really can't," Callum said, reaching for the bag with his free hand. "You *have* to give it back. You can't keep it, Mrs Smith. It's dangerous."

"*You* have to give it back!" Petra shouted. "Don't make us come over there!" Cyril the dog looked up at her and whined, his tail between his legs. I didn't blame him. The magic reeked, like potpourri covering rot.

"It's not *hers!*" Callum yelled at Petra. "I'm trying to *help*. For God's sake— *Ow!*" He dropped the bag straps and jerked away from Mrs Smith, bringing with him a rather glossy green snake that had its teeth firmly embedded in the fleshy part of his palm. He danced off the pavement and into the street, yelping and waving his hand about wildly, but the snake wasn't going anywhere. Its body flopped about like a rigid green streamer, and Cyril burst into hysterical barking, trying to drag Petra down the street away from the whole traumatic, magic-drenched scene.

Mrs Smith hauled the bag back onto her shoulder and sprinted for the building, and I bolted after her again, overtaking her as she reached the steps and lunging at her feet. Broken hips be damned – I couldn't let her get back inside with the book.

"Stop it," she screamed, dodging around me with far more grace than she had any right to. "Stop it, you horrible little furball!"

I shot straight at her, leaping for the bag with my ears back. I'd tear it off her shoulder and break into it myself if I had to. Mrs Smith swung the bag at me, knocking me sideways with one solid blow, and the most hideous screeching broke out all around us.

The flight of cockatoos roared down out of the trees, all of them screaming like cats with wet feet, and I didn't even have time to hit the ground before they snatched me up. Talons punctured the skin of my back and lit it on fire, and they hoisted me higher still. I bucked and twisted wildly, snarling as the wounds tore, cursing out the birds, their offspring, their ancestors, and avian species in general. I was thrashing as hard as I could, but my claws caught nothing except feathers, and my vision was full of harsh beaks and flat eyes. I yowled in fury and frustration, flung myself as hard against my captors as I possibly could, and finally managed to sink my teeth into a wing. The bird screeched and lurched into its companion, breaking both their grips as they squawked furiously at each other.

"Eat me!" I roared triumphantly as I fell away from them, but the joy of the moment didn't exactly last – I was upside down, in free fall, and I had no idea how high I was. Callum was yelling my name, but I ignored him. I had bigger birds to fry.

I twisted, angling my tail just so, looking for the ground, gaze coming around to find it, paws following, and … yep, there it was. Rushing at me so fast I thought I was in for a stubbed nose at the least. But I was moving into the roll faster than I realised, and even as I braced myself for the impact I brought my feet around and landed, belly dropping almost to the stone as my legs took up the shock of the fall.

I had about half a second to feel smug before the cockatoos thundered down after me like a plague of sulphur-crested vampires, and I bolted under the nearest car for shelter, screeching at them what their mothers had no doubt done to deserve such monsters. From the protection of the car I watched Mrs Smith run up the stairs of the building and vanish inside, the door slamming shut behind her.

"Hairballs," I said.

Running feet caught my attention, and I peered out

from under the car as Callum's tatty boots appeared on the street. He dropped to his knees and peered at me anxiously. "Are you okay?"

"I was just attacked by dinosaurs, Callum. *Dinosaurs.*"

He nodded. "Birds. You were attacked by birds. I mean, cockatoos, but still. Birds."

I hissed at him, and he looked around. "They're gone. You can come out."

"Are you sure?"

"Yes. I'll even carry you, if you want."

"I don't need *carrying,*" I spat, but I stayed very close to his feet as I crept out of shelter, peering around warily. The darkening sky looked clear.

Petra was still standing on the other side of the street, Cyril's lead wound around her arm and the dog pulled close to her side. She had a hand resting protectively on his head. She blinked at me, opened her mouth, shut it again, then finally settled for calling, "Is he okay?"

"He's fine," Callum said.

"Are *you* okay?"

"Yeah."

There was a pause, then she said, "You have a snake on your hand."

We all looked at it. The snake still had its teeth sunk in Callum's palm, and had managed to wrap coils all around his wrist, locking itself in place. As if realising we were looking at it, it tightened its grip, and Callum winced. "It's not too bad," he said aloud.

Petra nodded slowly, and said, "Do you train them as well?"

"What? No— I mean, yes. I train all sorts of things. Rats. Snakes. Cats."

I growled.

"And that lady stole your snake?" she asked. "That's what you were trying to get back?"

"Ye-es," he said, not sounding particularly convincing.

She looked at us for a while longer, not smiling, then said, "This is the weirdest place I've ever lived." Then she turned and walked away, Cyril doing his best to drag her along with his hobbling gait.

"She's got a point," I said. "We should move."

"Sure. Let's move. But can we get the snake off first?"

18

ADAPTABILITY & FLEXIBILITY

CALLUM TRIED UNWINDING THE SNAKE FROM HIS ARM, BUT all he seemed to manage to do was shift the coils a little closer together, making them tighter, and the snake bit him harder in protest. Eventually he gave up, blood dripping quietly down his fingers.

"Is it poisonous?" I asked, and he scowled at me.

"I don't know. It's the one biting me."

I glared at him. "You know what I mean. Venomous, then."

"How the hell do I know?"

"Well, does it feel venomous?"

"My heart hasn't stopped yet, so I suppose that's a good sign."

"I imagine so," I said. "Unless the venom's really slow-acting. Your hand might gradually rot and your fingers fall off, rather than your heart stopping."

He shook his head. "Thanks, G. That helps so much."

I shrugged. "Maybe if you put it in water it'll let go."

"Maybe I should go to the hospital. It's probably what you should do when a snake bites you."

"Sure. Then you can wait four hours in A&E before taking another couple to explain how you got a snake stuck to your arm, while all the time Mrs Smith and the book will be eating up the world with niceness and octopuses from another dimension."

"Octopodes." He fished around in his pockets, clumsy with only his left hand.

"*Octopuses.* You're having a *cigarette?*"

"Maybe I can smoke it off," he said smugly, and I turned my back on him.

"Come on. We have to come up with another plan."

"She's not going to give it to us, G."

"I kind of figured that. So we have to steal it. And quick." I nodded at the building.

The gentle ivy was swarming over it in the light of the lanterns, growing in all directions as we watched, sprouting slick spiked leaves and orchids and softly glowing chrysalises, and sending butterflies into multi-coloured flight while the bricks creaked and groaned with the pressure of it. A rusty old Ford parked a little too close had transformed into one of those rattly old-school cars where people perched on top and wore driving goggles and flowing scarves, and the pavement had turned entirely to glossy grass.

As we watched a crack appeared in the road, groaned, spat half a dozen penguins out then healed up again. The penguins blinked around, lifting their wings anxiously and shaking their heads in a manner that said very clearly that this was not what they had expected when they woke up this morning.

You and us both, penguins. Aloud, I said, "Things are getting squiffy."

"To put it mildly," a quiet voice said from under the car. Callum crouched down next to me as we peered at Susan. She seemed …

"Are you *pink?*" I demanded.

"With fuchsia ears," she said, and pattered out to sit on her hind legs, looking down at her sleek, softly rosy belly. It was the sort of belly you give kittens to cuddle, but only because you feel too old to cuddle it yourself. "I'm hideous!"

"It's not so bad," Callum said. "It's actually kind of cute."

She glared at him. "I am the Queen-Empress of the Lower Ways, you teaspoon. I am not *cute.*"

"Sorry," he said, and blew smoke on the snake. It glared at him, but didn't let go.

"The book?" I asked Susan.

"I rather doubt it's a coincidence that every rat in a one block radius has turned pastel. When are you going to fix this?"

"We're trying," I said. "Only he got bitten by a snake and I got attacked by dinosaurs."

She stared at me for a moment, then shook her head. "It was obviously a mistake to leave any of this with you two. I should have known. A cat and a human, I mean, gods. Do you even have a plan?"

"Well," I said.

"In a way," Callum started at the same moment, and we

both looked at each other. "No," he admitted. "Steal it back, I suppose."

"Just like that," she said.

"Well, no," I said. "But we'll work out the details on the fly, like. Adaptability and flexibility, you know?"

"Sure," she said. "Just like your bag snatch there."

"Okay, admittedly, we could have handled that better," Callum said.

"We'll get it next time, though," I said.

Susan rubbed her front paws together, a nervous little gesture. "There's not much time for next time. It's turning into a magical vortex in there, and that is not as fun as it sounds. I don't think you can handle this alone. We should call in the Watch."

"No!" I yelped. "No, that is the one thing we absolutely can't do."

"This is out of control, G," she said. "There's too much power flying around, and things are getting unhinged. It might not even be enough just to break the book's bond anymore. We need someone who can actually get rid of the thing. Either bind it, which means sorcerers, and I don't know any, or drop it in the Inbetween, and that means the Watch, as much as I'd rather avoid them too. Funny how cats like to set up treaties then have nasty little memory lapses."

I licked my chops. My back was stinging from the birds' claws, and I could feel the sticky damp of blood in my fur, but that wasn't what had my heart running too fast. "I can't do the Watch, Susan. They can't know I'm caught up in any of this." I looked up at Callum. "They *can't*."

"I know," he said, and reached out to pet me, forgetting the snake. I drew back, hissing, and the snake gave me a muffled hiss in reply. "Sorry. Look, we know sorcerers."

Old Ones take me, in all the fuss I'd kind of forgotten how the whole thing started. "Jones and Walker!"

"We start there," he said, fishing in his pockets. He bumped the snake's nose on a button, and it gave another, rather aggrieved hiss. "Sorry. If you just let go it'd be a lot easier on everyone involved, you know." The snake wriggled, which seemed to mean no.

"Trustworthy sorcerers?" Susan asked. "The book's completely feral now. You can smell it in the magic – it's just doing anything and everything. Power for the sake of power. The sorcerer's going to have to be strong enough to break the bond with the old lady, bind it to them, *and* not have it take them over entirely. Or, you know, get all carried away and try to turn the world into their own personal empire of cheese or something."

Not Walker, then. "Jones can do it," I said, and looked at Callum.

"Yeah," he said. "It was hers to start with, anyway. And Walker's bond's been broken by Mrs Smith, so the counter-curse should be lifted. Ms Jones is free to take it back."

"Great. So call her," Susan said. "Chop-chop, kids."

Callum scratched his stubble, and I looked at the penguins. One of them was attacking a solar lamp that was stuck in the grass, and the others were investigating some wildflowers, squawking unhappily. Maybe they prefer herring.

"You don't know how to get in touch with her," Susan

said, shaking her head. "You're just amazing, you know that?"

"I reckon if we get hold of Walker, he'll know," I said. "We've got his number in the file upstairs."

"I'm sure he'll be really happy to tell Jones where her book is," Callum said. "You know, after he stole it and counter-cursed it in the first place."

"And your bright idea is?"

He muttered something about problems with talking animals and thinking he'd rather stick with dogs in the future, then got up. "Let's go try."

IT WAS A GOOD PLAN, that held right until we got to the door. Or rather where the door had been, because now there was just an ivy-clad brick wall. Callum poked it as if he thought he only had to hit the right combination of stones for the wall to swing open, like the entrance to a millionaire's secret lair. But the wall just sat there, being a wall, and when a large hairy spider with several extra legs took a run at Callum he jumped back and stumbled down the steps.

"Can you get inside through a vent or something and let us in?" he asked Susan.

"Let you in what?" she asked.

"Well, maybe there's a door on the other side of the wall you could open."

She sighed deeply. "I don't think that's how walls work."

I looked at the ivy, then at the tree. It looked cockatoo-free, but who knew. They could be lurking anywhere. "You left the window open, right?" I said to Callum.

"Um. Yeah? I think so," he said, and peered up the side of the building. "Yep. It's open."

"Well, that's something," I said, and took off at a run before I could think too much more about it. Cockatoos or no cockatoos, it wasn't like we had a lot of choice at the moment.

I shot up the trunk, concentrating on nothing more than where my next claw-hold was. The branches were even heavier with growth and good health than they had been that morning, and the tree seemed to have grown a few metres taller and fatter. In the low light fireflies danced in the hollows, and when you got close enough you could see they were less flies and more ... well, dragons, not to put too fine a point on things. Very small dragons, turning teeny green somersaults and belching yellow flame at each other, singeing little scars in the bark and charring the leaves. I hoped they didn't burn the tree down before I got hold of the file and got back out.

Deeper in the shadowed parts of the trunk unseen things whispered and chuckled, and I could hear the scrape of claws on old wood. I didn't hang around to see exactly what they were talking about, or what they were. Certain things I did not need to know.

I scuttled up to where the branches thinned out, belly-flopped my way across the foliage, and tumbled out of the tree at the perfect spot to snag some ivy (which was lusher and more exotic than any ivy I'd ever seen, even in the botanical gardens), and scramble across to our windowsill. I paused there, breathing hard, and peered into the room. It had changed from hunting lodge decor to something involving a lot of purple velvet and gold braid, and there was a large mirror on the wall that looked troublingly *watchful*. But no spiders, snakes, or alligators that I could see. Or cockatoos. And the antlers were gone. Small blessings, you know.

There was a neat brown folder sitting rather invitingly on top of the desk, and I peered at it suspiciously. It seemed rather too convenient, when everything else had been tidied away so nicely. But something had to go our way at some point, right? And we were running out of time to go driving about the place looking for Walker. In fact, I had the feeling we were running out of time for a lot of things.

I took another careful look around the room, but it really seemed to be empty. Just heavy curtains and muted lighting, and what looked to be red satin cushions perched on the black velvet sofa. Classy. I jumped from the windowsill to the desk, pawing open the folder as quickly as I could, my ears back and my whiskers bristling, on guard for the slightest breath of movement around me.

The room didn't smell right. No damp walls or whiff of toast and cigarettes, no must of books. It smelt of cold thin places between the stars, of hungry magic and broken things, and my heart was running too fast and too loud. I flicked a takeaway menu aside. Where was the damn number?

Callum always said he liked to keep things handy, but what that really meant was that he never got around to filing things until the case was finished, and even then usually not for a week or so – or months – after. His notes would have been out on the desk still, but who knew what the book had done with them while reorganising. And if I had to start going through drawers we were out of luck.

I nosed hurriedly through the contents of the folder, and gave quiet thanks for Callum's disorganisation. It was evidently at such a level that even the book hadn't figured out how to counter it entirely. The folder was filled with takeaway menus, a flyer for a book sale, the dust jacket for a pirate romance novel, two cardboard coasters, three book covers featuring monsters, scientists, and spaceships, five bookmarks, a whole clutch of receipts, and Ms Jones' envelope. Evidently it was just all the bits the apartment hadn't known what to do with. I grabbed the envelope in my teeth and tried to worry it open, but it was one of those ones with a metal clasp holding it shut. I tried biting it, but it jabbed the roof of my mouth.

"Ow," I muttered, and tried a different angle. There was a little bit of give, and I bit it carefully, trying to make it bend. I didn't really want to lug the whole envelope with me.

Movement caught the corner of my eye, and I looked up, tail bushing – not that that was unusual at the moment. I seemed to be spending a solid half of my time pouffed up like a porcupine fish since the book appeared. The apartment was deeply shadowed, the heavy purple cloth draped on the walls muffling sound and light alike. Maybe I could manage to take the whole envelope. The air resistance was going to be a bit sucky trying to get back to the tree, but it wasn't a long jump. It might be okay.

I stared around the dim room, trying to decide what I'd seen. A reflection from outside in the mirror, maybe? The mirror looked perfectly blank, a deep and featureless lake that swallowed light rather than reflecting it.

I fumbled with the envelope, trying to get a grip on the long edge while not looking away from the room. I was somehow certain that if I did, something leviathan would creep into sight on soundless feet, looming up to fill the world and breathing the stink of the void on me.

The envelope was slippery, maddeningly difficult to get my teeth into. I held it down with one paw and scratched it with the other, finally looking away from the room long enough to see I'd pulled the corner up. I grabbed it in my teeth, lifting it as well as I could, and checked the room again. It was so *still*. No noise from the street outside or the other apartments. So silent the world outside could have ceased to exist. There was just my own breath, whispering across the paper, fast and harsh.

The luxurious curtains were still, although they were so heavy it probably would've taken a hurricane to stir them anyway. I stood there on the desk, the envelope gripped in my teeth, knowing I should run but waiting for something to reveal itself. Every hair on my body was making a concerted effort to part company with my skin, and I could feel my pupils stretched as wide as my senses, grasping at every shred of light.

I looked at the mirror again, oddly sure something would be staring back at me, or crawling out, all teeth and claws and raging hunger. At first I couldn't see anything except the reflection of the room. I was a shadow, so small as to be a memory, the envelope stark yellow against my chest, the window a square of fading light behind me. There was nothing else.

Then something crystallised slowly into being, like one of those instant photographs developing in front of your eyes. It was over me, clinging to the ceiling, *growing* from it, a long, multijointed limb that reached out to touch the window, ready to push it shut. Three more clawed and spiny limbs stretched toward me, drifting down soft and silent as predatory snowflakes, so slow I could barely credit them with movement at all. The thing attached to them was there and not, seeping through a ceiling that was no longer quite solid, no longer quite *real.* Behind it I could sense more than see howling, un-empty space, pressing against the creature's back like the sea desperate to breech a restraining wall. The envelope felt like it was suffocating me.

You know the term, reflexes of a cat? Well, for one very small moment my mind wanted to know what, exactly, was up there, and if it came from the Inbetween or somewhere deeper and more awful, and what was behind it, and what it would feel like when those slick spider-crab-whatever limbs touched me. For that horrible, endless moment I was frozen, and if it weren't for those aforementioned reflexes I'd be a … well, dinner, or gloves, or whatever the hell that thing wanted me for.

Instead I went from standing to airborne faster than any car or jet you want to name, spinning through 180 degrees as my front legs left the desk, back legs powering me up and catapulting me at the window. The envelope slowed me, and I stood on it with one front paw as I hit the windowsill, tripping myself so hard my nose hit the wood, but my momentum carried me on and I just went with it.

I somersaulted over the ledge and straight out into the dying light of the evening as the window slammed shut so close behind me I felt the wind of it, and heard a rumble of frustration that echoed in my soul as something vast missed out on its kitty snacks. Then I dropped the envelope, flung my legs wide, and tried to pretend I was a flying squirrel.

I hit three branches on the way down, and the fourth I tackled like a rugby player, digging my claws in as hard as I could and winding up hanging upside down with my ears back and my eyes wide, staring at a minuscule orange dragon and hoping it didn't decide to flame me. The envelope fluttered past and drifted softly to the ground.

"Gobbelino!" Callum yelled. "Are you okay?"

"Sure," I shouted back, and the dragon ducked away in alarm. "This is how I like to spend all my Friday nights."

"It's Saturday," he said, from directly underneath me.

"Days of the week are a human invention," I replied, and let go.

He caught me with one hand and one snake-y sort of mitt, and the snake let go of Callum with a hiss and tried to bite me. I bopped it on the nose and hissed back, rather more impressively, and it dived into one of Callum's pockets.

I looked at him. "You have *got* to lose the coat."

"I like the coat."

"It now has snakes in it."

"Stops pickpockets," he said, and put me on the ground.

I shook myself off and stalked around a penguin who was waddling toward me and grunting in a friendly sort of way. "Whatever. Let's just give Walker a call and get Jones here quick as we can."

"Any problems?" he asked, picking up the envelope.

"Nothing I couldn't handle," I said, and tried not to think of the thing seeping out of the ceiling, and the screaming dimensions beyond it.

Or the fact that we were going to have to go back into what was rapidly becoming a building with a very dubious grip on reality.

SORCERER-ER IT

So naturally, Walker was not in favour of calling Ms Jones. Callum squatted on the pavement across the alley from the building with the phone on speaker so Susan, myself, and the snake (which was peering out of Callum's pocket), could all hear him.

"You can't try and take the book on your own," Callum said, not for the first time. "You said yourself, you only learnt how to escape."

"Yeah, but I had to break the bond to do that," Walker said, his voice tinny. "Hang on, I'm just getting in the car." There was a pause, a moment of deadness, then he came back on. "You still there?"

"We're here. Walker, the book's gone feral. There's …" he waved vaguely at the building, as if not quite sure how to describe it. "Stuff," he ended.

Susan and I looked at each other. "Dude," I said, leaning over the phone. "There's a creature from the void in our ceiling, a cocktail-toting warthog in Mrs Smith's apartment, penguins on the street and dragons in the trees. I mean, little ones, but still. We need the big guns."

"I can handle it," he insisted, then muttered, "Dammit. I don't *want* GPS coordinates. I want postcodes. Stupid machine." There was a thump as he evidently slapped his nav system, because that always helps. "Do you know your GPS coordinates?"

"No, of course I bloody don't," Callum snapped.

"Can you get them?"

"No. Just call Ms Jones, alright?"

"I'm *not* calling her! The book's *mine.*"

"Then give us her number, pudding-brains," I shouted at the phone. "Then we can at least get her here in time to scrape your perforated hide off the pavement."

"You're as bad as her! You've got no faith in me—"

I swiped the phone out of Callum's hand and sent it skittering across the pavement. He watched it go, then sighed and went to fetch it. "That's unhelpful, G."

"*He's* unhelpful."

Callum checked the phone as he picked it up. We couldn't afford a flashy one, so it was ancient, had patchy internet that worked about three days a week, and did more damage to the floor than the floor did to it whenever we dropped it. Which was pretty regularly. "Well, you hung up on him."

"Good."

Susan sighed. "So what you're telling me is that we have some dentist – who probably can't tell a magic bean from a baked one – coming over to save the world."

"Pretty much," Callum said.

"If he finds the place," I pointed out. "Since he doesn't have the GPS coordinates."

She examined her pale pink paws. "Fantastic. We have to go to the Watch, Gobbelino. This is getting out of hand."

"No. We'll sort it," I said. "We will."

"With a *dentist?*"

"I promise." Although I wasn't enthused by the dentist idea either.

"You'd better be right," she said, and nodded at the building. "My distance vision isn't that good, but I can smell it. Things are getting wonky. And even I can see something's not right over there."

We turned to look back at the building. The sun had vanished behind the mass of the city, leaving the sky a high, pale grey and the shadows deepening. They seemed particularly deep in our corner of the world, extending about the place like a pocket of night even I couldn't see through at this distance. I looked up at Callum. "What's going on over there?"

"Um," he said, and fumbled the phone into his pocket on top of the snake, which hissed. "Okay, so you know how sometimes in the evening or morning, when the sun's up far enough to be bright but not so far that it's all white, you get the sun behind the clouds? And it spills out the sides all in shards of gold and orange, and it looks so perfect you think it has to be a painting, that nothing can be so textured and spectacular?"

"Kind of," I said.

"No," Susan said.

"Well, it's like that, but it's sort of a *bruised* light rather than a gold one, and I think it's actually the sky in front of it rather than clouds, so the weird light – or not-light – is coming from *behind* the sky?"

We were quiet for a while, because the only thing that sounded like to me was other dimensions busting through thin places in reality. And my time in the Inbetween was like a bunny rabbit's picnic compared to that.

"I really don't think the dentist is going to cut it," Susan said.

A SHINY BLACK car with fat tyres and tinted windows and too much chrome pulled up in front of our building, the engine rumbling excessively enough to make my ears twitch. Walker clambered out of the car, wearing sunglasses despite the fact it was almost dark, and pushed them up somewhat ostentatiously to stare at the crawling ivy-type stuff on the facade and what had been the old-style car parked just behind him. It had turned into a Cinderella-style carriage complete with four confused white horses while we'd been waiting. The horses had dragged the carriage over to the veggie stall and were currently eating all the lettuce, of which there seemed to be an excessive variety.

"Whoa," Walker said.

"Yes," Callum replied, crossing the road to meet him. "*Now* will you call Ms Jones?"

"No," Walker said, but he sounded uncertain.

I wished I could smack him just as I'd smacked the phone. Callum had been describing the bulging sky, moving like a sac about to disgorge a flood of unearthly spawn, all coloured in greens and purples and yellows and other colours that didn't belong to this world. I'd given up trying to make the fur on my tail calm down, and Susan was cleaning her whiskers incessantly.

"You've as much sense as a cauliflower," I said to him.

He sniffed at me. "Says the talking cat."

"What? What the hell does that have to do with it? Can you talk *Cat?*"

He ignored me, and leaned into the car to grab a tablet. "I've got all my stuff on here. Let me just pull it up before we go in."

"You don't know it off by heart?" Callum asked.

"It's very complicated!"

"Oh, I can see this going well," Susan said. "I'm going to evacuate the clan. We'll just have to put up with being pastel."

Walker stared at her. "You talk, too?"

"Most things do. Most people just don't listen." She shrugged. "And often aren't worth talking to anyway."

He frowned, then looked back at his tablet and tapped a couple of things. "Here we go. Alright, I'm ready."

"That's it?" Callum said. "Your tablet?"

"Yeah. What'd you expect? Chicken hearts?"

"This should be fun," I said, and looked at Susan. She lifted her front paws in a gesture of despair and scooted off down the pavement. I hoped she was going to be alright. I hoped we were *all* going to be alright.

———

THE WOUNDS on my back from the cockatoos were tight and sore, and I'd hurt a shoulder on the way through the tree. Everything had stiffened up while we'd been waiting, and I hobbled next to Callum as we walked to the foliage-encrusted wall where the entrance had been. Walker looked at it, then at us.

"Where's the door?"

"Looks like you'll have to make one," Callum said.

"There was a door. I remember it."

"Well, it's not here now," I said. "And, you know, there also weren't any penguins before. Or flamingos." They were new, stalking down the pavement looking confused. The horses were staring at them in astonishment.

"How're we going to get in?" Walker asked.

"You're the sorcerer," I said, and sidestepped a marching line of luminous green centipedes that were stomping past on bright yellow feet, waving small pink pennants from their pincers like cheerleaders. "Sorcerer-er us one."

"Oh. Well, okay. Sure. Hang on." He started scrolling on his tablet, while the building twitched and groaned above us, crenellations and turrets blooming from the walls and vanishing again, flights of polka-dotted bats swooping through the blooming vines and hordes of bright blue and yellow spiders scuttling from one clump of glossy green leaves to another.

"You could just call Ms Jones," Callum said. "I'm pretty sure she doesn't need a tablet."

"No, no, here it is." He tapped the screen, and a moment later someone's dulcet tones informed us that their cologne was going to make all the kitties purr, or something equally senseless. "Bloody ads," he muttered, tapping again, then the tablet said, "*Okay, so, like, as a sorcerer? You need to like, be able to make doors in stuff, you know? And, like, there are a few ways to do this, but this is totally easy and really cool—*"

Callum snatched the tablet off him, staring at the screen. "*This* is how you're going to get in there? A YouTube tutorial by a fourteen-year-old wearing his dad's dressing gown?"

"Give it back!" Walker yelped, grabbing at Callum's arm, but Callum held the tablet out of reach easily. "I need it!"

"Dude, that's sad," I said.

"It *works*," he insisted. "I learnt how to bind the book from that channel! Just because he's young doesn't mean he's not a good sorcerer – I'd never have got away from Polly without these videos!"

"Polly?" Callum and I said together.

"Polly Jones," he said, and tried to grab the tablet again. Callum pushed him away, not hard, just enough to stop the man scrabbling at him.

"That book *really* wanted free," I said. "There's no way it would've worked otherwise. It latched on to the smallest bit of magic and called it enough."

"It *did* work," Walker almost wailed. "Give me the tablet and I'll show you!"

"Gods. How long's the video, Callum?"

He checked, still keeping the tablet out of Walker's reach. "Five minutes."

"Give it to him. But if this doesn't work, you're calling *Polly*, alright?"

"Fine," Walker said, and snatched the tablet as Callum handed it back. "I'll show you!"

"Sure you will," I said, and wished the world wasn't ending, because this would've been a whole lot funnier if we hadn't been in danger of seeing the fabric of reality rip and our souls devoured by multidimensional monsters any minute.

IT WENT PRETTY MUCH how we expected. Walker waved his hands around a lot, poked the wall a few times (jumping away with a yelp and just about falling down the stairs when a glittery, six-legged lizard tried to poke him back), and chanted a lot of rubbish that didn't sound like any incantation I'd come across before. It sounded kind of like a cereal commercial run backward, to be honest. The wall actually did shiver a couple of times, and some vines fell off, but I think that was more due to the fact that the whole thing seemed to have started breathing, the masonry cracking and healing over and over.

Finally Walker stepped back, staring down at the tablet. "I don't understand," he said. "It worked before, when I broke Polly's bond. And it was definitely working for attracting more wealth. I got three more clients last week."

Callum looked at the ground. "You know the waiting list for NHS dentists is like six months, right?"

"*Private* clients," Walker snapped, holding the tablet against his chest. "It was working!"

Callum opened his mouth, probably to say something about lottery wins or mysterious inheritances, and I swiped his ankle with one paw, glaring at him. We didn't have time for him to point out Walker's failings as a sorcerer, numerous though they were. He subsided.

"Look," I said to Walker. "You were bound to the book when you were trying to attract wealth, so of course it worked. As for breaking the bond, maybe there was enough in what you learnt that when the book wanted its bond to be broken, it could be. But you don't have the book now, and the little bit of magic you have left in your watch will be pretty much gone. You don't have enough to tackle the book when it's in full power like this. You know that."

"Dammit," he said, running his free hand over his thinning hair. "I really thought …"

"Never mind," Callum said. "Just call Ms Jones, okay?"

"I suppose," he said, and looked at the tablet as if he wanted to throw it in the bin. I felt a teeny bit sorry for him, to be honest. The book had tricked him into thinking he was some great sorcerer, when he was really just a slightly paunchy dentist with surprisingly bad teeth. No wonder business hadn't been great.

Callum steered him back to the car and watched him send Jones a text, then we waited, listening to the night throb and pulse with magic around us. The penguins had decided they disapproved of their immediate environment and had headed off into the early evening, lurching along in a straggly line. The flamingos were hanging around the veggie cart, apparently hoping the horses turned up some minnows or sardines or whatever it was they lived on. And the rats were evacuating, a little pastel-tinted plague of them trotting off into the shadows with a chubby lavender female in the lead, their heads down and their whiskers twitching.

Susan ambled up to us, Abigail and Esther in tow. Esther was the egg-yolk yellow of an Easter chicken, and Abigail was a lovely shade of minty green.

"Come to say 'bye?" I asked them.

"Nah. You need someone with a little nous around here," Susan said. "Left to yourselves, you'll probably summon the great many-tongued demons of Payaroth."

"Where?" Callum asked. I didn't answer. I'd never heard of them either.

"And if the world's going to end, I'd rather watch," Abigail said. Esther just looked alarmed.

We waited.

I'M HONESTLY NOT sure where Ms Jones came from. I didn't hear a car or a motorbike, and as only faeries, cats, and the odd livelier gargoyle can shift, she didn't do that. And no, she didn't arrive on a broom. Come on.

However she got there – taxi, Uber, *not* a broom – I didn't see her arrive. One moment the only movement in the alley was a couple of zebras heading off in search of the big city (they'd emerged from the undergrowth on the wall, taken one look at the flamingos and decided it wasn't their sort of place), the next she was striding down the street with her head up and a multicoloured shawl hanging from her shoulders. Pink Doc Martens slammed into the tarmac with pure fury, and she seemed to have half a dozen pens stuck in the dark coils of her hair. Her scent swept ahead of her, musky and heavy with magic, both terrifying and intoxicating in a weird, head-spinning way.

She marched straight up to us, pointed at Walker and snapped, "Wait in the car, you … you *Tupperware lid.*" Then she turned to Callum and me without waiting to see if Walker followed her instructions, putting her hands on her hips. The pens bristled with rage. "One job. One!"

"Sorry," Callum said, taking a step back.

"It might have helped if you'd told us everything from the start," I said, keeping Callum between us. "Or, you know, given us a contact number."

She raised a finger like she was about to give me a very firm telling-off, then sighed. "I hardly thought you were going to make this much of a mess of things."

I opened my mouth to defend our truly excellent PI skills, then shut it again. She was right. We'd left the book in the office, unguarded, despite knowing it was a book of power, then it had taken us a day to realise our neighbour was the thief, by which time it was well and truly attached to her. And now reality was getting squiffy and the very foundations of the world were about ready to crumble.

It wasn't exactly our best work.

Ms Jones surveyed us for a moment longer, then clapped her hands together. "Time for all this later. Let's get my book back before anything gets worse." She nodded at the rats. "Nice colours."

"I like her," Susan observed.

"You would," I mumbled, and Jones shot me an amused look, then glanced at Walker, who was hovering behind us.

"I thought I told you to get in the car."

"I don't *want* to," he said. "And it's my book, anyway."

"It's not your book," she snapped. "It's mine, and I'm taking it back."

"It's not either of yours anymore," Callum pointed out. "It's Mrs Smith's book, and we need to get the damn thing under control one way or the other before, you know, multi-universe disaster."

"Multidimensional," I muttered, but he was close enough.

Jones looked at Callum. "If this sorry excuse for a dentist touches it now, it'll tear him apart. He doesn't have the training for it. The only reason it didn't destroy him before is that I'd tamed it."

"I'm right here," Walker said. "And you're so wrong. I was handling it just fine!"

"Sure," Jones snapped. "That's how these two amateurs nicked it from right under your stubby little nose."

"Hey. We're *professionals*," I said, although maybe without quite as much vehemence as I might have.

Callum nudged me with the toe of his boot. "It's not tame now. Can you get it back under control?"

Jones looked up at the bulging sky and watched a fall of birds with serrated wings and suckers for faces tumble out of the clouds. "I hope so," she said. "Has anyone been inside?"

"There was half a jungle in there this afternoon," Callum said. "God knows what's in there now."

I looked at Susan. She shrugged, and said, "We can scout."

Jones gave her a sharp nod. "I always liked rats."

"Okay, if you get us in, Susan and her team can scout," I said. "The rest of us will run interference as much as we can, keep the way clear for you, and you shut the book down." I looked at Callum, and he nodded, like it was going to be just that simple.

"Sure. Sounds like a plan."

"Alright," Jones said. "But no one come running to me complaining if you're caught in the crossfire and turned into a frog."

"That would suck," Abigail observed, and Esther ducked behind her.

"What about me?" Walker asked. "I'm not staying out here when you're after *my* book."

"Bait?" I suggested, and Callum gave me another nudge. I glared at him. "What?"

"You can come if you do exactly as we tell you," he said to Walker. "Don't go near the book. Keep any critters away from Ms Jones."

"Fine," Walker mumbled, and I narrowed my eyes at him. I trusted him about as much as I trusted his dental hygiene.

"Just stay out of the way," Ms Jones said, and turned to the wall. She raised one long-fingered hand and barked a command that echoed in the bones of my ears and under my feet, shaking my teeth in their sockets. The wall blew apart with the roar of a felled tree and she marched in, ignoring the dust and centipedes and cockroaches raining down all about her.

Callum and I looked at each other.

"After you," he said.

20

STAIRWAY TO NOWHERE

INSIDE, THE WALLS WERE BREATHING. I DON'T MEAN LIKE some sort of horror movie rubbish, where they'd transformed into raw and vaguely suggestive flesh, heaving squelchily about the place. No, they were still old red brick, the plaster sloughing off and falling to the floor in sheets, smashing on the torn lino that had reasserted itself. The brick swelled and creaked and groaned, the mortar crumbling and spitting as the building shifted muscles it shouldn't have had, and drew breath that it shouldn't need.

The fluorescent lights were shattered, the entire hall drowning in moving shadows as the dark drew down. There wasn't a trace of the fancy lamps or skinny side tables left, no expensive but dubious murals. Not-nice was reasserting itself as the power moved elsewhere.

Jones stalked into the centre of the moving, crumbling foyer as Susan, Abigail, and Esther shot past her and vanished through the warped door to the stairwell. They didn't seem to be too keen to use any of the many gaps in the walls, and I didn't blame them. Those gaping spaces looked unpleasantly hungry.

Jones pointed at Callum. "Torch?"

"Um, no," he said, and she gave him a look that suggested he'd let the whole side down.

"I've got my phone," Walker said, fumbling in his pockets. "Let's see, there's a button, I know there is, it's just … this one?"

There was the click of a camera shutter, and Jones glared at him.

"No, not that. Maybe this?"

"Hello. This is your Google assistant. How ca—"

"There is one in here. Hang on."

Jones took one of the pens out of her hair, mumbled a couple of things to it, and light bloomed around the end. She shone it in the eyes of both men. "This is not what I should be using my magic for, you know? I'm going to need it."

"Sorry," they mumbled, and she turned away from them.

"Try and keep up." She strode to the stairs, hauled the door open and started inside.

I looked up at Callum. "I might have to trade you in."

"As if anyone else would have you," he said, and we followed Jones with Walker trailing behind us, still poking his phone and muttering.

The stairwell had reverted to its old, stinking self, mysterious stains running down the walls and the handrail too sticky to be used. There were some new, even less pleasant changes too, like the howling winds that blew through cracks in the bricks, reeking of distant dimensions and twisted worlds, and unseen things that clawed at the gaps. I could hear them plucking at the fabric of our reality, a thin sharp sound that rang in my bones like angry harmonics.

I kept close to Callum's feet, less in the hope that he might protect me and more on the vague assumption that he was a bigger target than I was, so any inter-dimensional monster munchers might go for him first.

Jones slowed, playing her light over the stairs above us.

"What is it?" Callum asked.

"The book doesn't want me here," she said, and there was hurt in her voice, a bone-deep betrayal. I wondered how long she'd walked the world with that conqueror's stride, watching humans move from magic to iron, the Folk from feared to forgotten, building her power and sinking her excess magic into the book that she'd had every right to think was hers forever. I mean, cats don't do lonely, but it sounded lonely anyway.

"Of course it doesn't want you here," Walker shouted from behind us. "It's *mine.*"

Jones ignored him. "So much of me in it," she said, her voice so low I had to twitch my ears to hear her. "What do I have left?"

"Enough to shut the damn thing down?" I suggested, and she gave me a dirty look. Well, a self-pitying sorcerer was going to be no help to anyone. "Just asking. I mean, it'd be good to know if we're marching in here with a gun but no bullets, so to speak."

"It's fine," she snapped. "I was a sorcerer long before I created the book." But there was something in the line of her mouth, in the way she looked at the walls, that didn't sit right. Something which suggested that, in a world where magic was lost and passing as human was easier than finding the room to stand apart, putting most of your power into something you could lock away in secret might seem like a good idea.

Joy.

Two flights of stairs. Not a lot, right? I could have run up them in under thirty seconds, easy. Hell, even Walker could probably have tottered up in under a minute. But Susan was right. Things were getting a lot more than just squiffy. Reality was warping and twisting. One moment we were stumping up the bare, grubby stairs, the boards creaking under our feet, the next we were clawing our way up a cliff face that fell to shrieking, unmeasurable depths below, while half-seen shapes flashed in and out of the clouds that roiled behind us. I dug my claws into rock and crumbling earth with a squawk, trying to avoid being battered about the head by Callum's coat as it flapped and thrashed in the wind.

"Keep going!" Jones yelled from above us, and I could dimly see her pink boots scrabbling for grip. "It's not *that* real. Just keep going!"

"Not *that* real?" Callum shouted back. "So we won't die *that* much?"

She ignored him, which was fair enough. It wasn't like platitudes were going to help at this stage. Walker was shrieking that he didn't like heights and his shoes weren't made for this, but he was also clawing his way up the cliff at a surprisingly impressive pace. He passed us to the right, still shrieking, and Jones started yelling at him to shut his mouth before he brought all the not-that-real monsters in the clouds down on us. Callum looked at me as he fumbled for a new handhold, the wind tearing at his hair and making his eyes run.

"We should consider a new career."

"I second that," I said, and kept clawing my way after Walker and Jones. The cliff wasn't impossible to climb, but the clumps of feathery grass were slick under my paws and the rocks loosely anchored, and I found myself thinking of the ivy rather fondly. At least you knew what to expect with ivy. This stuff, you had no idea if it'd shear away in an instant or if you could swing from it like a trapeze.

Callum let me go past then climbed after me, grabbing a root here, an outcropping there, and digging his fingers into crevices in the face itself, hauling himself up with the ridiculous coat tugging him every which way in the petulant wind. Vast things with echoing voices called to each other in the wet reaches of the clouds, and once something grey and sweating passed so close that Callum buried his face in the cliff, as if to look at it would bring its attention down on us. It flapped clumsily away again, greasy and uninterested, and in its wake the air turbulence formed tornadoes that plucked me from a ledge I'd been sheltering on. I spun into the abyss with a shriek and some rather colourful cursing, and Callum snagged me as I went past, almost losing his own grip on the rock. He deposited me on his shoulder and went back to climbing, and I settled there to watch for more of the sky creatures. It was a better use of my time and energy, after all.

Jones' pink boots and Walker's socks led us on – he'd apparently kicked his shoes off, which wasn't the most ridiculous thing I'd heard of. He might have more sense than I'd credited him with.

Then Jones yelled, "*Hang on!*"

Callum flattened himself to the cliff as a roar of sound rose from above, a jet engine firing up or a train screaming into a tunnel or a tornado coming to ferry us to Oz, and I latched myself into his coat as firmly as I could. I looked up to see a deluge of water and rock and broken plants thundering toward us, carrying Jones with it. She was grimly silent, her face set in hard lines, her hands scraping at the cliff as she came like a crab skittering down rocks in an outgoing tide. She snagged an outcropping, coming to a halt that jerked a curse out of her, and the water roared on, cutting around her head as if around a boulder in a river.

I buried my snout in Callum's collar as it hit us, cold in a way that sliced to the bone, that threatened to drown you right through the skin. He was shaking from the effort of holding on against it, and I could feel his pulse racing under my nose. I clawed my way closer to his neck, struggling to find some pocket of air in the folds of the coat, but the weight of the water carried everything with it. I couldn't see, couldn't breathe, couldn't hear anything but the endless, crushing downpour, pressing us into the rock and into each other, and I had time to think that death by drowning on a cliff in a stairwell was a pretty crappy way to lose a life.

Walker went sliding past us, spluttering and yelping, and Callum somehow let go with one hand and grabbed the collar of the dentist's trendy leather jacket, dragging him to a halt. That unnecessary heroism almost dragged us off our perch, too, but the water was lessening, the flood becoming a filthy, spluttering flow of muddy water and debris, more petulant than devastating. Callum shoved Walker against the cliff face, and he managed to find something to hold onto.

"Thanks," he gasped. His face was scratched and muddy, and he'd lost his sunglasses.

"We charge extra for rescue services," I told him, and he scowled at me. Callum started climbing again, pausing to check on Jones, who gave us a thumbs up. Her pens and her bright shawl had been swept away, and her loose hair was festooned with twigs and mud. She looked like pretty much any cat caught in a rainstorm.

In other words, she looked ready to kill someone.

"Alright?" Callum asked her.

"Super," she said. "I'm so glad I hired you two. This sort of eventuality was just what I had in mind at the time."

"Full disclosure," I said, "we're not so happy we took the job, either."

"I think it's levelling off," Callum said, ignoring both of us. "Come on. Before we get another flood."

He led the way as the cliff slowly eased its angle, and we went from clawing up the vertical face to scrambling on steep, rock-crowded ground, to eventually standing. I settled myself more comfortably on Callum's shoulder and looked around suspiciously. The landing was bigger than it should have been, and the stairs hadn't reappeared behind us, but ahead there were tatty walls and peeling wallpaper enclosing an area of rocky, uneven ground, all patched with grass and a couple of stubby shrubs. Water was still washing steadily past, but it wasn't the deluge it had been. Across the landing, a door sat blandly in the wall, a swathe of threadbare grass leading up to it.

Walker staggered up next to us. "Thank God," he said. "Is my book in there?" He headed for the door.

"Wait," Callum said, but was drowned out by Jones.

"Malcolm Walker, don't you *touch* that door," she snapped.

He glanced back at her. "Or what? It's not yours anymore. It's *mine!*"

"It's really not," Callum said, but neither of them were listening.

"You don't know what's behind that door!"

"My *book's* behind that door!"

"It's not," Callum said again.

"You have no *idea* what you're doing!" Jones spat. "I should've just left you outside!"

"I'm not your pet poodle, no matter what you think!"

"It's not this door," Callum said, and they both ignored him.

Jones ran after Walker and grabbed his arm, jerking him to a stop. "*Do not open that door!*"

"You can't tell me what to do!" Walker yelled, and tried to shove her away. We watched with interest as they had a brief, enthusiastic grapple, then Jones headbutted Walker.

"Ooh," Callum said.

"Nice," I agreed.

"Not what I meant," Callum said.

Walker yelped and staggered back, then tripped on a hummock and fell over, smacking the side of his head against the wall. "*Ow!*" he howled, clutching his nose in one hand and his head with the other. "Jesus *Christ!* You—"

"Don't," she said, her voice hard.

"Ow," he repeated, staring at his socks, and Jones opened the door.

There was a blast of heat and wind that swept her off her feet, carrying her a good couple of metres and dumping her in a rocky puddle. I flattened my ears against the furnace breath that washed over us, and Callum raised a hand to shield his face. Beyond the doorway, a large fiery eye glared at us, and one molten claw reached out to hook the door and slam it closed again. Then the whole thing disappeared with a shiver, taking the walls with it and leaving behind nothing but barren wasteland stretching to purple horizons in some indeterminate distance.

The heat vanished, other than a few smouldering tussocks, and Callum flicked some ash off his coat. "I did say it wasn't our door. We're on the second floor."

Jones climbed to her feet, dusting her hands off. Her hair looked a little crispy at the front. "Well, why didn't you speak up, then?"

"Yeah," Walker agreed. "You should have been clearer."

Callum shook his head. "Shall we keep going?"

"Sure," I said, and glanced around. At some stage after Walker had made it up to the landing, the cliff behind us had vanished, leaving the dim-lit stairs prowling innocuously – and somewhat invitingly, considering what probably lay ahead – down to the foyer. Up here, with the door and walls gone, the strange grasslands rolling away from us were empty and desolate, and a cold wind came off them, smelling of stale, derelict worlds. The only signs of life were birds of prey wheeling hungry above us in a grey sky. "How, exactly?"

"The stairs up have to be here somewhere," Jones said. "We just have to find them."

We spread out, the humans kicking their way across the rough ground and waving their hands about like cut-rate magicians. Jones, not being human, didn't bother with that, and just stood there with her eyes half-closed and one hand out like the stairs were just going to appear under it. I jumped off Callum's shoulder and prowled after him, trying to look at things sideways. Sometimes a different angle was all that was needed, and Jones was right – the stairs had to be here. We just had to figure out how to see them.

But it was Walker, of course, who stumbled on them. Literally. He stuck his foot in a rabbit hole or vole burrow or whatever interesting variant of those creatures the building had conjured up and pitched forward with a squawk, then stopped at about 45 degrees, his outstretched hands braced on the air.

"*Ooh*," he said, and we hurried over to him.

"That's them," Callum said, running his hands across the air and making the shape of a step. "Let's go."

I petted the invisible shape a couple of times, turning my head this way and that as I tried to get the stairs to come into focus. I could feel them well enough, but they were stubbornly invisible, not even a ripple of distortion in the air to betray them. I put one paw on the first step, then another, and stared past my claws at the ground. Then I looked up at Callum, feeling his way slowly up, already a good metre off the ground. I could see the worn tread of his boots perfectly, just floating about the place. I closed my eyes and bolted after him, tail stiff as a signal flag. I overtook him and ran until I hit an unseen wall, peeked around, then ran again, hoping the stairs didn't suddenly change their minds about existing.

That's always the problem when reality gets dodgy. You can't rely on anything to keep existing.

Behind me, Callum, Jones and Walker climbed steadily above the boggy plains, all of them trying not to look down, hands outstretched to follow the turns of the invisible stairwell, and still the stairs went on, and on, and on, the air getting colder and thinner and the wind more and more cruel. I started to keep my eyes open, because I was worried I was going to miss the door and just keep climbing until the air ran out. Wisps of cloud drifted past us, and once a bird of prey wheeled by so close I could see its tiny, humourless eyes fixed on mine. I bared my teeth at it and kept going.

The humans were slowing down, Callum wheezing so pitifully I almost felt bad about pointing out how much better he'd be feeling right now if he didn't smoke. His expression suggested he didn't appreciate my concern, but was too breathless to actually say anything. Walker had gone so red I thought he might be on the verge of cardiac arrest, and Jones had passed both of them, her eyes fixed on me as she climbed. I could see her legs shaking just slightly in her skinny jeans, and I risked a peek all the way down. There was nothing below us at all, just empty greyness, and when I looked up I could see the featureless sky darkening slowly to night, moonless and starless.

"Almost there?" I offered, and they all glared at me. I shrugged, and started up the stairs again, and they trailed after me, panting.

I'D BEEN WRONG, actually. There was a star up there. Or a moon. A weird, sort of square moon. Rectangular, maybe. Sort of … "Door!" I yelled. *"Door!* We're almost there! For real this time!"

"If you're lying, I'll skin you," Jones snarled, and I scooted toward the distant window of light, figuring it was best to stay out of reach just in case.

It took both a long time to get to the door, and nowhere near as long as it should have taken, considering how far away it had seemed when I first spotted it. I suppose space and time get a bit squiffy too, when reality starts to twist. There was a small shape sat on the doorway, like a doorstop or a dropped wallet, and I kept my eyes on it as we struggled on. Grey gave to deep shadows gave to utter darkness around us, the wind plucking at my fur, but considering we hadn't been able to see the steps in the first place, the lack of light didn't make much difference. Then I was level with the door, and Susan was sitting in the frame with her nose twitching violently, not twenty metres from me.

"Susan!" I yelled. "We're here!"

She didn't respond, and I started to trot toward her. I made it about a metre before the ground vanished beneath my front paws and I plunged nose-first into the abyss. I screeched, trying to push myself back, to find any sort of purchase for my back legs, but it wasn't working. I pitched into the dark, yowling fury and despair while Susan still sat there, looking at nothing.

21

NOT REALLY PHYSICS

MY BACK PAWS SCRABBLED USELESSLY AT THE SLICK SURFACE of the stairs as the front half of me plunged into the void, and I tipped into a somersault with no hope of recovery. Emptiness reached up to grab me, the floor beneath too far off to be even a suggestion in the shadows, and I decided to accept my fate with grace and dignity. Or I would if I could stop screeching like a kitten. My back legs flipped off the edge and I crashed into free fall, wondering how long it would take before I hit the bottom – an eternity? A stairwell's worth of time? – and I tried to think of some heroic last words to scream as I fell.

Then someone grabbed my tail and I yowled with outrage.

"Calm down," Jones said, and I peered past my splayed toes at her. I could see the whole stretch of her body flattened to nothing, one arm reaching back to hold her in place, the other hand gripping my tail uncomfortably tightly. "Or I can let go, if you prefer?"

"No thanks," I managed. My heart was uncomfortably

loud and fast in my ears, and I was fighting the urge to chuck up a hairball. Although it might have been the charred mackerel, too. "I can be calm."

"Good." She pulled me up, which made it feel a lot like my tail was about to part company with my body, but I decided it was best not to complain. She deposited me on the ground just as Callum staggered up next to her.

"Guh … Gobs," he managed, then put his hands on his hips and gulped air. Apparently that wasn't quite enough to allow him to cope with the severity of the situation, as he sank to his knees and peered at me. "'Kay?" he managed.

"Yeah," I said, and looked at Jones, who was waving her hands in the gap, trying to see if she could feel the other side. "Thanks, y'know?"

"Sure," she replied, and sat up. "I can't tell how big this thing is."

I looked across the dark chasm at Susan, still sitting in the doorway staring blankly toward us. "Suze!" I yelled. "We're *here!*"

She jerked her head to look behind her, then back again. For a moment I thought she'd heard me, the movement was so fast, then I realised she looked like one of those freaky stop-motion ghosts in a movie. Her ears were moving so quickly they were almost a blur, and she still stared steadfastly, if blankly, into the stairwell.

I wondered what she was seeing. If it was the old, threadbare landing outside the stairwell door, or if she was looking into some sort of murky void, hoping we'd appear out of it like ghosts. I measured the distance between us. It was tricky to be sure of anything, the darkness making proportions odd. Plus, the whole space/time squiffiness thing wasn't helping.

Callum sat on the edge of the gap and dangled his legs into it, then kicked out as far as he could. "I can't feel anything."

"It could go all the way to the door," Jones said. "How the hell do we get across that?"

"*Gurk*," Walker said, or something like that, staggering up the last steps and slumping to the ground behind them.

I eyed the gap again. Theoretically, we were still in the stairwell. I knew we'd climbed what felt like Everest's smaller, less icy indoor cousin, but we were still in the stairwell. Time and space. Maybe space hadn't expanded. Maybe time had. Maybe we'd just climbed very, very, slowly, all the while believing we were going at a normal speed, just for a really long time. Which is why we'd rocked up exactly where we should be, two flights up in a scrapheap of an apartment building, and not at the top of Snowdonia.

Although, seriously, even Wales' tallest peak wasn't big enough to justify taking as long as that climb had. Or had felt, anyway.

"Squiffy," I said, and Callum looked at me.

"What?"

"It's all gone a bit squiffy. Time, space. Reality."

"You only just noticed that?" Jones asked.

"But it can't be *entirely* squiffy," I said. "Or else it all would have collapsed already. You know, things must still be holding relative to each other somehow."

"Is squiffy a technical term?" Callum asked. "Only I can't see them using it at the Large Hadron Collider."

I got up and strolled back down a few stairs. "So if we were still going at our usual speed, but it took us longer to get up here, then either time or distance – space – is the problem. Susan's moving like she's on fast forward." I nodded at her, and they all stared at her, then back at me. "So our *time* slowed down, or expanded, or whatever you want to call it. Which means space stayed the same. Or even compressed. And we just moved very slowly across the same distance. You know, speed equals distance divided by time, or whatever."

"Does your cat fancy himself a physicist?" Jones asked. "Because I'm pretty sure it doesn't work like that."

"He definitely fancies himself," Callum said.

"Doesn't," Walker panted. "Doesn't work. Not same."

I ignored them all and bunched my legs under me, feeling the ache where I'd hit the tree about an aeon earlier. "Which means this is no further across than the stairwell, because it can't be."

I broke into a sprint before I could think about it any further, because it wasn't really about physics. It was about reality coming unstuck, and that made it about belief. I ignored Callum's yell, feeling the whisper of his hands closing on empty air behind me as I launched myself off the unseen edge and sailed across the abyss.

It's one thing to know – okay, to be mostly certain – that reality has just got a bit soft and unreliable.

It's quite another to make the leap and trust in physics to catch you. Particularly when you're a cat, and so have a pretty casual relationship with physics anyway. In fact, physics probably wants to have a stern word with you, likely involving mass, velocity, and force.

But, in the end, I was relying on a belief in physics more than physics itself. There was absolutely nothing remotely related to normal reality happening in this building right now, and if I didn't do something we'd be stuck out there in the void until reality collapsed completely, which was no doubt the book's plan. Besides, Susan might be a rat and therefore twitchy by nature, but this was far beyond twitchiness. She was moving at a speed reality definitely wouldn't approve of. Unless she'd got her paws on some sort of ratty accelerants, but that wasn't her style.

So I was in the region of 90 percent sure I had this right.

I soared into the darkness, my whiskers flared against the movement, my eyes on Susan. My body moved across the void in a rising arc, legs outstretched and tail streaming behind me, and the moment seemed to unfurl forever. It was glorious and terrifying, the weightlessness of my body, the false night of the stairwell expanding forever around me, the air thick with magic and doubt. My forward movement carried on and on, until I started wondering if this was how an astronaut felt as they fell untethered from their ship, unable to turn around or reach back, and then I remembered that was just in movies and books, and started wondering if it was like that at all.

Then I hit midway, reality slapped me across the snout, and I started falling, promptly forgetting about astronauts. Callum's shout crashed to roaring silence behind me, and everything – the stairs, the void, the hall ahead, *reality* – concertinaed in a weird crumpling movement. Perspectives shifted and shortened and reasserted themselves, and Susan's gaze snapped to mine as I plunged toward her, feeling suddenly very heavy and likely to bump my nose on something.

She gave a squeak of alarm and dived out of the way as I accelerated out of the stairwell, and an instant later my forepaws hit the ground where she'd been standing. I managed not to bump my nose, but there was so much power still in my leap that I had to run on a few steps to recover myself, then trot back.

"Hey," I said to Susan, who glared at me.

"Where the hell did you come from?" she asked me. "And where have you *been?* You were right behind us!"

"It's kind of hard to explain," I said. "But we should probably stand clear of the door."

We shuffled up against the wall and waited. I peered into the stairwell, the banisters looking a bit uncertain and wavery in the low light, but nothing else seemed out of place. I couldn't see anyone, and I kept not seeing them until the air *bulged* suddenly, and Callum flew out of the stairwell with his legs out in front of him like he was competing in the long jump. He stumbled as he landed and went into a clumsy roll that pitched him into the nearest wall, then scrambled to his feet and stared around.

"It worked," he said, and grinned at me. "It worked!"

"Of course it did," I said, and he scritched my ears, then flattened himself against the wall with a yelp as Jones came tumbling out of the stairwell with her legs still going like a hamster on a wheel. Walker came next, belly-flopping painfully onto the landing with his legs still lost in the murkiness of whatever weird dimension stuff was going on. He shrieked in alarm, and Callum ran onto the landing to drag him to safety. Walker's legs reappeared flailing and kicking as if he were being pulled out of thick grey water, and I half expected him to be dragged back at any moment, but the stairs let him go.

Then we were all in the hall, the door to the stairwell pushed firmly shut, everyone a little breathless and dishevelled except Susan.

"You took your time," she said. "I've been waiting here for five minutes already."

We looked at each other. My shaky legs suggested five hours was closer to the mark, as did my hungry stomach.

"It's further than it looks," Jones replied, and dusted her hands on her jeans. "What've we got?"

"Tigers. Snakes. Alligators. Tears in the skin of the universe." Susan shrugged. "I think I saw a kraken in the sink, too."

"Great," Jones said. "Let's get this done, then."

Susan started down the hall on quick sure feet, ignoring the way the wallpaper swelled and shapes beneath it crawled after us, and I fell into step with her, my tail up and my head high despite my aching back. Hey, I'd just believed our way out of a rift in reality. Damn straight my head was up.

Callum followed with his damp, muddied coat flaring around him, and Jones strode next to him, her hair a dark mane and her pink boots still shining despite the muck. Walker pattered on behind in his filthy socks, and our shadows stretched long and treacherous before us, while reality tripped over its own rules and turned backflips on all it knew, and something growled deep within the walls.

Mrs Smith's door had grown into the wall and the frame had become smooth and membranous, like a skin of mould on old jam. Walker reached past Callum and grabbed the handle, then spluttered in disgust and let go, looking around for somewhere to wipe his hand.

"That's gross," he announced, looking at the black sludge on his fingers.

"And probably highly poisonous," Jones said, handing him a tissue from her pocket.

"*Ew.*" He scrubbed at his hand anxiously. "How poisonous? Will it seep into my bloodstream? Is there an antidote? Is—"

"Just don't lick your fingers," she said, and looked at Susan. "How do we get in?"

Susan looked at the door, then back at Jones. "Gee, I dunno. I mean, you got in the building without there even being a door there."

Jones snorted. "Do you want to be a familiar? I could do with a good familiar."

Susan sniffed. "I am the Queen-Empress of the Under Paths. I will never be *anyone's* familiar."

"Fair enough," Jones said, and turned to the door, raising one hand just over the surface.

I looked at Susan. "I thought you were the Empress-Queen of the Lower Ways."

"Whatever. People'll believe anything if it sounds posh enough."

There was a click, and Jones smiled as the door swung softly off the latch.

"Nice," Callum said.

"No point announcing ourselves," Jones said, and pushed the door wide.

It didn't look like a jungle anymore. Or it did, but not a glossy, BBC, look-at-the-lovely-critters-type jungle. This was the sort of jungle you might find on an alien planet, or in a journey to the centre of the earth. Things hissed and spat from the cover of the leaves, and thorned vines slithered through the branches. Leaves clattered together like waiting teeth, and fleshy flowers opened wide maws, dangling bait from their stamens. Susan shuffled away from a buttercup that nibbled at her toes, and I stood on it for her. She gave me an unimpressed look, which seemed a bit ungrateful. Then the buttercup nipped the pad of my paw and I jumped back, swearing.

"How do we get through it?" Walker asked.

"Carefully," Callum said.

"Quietly," Susan said.

"And carrying a big stick?" I suggested, but no one laughed. Fair enough. It had been more a serious suggestion than a joke, anyway.

Jones stepped slowly into the foyer and Callum followed her, stopping to free an umbrella from an overgrown stand. I skirted the buttercup and padded after them, the moss thick and giving under my feet, making my steps soundless. The place was heavy with the reek of magic and mould, and the tart torn scent of things going wrong at the edges.

We moved quietly, ducking under things that might have been banana palms if the fruit hadn't been fanged and clawed, and stepping gingerly over coconuts that rolled to watch us go with staring eyes. Nothing moved to stop us, and I hadn't seen any actual animals yet.

"Where's Mrs Smith?" I whispered to Susan.

"In the centre," she whispered back. "It's weird. It's like she's just sitting there waiting for you."

That sounded more alarming than weird, if I was honest, and I passed it on to Callum. He just nodded. "Not much we can do. We've got to face her if we're going to take the book back."

"I," Jones said. "If *I'm* going to take the book back."

"It's not your book," Walker insisted from behind us, then fell into an overgrown, fleshy pineapple with a screech.

Callum just shook his head at both of them and used the umbrella to nudge a vine. It wriggled out of the way obligingly enough, and we tiptoed on through the jungle, listening to the drip of water on leaves and breathing thick, gunky air that sucked at my lungs and made my head spin. I glanced at Susan in time to see her stumble, pitching nose-first into what looked like a sea anemone, which flared its arms wide then wrapped them tightly around her. She gave a half-hearted squeak and a wriggle, and I threw myself at the plant, clawing it frantically with both paws and sending shredded vegetation scattering. I had the thing half dug up before it finally relinquished its hold on Susan. She plopped to the ground and blinked at me, bewildered. A vine sneaked around behind her, aiming for her tail, and I picked her up like a kitten.

"Hey," she protested. "I'm … I'm a queen."

"So act like one and let your subjects carry you for a bit," I said, somewhat indistinctly.

"Fair enough," she said, and curled her tail around her, safely out of reach. We padded on through the jungle.

I don't think we actually walked for that long, but in the heavy, stale air my flanks were soon slick with moisture, and I could see sweat coating Callum's face long before we stumbled out of the trees and into what had once been Mrs Smith's living room.

When I say we didn't walk for long, I mean it was much further than it should have been, given the size of the building, but it wasn't the long haul of the stairs. Whatever. Her living room had truly become a tree house, glassless windows looking out over a vast forest canopy, where flocks of brightly coloured birds swept from tree to tree, and monkeys screeched at each other happily. Or furiously, I couldn't tell. Hell, I was only assuming they were monkeys. The room was crowded with exotic flowers, and a leopard looked up from beside the coffee table and grumbled at us. The warthog was still wandering around with a tray on its back, and Mrs Smith was reclining in the coils of a very large snake. Her jungle explorer outfit looked immaculate.

She looked up as we emerged from the trees, and swung her feet off the snake, straightening up. She stared at us, and shook her head gently. "Again?" she said, and the leopard rose to its feet. A tiger lifted its head from the other side of the table and blinked at us lazily.

"You need to give the book back," Callum said.

"I was very clear, dear," Mrs Smith said. "I don't want to hurt you, you know. I never want to hurt anyone."

"I know you don't," Callum said. "But you *are* hurting things, doing this. Hurting everything. Please, just give the book back."

"That's not possible," she said. "Now, how about a drink? We can all sit down and have a lovely chat."

"Mrs Smith," Callum started, and a tall, rather elderly gentleman with a shock of pale hair, no shirt, and very small khaki shorts emerged out of the trees, a martini glass in one hand. We all stared at him.

"Fascinating," he announced. "Not observation in the natural habitat, exactly, but the adaptations make for most interesting behaviour." He wandered back into the jungle, his broad back a little saggy and festooned with flowers.

Callum looked at Mrs Smith. "Was that—" he started, and she smiled.

"It doesn't matter, dear," she said. "Come sit down and have a drink. Maybe a bite to eat?"

"Mrs Smith," he started again, and Jones pushed him out of the way.

"That's my damn book you've got," she hissed. "And I will *have* it." She clicked her fingers together, and there was an eruption of cushions and plants from the cane sofa, scattering leaves and stuffing like confetti. The book spun into the air, the dim green light glassy on the old skin cover, and Jones held her hand out for it, grinning. Mrs Smith shrieked in fury, and Jones' smile vanished as the tiger came over the table in a rush, teeth bared.

Callum grabbed Jones, hauling her sideways and

rolling to the ground as the leopard charged from the opposite direction, and the two big cats collided with a body-shaking thud where the sorcerer had been standing only a moment before. Walker used Callum's back as a step and threw himself on the book as it crashed to the leafy floor, clutching it to his chest and rolling into the undergrowth while the jungle shook and Mrs Smith screamed, and the two big cats spun away from each other and lunged for the dentist.

I dropped Susan and said, "Hairballs."

THINGS GET SQUIFFY

THE WHOLE BUILDING QUAKED. I'VE NEVER BEEN IN AN actual earthquake, so I don't know if it was comparable, but I can definitely say that I have no desire to feel anything like it ever again. The floor shuddered and pulsed, suddenly untrustworthy, and somehow that failing of something I'd always been able to rely on was worse even than the treacherous stairs.

I stumbled as I started toward Walker, my claws out and my ears back, and a couple of the fanged banana trees toppled over with plant-y screams. I didn't even know what I was going to do when I reached him. If he had control of the book, maybe I could talk to him, convince him to calm everything down.

The jungle juddered, there and not there, and the two big cats stopped before they reached Walker, shaking their heads as if someone had bopped them on the nose. There was a pulse, a *pop* of air pressure abruptly changing, and the heavy leaves and multicoloured toadstools vanished as dark wood walls reared up around us. Dull yet expensive landscape paintings and overly detailed portraits peered down from among hangings of dark velvet and gold braid, and white tablecloths were attended by dripping champagne pyramids and young women in skimpy dresses. It smelt of old cigars and arrogance and musk, and it might be what Walker aspired to, but it also said he wasn't even slightly in control of what the book was doing.

"Extraordinary," the elderly man muttered, examining a butterfly with antlers and six bulging eyes. It bit him, and he winced, then said *extraordinary* again, although in a slightly strained voice.

Mrs Smith shrieked and threw herself at Walker as he sat up, the book clutched to his chest. *"It's mine!"* she screamed, and grabbed the sides of the book, throwing herself back like a small, determined dog in a tug of war. *"Give it to me!"*

"No!" Walker yelled. "You don't know how to handle it!"

The room started to stutter again, faster this time, flashing from jungle to velvet rooms and back, the trees and champagne stacks there and not there, the big cats looking about in confusion and the plants blossoming violently every time they reappeared.

Jones was roaring, one hand outstretched toward the book, and Callum was trying to stop her joining the scuffle on the floor. She elbowed him in the nose and shoved him away from her, hard enough that he stumbled to the ground and fetched up against a large, bulbous plant. The plant promptly flung sticky tendrils all over him and started trying to stuff him into a maw that yawned alarmingly wide in its trunk. He flailed at the plant, trying to scramble away in the moments it gave way to the velvet rooms, but it kept reappearing and grabbing him again.

Jones was trying to haul Mrs Smith off both Walker and the book, but our neighbour was proving more tenacious than Callum, and the big cats had decided to ignore their stuttering surroundings and were creeping closer to the wrestling sorcerers (well, sorcerer and two wannabe sorcerers), their bellies low to the ground. No one was paying them any attention.

Callum was vanishing into the trunk of the sticky tree, so I was just going to have to hope no one got their face bitten off too quickly. I ran for the plant, Susan scuttling after me, and we attacked the body of the thing as the room shuttled between realities around us. One moment we were surrounded by thick green growth while we scratched at the stem of a rather nasty-tasting tree, the next a stern butler-type was striding across a dim-lit room toward us with a spray bottle in his hand, and we were tearing into something that looked antique and probably priceless.

"I'm out, I'm out," Callum yelled, and grabbed us both, legging it away from the plant before it could attack him again. The butler shouted something and waved his spray bottle threateningly, then vanished behind a wall of greenery as the jungle returned.

"The cats!" Susan shouted. "They're going to attack!"

The big cats were crouched low, yellow eyes intent on Jones as she kept trying to haul Mrs Smith off the book.

The leopard's mouth dropped open slightly, and I saw his muscles bunch.

Old Ones take me, I have no idea why I did what I did. Life would be much easier without sorcerers, and Mrs Smith had kind of used up her chicken-based goodwill by siccing a jungle on us. But I jumped from Callum's grip and took two perfect bounds, the first one bouncing me off the coffee table and the second carrying me straight into the leopard as he crouched to leap.

I had all teeth and claws bared, and I buried them into the monster's snout as hard as I could, trying to ignore the fact that I could feel his own massive teeth pressing against my belly as I hit him. Hey, we were cousins, right? So hopefully he wouldn't actually eat me. Just a mild maiming, perhaps.

"Gobs!" Callum yelled behind me, and I glimpsed him snatch the spray bottle off the butler (who had just pushed his way out of a stand of mangroves and was gazing in astonishment at Callum's carnivorous tree, which promptly slapped him across the face with some tendrils).

The leopard snorted and stumbled to a stop before he could jump, shaking his head and giving an alarmed little cough.

"Give it up!" I yelled in his ear. "Come on, cuz. You're a wild animal, not a guard dog!"

The leopard huffed, confused, and tried to shake me off. I clung on. It seemed safer than letting go.

"Go eat some monkeys or something! A cockatoo. Cockatoos suck. Go on – have you ever eaten cockatoo?"

"Are you alright, Claude?" a rather cultured voice enquired.

The leopard huffed, then said, "I'm not sure. This miniature panther wants me to eat a cockatoo, whatever that is when it's at home."

I peered over my shoulder and spotted the tiger. Well, I spotted his teeth. He was too close to see much else. "Hey," I said.

"Hay?" the tiger said. "Hay is what elephants eat."

"Horses," Callum said. He was poised over the tiger with the spray bottle aimed at him, looking a little uncertain. "Hay is what horses eat."

The tiger looked him up and down, lifting his whiskers at the spray bottle. "I'm sure."

"Would you mind getting your claws out of my nose, tiny panther?" the leopard asked.

"Are you going to eat me?"

"Not if you get your claws out of me," the leopard said, with a rather threatening edge to his voice.

"Sorry." I let go and dropped to the ground. Callum was shifting the aim of the spray bottle from one big cat to the other, and the butler tapped him on the shoulder. Callum shrieked, spun around and sprayed the butler in the face. He staggered back with a yelp, waving his hands in front of him.

"Sir, *please*. That's vinegar for the glasses!"

"Where'd he come from?" the leopard asked.

"Worlds collide," the tiger said, nodding solemnly.

"Sorry," Callum was saying. "I thought you were that plant again."

The butler snatched the spray bottle off him. "I *was* polishing the glasses." He looked around and frowned. "Somewhere."

"Attack her!" Mrs Smith screamed, kicking Jones wildly. "Kitties, *attack her!*"

"Please don't," Callum said.

"What on earth are we doing here?" the tiger asked. "I'd just caught a very tasty calf, then suddenly here I was, doing whatever that woman wanted. And she keeps calling us *kitties.*"

"I'm as confused as you are," the leopard said. "I was snoozing in my favourite tree. I left most of an antelope behind. And now I've been attacked by an undersized panther." He nudged me with one enormous paw, and I almost fell over. "What *are* you? Did you shrink in the wash?"

Both big cats broke out in hearty guffaws, and the butler ducked behind Callum.

"Why on earth are there *wild animals* in the club?" he demanded, peering around Callum's shoulder.

I glared at them all. "Callum? Don't we have something to do?"

"I don't know what to do," he said. The club seemed to be winning out at the moment, Walker retaining his hold on the book as the two women struggled. We were lingering in the dark walls for longer, and the elderly gentleman was frowning around with the butterfly still held in his cupped hand while an uncomfortable-looking waiter offered him a shirt. The warthog had made a run for it, and was currently chasing two young ladies in unsuitable footwear across the rich carpet. "Who do we want to get the book again?" Callum asked me.

"Jones?" I said. "She might be able to get it under

control. Walker seems to be entertaining delusions of grandeur already."

"Right." He took the spray bottle off the butler again. "Thanks, old chap."

"I say, that *is* mine," the butler said, but Callum shoulder-bumped him out of the way. The butler took a step back, tripped over a large Galapagos tortoise that I honestly hadn't even realised was there, and pitched into a thicket of pampas grass with a shriek of alarm.

"*Ooh*," the leopard said. "Shall we stalk him?"

"I'm not much for humans," the tiger said. "They're a bit greasy."

"Oh, we won't nip him," the leopard said. "Just a little casual stalking. You know, for fun."

"In that case …" the tiger said, and they both dropped to their bellies, slinking away while Mrs Smith screamed at them to come help her.

I wondered whether to warn the butler, then decided not to bother. We had more than enough to deal with, and it didn't sound like he was going to get eaten. Well, not by the big cats, anyway.

Abigail and Esther appeared out of the undergrowth, looking dishevelled and rather damp, and Susan looked up at me. "What now?"

"Cross your toes," I said, and followed Callum.

WALKER AND MRS SMITH were still squirming across the floor, both of them clinging to the book desperately and screaming for the other to let go. I'd have thought Walker would be doing better, being younger and larger, but apparently dentistry doesn't do much for upper body strength. Jones had Walker in a chokehold with one arm, and her other hand was buried in Mrs Smith's hair while she alternated between squeezing the one until he spluttered and shaking the other until she squawked. It made sense that she wasn't about to unleash too much actual magic in here – it'd be like lighting a flare in a fuel depot. Crispiness would ensue.

"Give me my book!" she bellowed.

"It's not your book!" the others roared back, and then all three fell to clawing and pulling and squeezing and kicking again.

"Everyone let go of the book!" Callum shouted, which went as well as can be expected, so he started squirting them with the spray bottle, for all the world as if he thought they were some scrapping dogs he could break up easy as you like. They ignored him entirely.

"Nice work," Susan said, and he scowled at her.

"You have any better ideas?"

"Sure," she said, and nodded at Abigail and Esther.

The rats swarmed forward, little feet fast and sure, and took one human each. They raced up legs and nipped at waists and ears and wrists, and the fighters swore and writhed and yelled threatening things about rat-catchers.

Mrs Smith took one hand off the book to try and bat Abigail out of her hair, and Walker wrenched the volume away from her with a triumphant roar. Mrs Smith wailed and lunged at him, and Abigail darted down the front of her safari suit, setting her dancing and jumping and trying to pull her jacket off. Esther and Susan were racing all over Walker, delivering solid little nips, but he ignored them, concentrating on keeping hold of the book as Jones let Mrs Smith dance away, stripping out of her jacket as she went. Jones turned her full attention on Walker instead, tightening her chokehold and trying to wrestle one of his arms off the book, but Walker flung his head back and smacked her in the nose. She yelped and let go, and he scrambled to his feet, the book grasped above his head victoriously.

"*Mine!*" he shrieked. "*It's mine!*" Then he bolted for the door, ignoring Esther biting his ear and Susan scratching at his neck desperately.

Jones sprinted after him as the rats lost their grip and tumbled to the floor, and Callum shot after the sorcerer and the dentist, shouting for them both to stop.

"My book!" Mrs Smith wailed, and danced in the general direction of the door, still trying to extricate Abigail from her clothing.

I looked at Susan as she picked herself out of a coat rack. She shrugged. "Still worked better than the spray bottle."

"Fair point," I said, and raced for the door as the last of the grassland melted away and the butler hid from the big cats behind a large set of leather sofas.

EVERYTHING WAS SHAKY. The apartment door was there and not there, the walls shining with heavy wood panelling that had grimy plasterboard floating through it. The hall itself had yawning gaps that I wasn't sure actually existed in this reality, and the tears in the walls had massive eyeballs with triple pupils pressed against them.

Their unnerving gaze followed us as we raced down the hall, Walker crashing into the stairwell first with Jones in hot pursuit. Mrs Smith reached the door just after them, but Callum grabbed her and pulled her back. There was a momentary tussle, and he seized her around the waist, lifting her clear of the floor and shouting, "Gobs!"

I leaped at the nearest apartment door while Mrs Smith kicked and spat and cursed impressively. I caught the curved handle under my paws and dragged it down, hoping locks were having some reality issues along with everything else. The latch ground, then gave a reassuring click.

"Open!" I yelled, and the rats threw themselves at the door as I struggled to keep my grip on the handle. They forced the door open a crack before the latch could slip back into place or I could fall off, and Callum struggled over to kick it wide. He hefted Mrs Smith bodily through, setting her down then jumping back to slam it closed in her face. He tore a piece of loose wood off the wall and jammed it through the handle and across the door, bracing it in place while Mrs Smith yelled and pounded on the other side, screaming her frustration. Callum checked it was going to hold then took a step away, wiping his forehead with his sleeve and giving us all a relieved grin.

Then he stumbled over a bulge that blossomed out of the floor like a molehill, narrowly avoided putting an arm through the gaping hole in the wall his board theft had left, which now groaned and gnashed splintery teeth, tripped again and sprawled to the ground, catching his knee on a broken floorboard.

"Ow," he said, then yelped and scrambled up as a long, spiky tongue slipped out of the wall and licked his face. "What the hell was *that?*"

"Could be anything. Could actually not really exist," I said. "Come *on!*"

I sprinted past him and slipped through the door to the stairs, taking them as fast as I dared. I could hear the clatter of the sorcerer's feet below us, Jones shouting at Walker to stop, and the rats flowed fast and silent beside me. The building was sobbing, the magic that had so distorted it flowing to other interests and leaving it broken and crumbling around us, with just enough self-awareness that it knew what was happening.

I leaped a gap I could barely see, shouting a warning to Callum as he charged after us, and heard him curse as he jumped it clumsily and slipped down two steps. The door at the bottom of the stairwell slammed open, letting faint light in, and I ran out into the foyer just in time to see Jones barge through the main doors. She was still screaming for her book, and there was something so starving and shrill in her voice that I wondered if she should really be allowed to have it back. But she was our best hope. For what that was worth.

Walker was standing in the middle of the street with his feet planted wide when I emerged onto the steps, and Jones was stopped a few paces from him. She had her hand stretched out to him, and I could see the lines of strain etched on her face.

"Give it to me!" she ordered.

"It's *mine!*" he shouted back, the book held out in front of him like a shield. It was pulsing with uncanny colours, bruised light and torn shadows snaking over his arms and spilling to his feet, and lifting into a sky I couldn't exactly see. I could feel it, though, the starving, contorting weight of it pressing down like a hurricane of unreality waiting to be born.

"You *stole* it!" she said.

"It wanted to be mine." He was shaking, and I could see fear on his face. The thing was already eating him alive and he knew it. But he loved it a little, too.

"You can't control it, Malcolm. Give it to me." Jones lowered her arm as she stopped trying to take it by force. She turned her hand palm-up instead, a powerless supplication. "It'll destroy you. You know this."

Callum had joined me on the steps, still clutching his spray bottle.

"No!" Walker protested. "No, I won't go back to before! I won't be *useless!*"

"You were never useless," Jones said. "But the book will make you that way. Give it to me. Give it to me and we'll try again. We were happy, weren't we?"

He twisted, the weird light of the book clawing at his face. "No. No, I—"

"Malcolm. Please." Her hand was still open, willing him to give her the book. Her face was human and vulnerable-looking, and there was a softness in her voice. "Now, Malcolm. Before it's too late. Don't let it hurt you. I couldn't bear it."

He took a hesitant step toward her, and now he

seemed to be offering the book to her rather than using it to fend her off.

"That's it. We'll be so happy. I know I was harsh sometimes. I'll try harder. I will." Her hand was almost on the book, but she wasn't looking at it. She was watching his face instead, a smile curving her lips. There really is no accounting for taste.

"Me too. I'll try harder," he said, and closed the distance between them, ready to press the book into her hands. "Take it. Please take it!"

And Mrs Smith ran screaming past us, her hair wild and her hands out. "*It's mine!*"

"No!" Callum yelled, and lunged after her, but she was moving so fast his hand just slipped off the soft fabric of her shirt. She collided with Jones and Walker and the book flew up into the night sky, spinning softly, light and dark sparking off its pages. It ran with power, calling magic out of the air and laying fury around it, and the whole street caught its breath as it began to fall again. Hell, maybe the whole city did. The whole world. Everything hinged on whose desperately clutching hands it fell into.

And then it slammed sideways as if caught in an ocean current, and straight into the outstretched hands of Petra, coming back from wherever she'd taken her three-legged dog. She looked at the book in bewilderment for the space of a breath, while her dog backed away then lifted his nose and howled, a panicked sound that would have raised the hair on my spine if it hadn't already been up.

Then the book exploded with power and Petra started to scream.

23

DESPERATE MEASURES

"*No!*" Callum yelled, and there was a witch's chorus of pretty much the same from Jones, Smith, and Walker. The night was tearing apart, light and not-light in hues that hurt the mind pouring through rents in the sky. Buildings shook and stuttered in and out of existence, and vast things screamed on the edge of reality. Wind tore across the street then channelled straight into the earth, shattering tarmac and dragging dead leaves and broken bottles and the corner of Walker's car with it. A horde of creatures, horses or overgrown dogs with horns and too many legs charged in panicked formation past the intersection, pursued by something that tore the tarmac with hungry, serrated limbs. A moth the size of a small jet plane threw itself at a streetlight and crashed to the ground with it, giving a wail of despair as the bulb shattered.

Everywhere angles shifted and distorted, dimensions bulged, things were misshaped and misplaced. The book was disgorging power into the night and sucking reality in, turning trees inside out and cars into monsters, sending a billboard stalking off into the darkness and weeds into battle against the city, tearing the pavement from its bed. The world was shattering.

Petra had fallen to her knees, still screaming, her hands locked onto the book and the thick dark curls of her hair unravelling and pulling toward it as it fed on her. Callum jumped down the steps and ran into the road, shoving Walker out of the way.

"Petra!" he yelled. "Catch!" And he flung the snake at her.

The little green snake curled through the air with a startled hiss, tumbling toward Petra. She lifted streaming eyes to it, tears stitched down her face, and instinct pushed past the grip of the book. She raised one hand to fend off the snake, the other still frozen on the cover. It wasn't enough. She couldn't let go entirely. The book was too strong.

And Callum knew it. The snake was nothing more than a distraction, something to pull her attention away from what was happening, because even as she caught the snake he was still moving, charging toward her with his face set and his horrible coat flaring behind him.

"Callum, *no!*" I roared, and sprinted after him.

He was almost there, shouting her name, but Petra didn't look up. Her attention was already wavering from the snake and back to the eruption of power in front of her. I could see her skull through the skin, see the way her flesh seemed to be melding to the book as it tapped her for every scrap of power she had. As it showed Callum what it would do if he didn't stop it. The snake flung itself to the ground and wriggled desperately away from her, and I wished Callum had half the sense the damn reptile did.

I was too far behind him, he was going to grab the thing before I could stop him, and that was what it *wanted.* I could feel the book's desire like the pull of a river in flood, a hunger that was beyond understanding. It was the sort of desire that drove dogs to fight to win the pack, and humans to slaughter others over a crown. It was raging, unreasoning, and was going to lead to blood.

"Callum!" I yelled again. He ignored me, but I saw the flashing pastel bodies of the rats arrowing toward him. They tangled around his feet, making him stumble and curse, and although he recovered himself almost immediately, it had slowed him. Not much, but maybe it was enough.

Bollocks to this book. It didn't want to be possessed by Jones, to have its power held in check. To be *tamed.* It had grown sentient enough to escape, to get itself into the grip of one misled dentist and two complete innocents, moving from one to the other as it searched for more. More power, more freedom, more chaos, just *more.* And now it was one step away from getting hold of Callum, and it was too strong for him. Or he was too strong for it. He'd think he was resisting it, maybe even guarding it, probably *using it to make things better*, even as it hollowed him out from the inside. All that magic in his bones – no wonder the damn thing was basically salivating.

And I was having *none* of it.

I still probably wouldn't have been quick enough, even with the rats running interference, but Cyril, the three-legged dog, obviously decided Callum was the one doing Bad Things to his human (reasonable, considering Callum had just thrown a snake at her). The dog had backed away when Petra dropped his leash, whining in fear and rolling his eyes at the stench of the book, which just goes to show dogs are smarter than humans. But as Callum reached for his human, Cyril came baying out of the dark at an astonishing pace, threw himself at Callum, and bit his leg with great authority.

Callum howled and staggered away, trying to shake the dog off, and I ran straight past him. I hit Petra's chest with all the weight I could muster, and spilled her backward off her knees and onto the ground. She only had one hand on the book, but she was still screaming, a terrible, helpless sound, and she stared straight past me up to the sky, seeing things none of the rest of us could, and that no one would ever want to.

I said, "I'm sorry."

Then I bit her wrist harder than I've ever bit anyone, feeling tendons crunch under my teeth, and her scream took on a suddenly more human note as her hand jerked open and the book fell to the ground. I dug my claws into its slick, greasy cover, ignoring Callum shouting my name and the book howling in my ears as it tried to bring all of reality down on me. I didn't intend to be here long enough for it to reach me.

I hoped I still remembered how to do this. Hoped I wasn't about to just fall through the tears in reality and be turned inside out by a different dimension. I closed my mind against the terror hammering in my chest, against the memories that were worse than anything the book could throw at me, and took one not-quite-physical step sideways, the book still firmly clutched in my claws.

I emerged into the Inbetween.

YOU NEVER FORGET.

Never forget the way the world releases you and you pass into the space that runs between it, or behind it, or maybe between all the worlds, that great and eternal void. There's utter stillness in there. Utter blackness. You can't hear anything, even when you're screaming because the beasts have found you and are tearing you to pieces.

You can't hear them coming for you.

I suppose I could have stepped in and stepped straight out again somewhere else, hidden the book and brought Jones back to it later, hoping she could control it. Or just stashed it somewhere no one would ever find it, maybe sneaking it into the foundations of a building site, burying it under a tower of concrete. Or thrown it into a dam in a weighted bag, or sealed it up in a tomb with a bunch of locks and warnings and skull and crossbones on it. You know, all the classic things you do with cursed objects and things you want to remain unfound.

But even regular secret objects have a way of drifting to the surface. And this book *wanted* to be found. It wanted to be used. It would call to people, beg them to uncover it, promise them all the riches of the world, their heart's desire. And so it would return, again and again, growing more and more powerful, searching for people with magic in their bones. And then we wouldn't be able to stop it. Of course we wouldn't. We could barely stop one old lady with a penchant for nature documentaries, never mind some minor sorcerer or natural magician with a hunger for power.

But there was a way to get rid of it forever.

I couldn't just drop it into the Inbetween, because a book like that is *lucky*. A passing cat would bump into it, bring it out with them. They'd likely know it for what it was, and take it to the Watch, but maybe not. Not all cats are trustworthy, Watch or not. Maybe they'd take it to someone else, someone who'd use it. A sorcerer who'd pay handsomely for it.

Or maybe a gargoyle would catch it in their clawed hands, and take it with them. Horde it in the gutters of some old church to read and ponder in their slow stone way, and from there it'd fall to the ground. And suddenly some pastor would be having record turnouts, and maybe sinners would be getting a little gentle smiting, or not so gentle, and the next thing would be angels and demons battling it out on the streets because that was what the pastor believed would happen.

Or a faery might grab it, as they're the only other creatures that can shift. And better the Old Ones take us than a faery get their hands on a book of power. That does *not* bear thinking about. I mean, the book would be upset, because it can't control a faery. But for the faery, world domination would only be step one.

So, yeah. I couldn't just drop it. Not and be sure.

And I *had* to be sure.

So I let myself fall into the darkness. Let the momentum of my step grind to nothing, so the stillness and silence was so absolute I could almost believe I'd ceased to exist. I closed my eyes – not that I could see anything anyway – and let my whiskers tell me all they could.

They were coming.

I didn't need my whiskers to tell me that, but they did anyway. It was in the tremble of the long, slow currents of the place. They were eternal, those currents, so deep and slow they were almost undetectable, but cat whiskers are delicate, and I was listening to them with all my heart. My body ached and screamed with the memory of a previous life, a previous death.

You don't forget the pain of dying, especially when your own kind hold you to the beasts. You don't remember the oblivion, but you remember what came before it, and I wished I could breathe in here, that I could take a great gasping breath and remind myself I was alive, but no one breathes in here. Your heart doesn't beat. You're silent, suspended in time, and my whiskers told me *they* were schooling all around me, all teeth and tentacles and shredding claws, and still I didn't dare leave too soon. Not and risk this book being found. It was feral and hungry for the world, just as the beasts were hungry for me.

I waited.

I felt the first pass, a tremble that was closer than breath.

Another, and something touched my whiskers, brushing through them, and suddenly they weren't telling me as much anymore. I bristled the ones on the other side, felt a slice of pain along one leg.

Come on you flea-ridden doilies! I screamed, although no noise came out. *Come on and get me!*

Another pass, closer, and I tumbled in the turbulence of the motion. Almost, almost. A flick on my ear that burned, a tweak of the tail that would have made me cry out if I'd been able. Still I hung on.

There. There it was, what I'd been waiting for. A pressure wave, rising out of the depths of this dimension-less place on the nose of something fast and hungry, something vast and starving for me. It would catch me on its teeth and fling me to its brethren, and then the real fun would begin. This was it. This is what would swallow the book, what would carry it forever in the dark and depthless places, far beyond the reach of anyone. The only safe place for the thing. It was time.

I let go of the book, my paws grimy and aching, and threw myself out of the Inbetween.

Nothing happened.

That pressure wave was growing, coming closer, and *nothing was happening.* I tried again, clawing wildly at the void, suddenly aware that I was motionless, that I had no way of propelling myself. Cats *moved.* We stepped through the Inbetween and out again, carried on the wake of our own momentum. And now I had none. I was just here, and the beast was coming for me, and this was going to happen all over again. The endless, shrieking pain.

Well, I'm going to give you some hellish indigestion, I said to the rising beast, because there was nothing else I could do. I couldn't get out. I was as trapped as I had been when the Watch had held me in here. These things were too unknowable to fight. All I could do was know that the book would be gone too, because the beast would swallow it when it swallowed me.

It was almost upon me, and I fancied I could hear the rush of it coming, the whistle of void against its teeth. I wondered if it was better or worse to not being able to see what ate you.

I rose on the pressure wave, helpless as flotsam, and readied myself for the pain.

And in that moment something small and fast hit me, sharp teeth locked into the scruff of my neck, and the darkness shattered as I was carried out of the Inbetween and back into the world, half-thinking I could hear a roar of frustrated fury rolling out of the abyss behind us.

I TUMBLED ACROSS THE ALLEY, thrown away from whoever had grabbed me by the force of our landing, and the night twisted at strange angles around me for a moment before resettling itself. I stayed where I'd fallen, not quite sure if I was upside down or sideways, staring at a discarded beer can and panting hard while I tried to remember how to breathe properly. Something was making weird little squeaking noises nearby, which was annoying, and there were loud thuds coming from somewhere, echoing in my brain. Something grabbed me, removing me from the nice, familiar ground. I mewled in wobbly protest and pushed at my attacker with half-hearted claws, then Callum said, "Gobs? Gobbelino?"

I blinked a couple of times, trying to get the strange dimensions of the world to settle, and realised he had me cradled on his lap, hands cupped around me. It was how he'd held me when I'd been small and hurt, when he'd rescued me from both the beasts of the Inbetween and the human ones, and his hands smelt of the same reassuring mix of magic and cigarettes and stillness.

I closed my eyes and considered just staying there, resting my aching limbs and nursing the screaming dark at the centre of me, the memory that would never go away. His hands closed over me, gentle and warm and *real*, and I thought I could feel the cold of the Inbetween fading beneath them.

Then a smooth voice said, "He in one piece?"

I struggled off Callum's lap, falling over twice and batting his hands away as he tried to help me, and managed to get myself standing (albeit with a bit of a wobble) to meet the odd eyes of Claudia, the Watch cat. "You? You pulled me out?"

"Sure," she said. "I came by to see how things were going – not great, I might add – and saw you take the book. I figured what you'd do, but it took me a bit to find you in there."

"Thanks," I said, not quite sure if this was a good thing or a bad thing. I mean, the being alive was good, of course. The being in debt to a Watch cat, not so much.

She sat down and inspected a row of sucker marks burned into her shoulder. They matched a row on my chest admirably. "It's okay. Probably the best thing for that book, by the look of things."

"Yeah," I said, with as much confidence as I could muster. It wasn't a lot, considering I was still having trouble standing up. "It was my plan all along."

Claudia looked up from her wounds. "You waited long enough. There's a bunch of flamingos trying to eat very small dragons out of the tree over there."

We all looked. The tree was burning in patches, and behind it our building looked a little lopsided and shell-shocked. I could sympathise.

"It may have taken a little longer than was perhaps ideal," I admitted. "But, you know. All sorted."

Claudia just looked at me. The snake wriggled past my feet, heading for Callum, and a straggling penguin waddled after it, squawking hopefully.

"Gobbelino pretty much saved the world," Callum said, and Claudia looked at him instead, which was a relief. "I'm serious. That book was completely out of control."

"It was," Jones said. She was holding Walker up with one arm, and he seemed to be enjoying it. "I still would've liked it back, though."

"I suppose this means we don't get the balance of the fee?" I asked.

She squinted at me. "You just dropped my book in the Inbetween."

"Yeah, but we did get it off him," I pointed out, nodding at Walker. "Probably saved his life."

"He wouldn't have needed saving if you'd just looked after it properly in the first place," she said, and shifted her grip on Walker. "Come on. Let's get you home."

He said something unintelligible, and she staggered off to lean him against his car, which the ground had spat back up. It looked rather the worse for wear, though. The only glass left was in the back passenger window.

I decided to ignore Claudia for now, and looked up at Callum. "Mrs Smith?"

"Looking after Petra." He nodded at the building, and I peered past him to see our neighbour sitting on the steps, her hair a silver mane that fell to her waist. She was rocking the waitress gently while Cyril whined and nudged them.

"Are they okay?"

"Not sure," he said, and looked at Claudia. "What about us? Are we okay?"

Claudia shrugged, a liquid motion. "Personally, I've no quarrel with you. Pretty down to the wire, mind, but I can ignore that. I'll just have a word with your ladies there, make sure they realise this was nothing more than a gas leak and a bit of an explosion."

"I mean Gobbelino," Callum said. His voice was calm, but I could feel the tension strung in him. "He just went into the Inbetween to save all of us. What's the Watch going to do about him being involved in all this? And not just this – the PI business? He's done nothing but help people, you know. He's *good* at it."

If I could have blushed, I would have.

Claudia looked at me. "As far as I'm concerned, the matter's closed. That's what I'll tell the Watch leader, too. Sometimes we need people who know how to walk the line of both worlds."

"What about the rest of the Watch?" Callum asked. "The ones that don't agree?"

She shrugged. "You'll have to deal with them if you come to them, won't you? You should be able to manage that, professionals like yourselves." There was a little twitch to her mouth as she spoke, but other than that she was unreadable.

We were silent for a moment, then I said, "That's it?"

She tipped her head. "What do you want me to do, bite your toes?"

"Only if you want to," I said, before I could stop myself, and Callum gave a startled bark of laughter. Claudia stared at me, then snorted.

"You'll need to do more than save the world for that," she said, and ambled off toward the women on the steps.

Callum looked at me. "Want a lift?"

"Why not," I said. "It's been a rough day."

"You're not wrong," he said, and picked me up. I leaned into his coat, for once the wet dog smell less distressing and more calming. Familiar. I started to close my eyes, then the snake poked its head out of a pocket and hissed at me.

Well. Couldn't have things be too relaxing.

24

LUCKY

THINGS WERE STILL SQUIFFY FOR A WEEK OR SO. OUR apartment, unfortunately, bounced back to normal pretty quickly. I missed the sofa, and Callum missed the shower, and we both missed the fridge. But, on the other hand, there weren't any dead animal lamp shades or ceiling monsters from another dimension looming over the desk and admiring themselves in the mirror. Which was nice.

Mrs Smith's apartment took a bit longer to recover. There were still ferns growing out of the walls, and a large frilled lizard had taken up permanent residence in the bathroom, but she quite liked them despite not knowing how they got there. Claudia had done some tidying up with Mrs Smith and Petra. Certain cats have a way of doing that, see. It's a talent, like any other – I can get people to forget little things like misplaced hairballs and missing tuna steaks, but Claudia obviously has the knack for the big stuff.

You'd probably call it hypnotism, but that always sounds so tacky-holiday-stage-show to me. We can just …

suggest things. Like maybe there hadn't been a jungle in the apartment, and maybe a book of power hadn't tried to eat your soul. There had been a gas leak, though. And hallucinations. Very vivid, very *real* hallucinations. Terribly dangerous, but I'd alerted Callum and he'd helped everyone to safety, and the only reason it wasn't in the newspaper was Conspiracies.

I liked the heroism aspect Claudia had thrown in for the two of us. It was a nice touch. Mrs Smith was over twice a day with cakes and sandwiches and salmon, and Petra put extra bacon on our plates and wouldn't let us pay for breakfast. Or didn't *want* to let us pay, but, of course, Callum insisted. I told him we should take what we could get, considering we'd lost out on both the rest of Ms Jones' fee *and* the extra I'd been negotiating out of Walker, and our apartment was back to trashed, but he said it wasn't right. *Morals.*

Of course, some things stuck around and were harder to ignore. The book had just moved a lot of stuff from where it should have been, rather than inventing it out of nothing – hence the lizard in the bathroom. I was pretty disappointed that had stayed and not our fridge, to be honest, but there we go. I was also slightly worried about the tiger and the leopard, but a couple of news items popped up about giant cats seen out in the Yorkshire moors, so I think they found some wide-open spaces. Hopefully they don't eat too many sheep. The cockatoos, much to my disgust, were still living in the rapidly wilting tree, and the penguins had been taken to the bird thingy at Harewood House, where they wandered about looking just as confused as they had before. No one was quite sure where the flamingos and dragons had gone.

Otherwise, things were healing. The building itself should probably have been condemned before any of this happened, so not much had changed there. There was one gap at the bottom of the stairwell that I didn't much like, and we kept finding piles of bones outside it, but we just stepped over them and pretended they weren't there. Some questions are best never asked.

The butler lived in Mrs Smith's wardrobe for three days before we persuaded him it was safe to leave. Mrs Smith fed him egg mayo sandwiches and asked us in a hushed voice if it was the gas making him think there were giant cats hunting him? Callum agreed that it very probably was, and she should just humour him. My contribution was to purr hopefully until she gave me some egg and scritched my ears.

Now Callum was sitting in a rickety chair we'd picked up from the local charity shop, his feet up on the increasingly lopsided desk and a book in one hand. A cup of tea sat on the desk (the surface at a slight angle), and a cigarette smoked in a yoghurt pot on the sill of the newly repaired window. I'd have to start putting my paw down about the smoking inside thing again soon, but given everything else that had happened it didn't feel that urgent. I inspected the scars on my back from the cockatoos. They were healing well. My whiskers were growing back too, although the burns from the beasts of the Inbetween were slower to heal.

But we were surviving.

Sometimes that's all you can ask for, right?

THERE WAS a sharp knock at the door, and we both looked at it. Heavy perfume was seeping into the room, all but masking the scent of peppermint mouthwash, and I wrinkled my nose.

"Recognise it?" Callum asked me, one hand on the cricket bat leaning next to the desk.

"Jones," I said. "Walker too, unless she's been at the mints."

"Oh, good," he said. "Maybe they can ask us to exorcise a demon for them or something. You know, just an easy job."

The knock came again, somehow sharper than before.

"Maybe they're bringing us flowers," I said. "Or a gift basket. You know, as a job well done thing."

"Sure," Callum said, swinging his legs off the desk and crossing to the door. "That sounds highly likely."

He opened the door on Ms Jones with her hand raised to knock again. She looked him up and down like a drill sergeant checking for missing buttons – he didn't have any buttons to lose, so that was okay, but there was a tea stain on his jeans and a hole in the elbow of his jumper – then said, "Callum."

"Hi," he said, and waved them in. "Gobs, get out of the chair."

"It's *my* chair," I said, but jumped off the cushion onto the desk anyway. There had never been enough room for a second client chair, even if we could afford one, so Walker plonked himself down on our armchair bed, which promptly unfolded under him. We hadn't been able to fix that.

Jones looked at the chair I'd just vacated and said, "Will it hold me?"

"Not sure," Callum said. "No one's sat in it yet."

She poked it a couple of times, then sat down. The chair creaked but held, and after a moment she relaxed enough to cross her legs at the ankles and look around. Her Docs were embroidered with red roses today. "Business slow?" she asked.

"About the same as normal," Callum said, which was to say, *yes*. "Tea?"

"Please," she said. "Milk, no sugar."

"Milk, four sugars," Walker piped up, which explained his teeth. Gods, you'd think a dentist would know better.

"You really need to cut back," Jones said, shifting in the rickety chair a little so she could look at Walker. "It's not good for your blood sugar."

He looked sulky. "I don't like sweeteners."

She sighed, and reached over to pat his knee. "I know."

Callum made tea in three mismatched mugs and handed them out, putting a packet of brand-name digestives on the table. A bit flashy, but he said we had to look after clients. I'd probably be more miffed if we actually had clients to eat the biscuits, but as it was, he'd be able to trot the same pack out for a few months at least.

"How can we help?" he asked, looking at Jones.

"I'm not going after the book," I said. "It's gone. Vamoosed. Done like a tree and, uh, leafed."

Jones smiled. I couldn't decide if that made her more scary or less. The perfume tamped down her own scent, but she wasn't wearing enough to drown it entirely, and I could still smell the raw, muscular power of her. She'd lost a lot with the book, but not everything. Far from it. She was ancient, and she'd continue on long after the rest of us were gone, rebuilding her strength and spinning her magic. There was no grief or longing in her. She'd lived long enough to know what was lost was lost, and no amount of fury would bring it back.

I was still slightly concerned she was going to turn me into a Persian or one of those squishy-faced cats, though. Or, worse, a lap dog. I didn't fancy it.

"I know the book's gone," she said. "Maybe it's even for the best. I'd put too much of my power into it for too long, and it was spinning its own magic, looking for escape. I should have realised sooner."

"Well, yeah. That would've saved a lot of hassle," I said, and Callum poked me.

Jones took a sip of her tea, then dipped into her bag. She pulled out a rather familiar-looking envelope and put it on the desk, where both Callum and I stared at it like it might bite us.

"Ah … we'd need full details," Callum said.

"*Full* details," I agreed. "Not like, *this book is a family heirloom*. More, you know, *this book wants to tear apart reality*."

"Honestly, I can't believe you hired them," Walker said. He was struggling to reach his tea from the depths of the armchair, and eventually just got up and stood sipping it next to the desk. "They're amateurs, Polly."

"So are you," she said. Harsh, but fair. Well, assuming

she was talking about sorcery and not dentistry. Although the jury was out on that one, too.

Walker spluttered on his tea. "I got that book off you! I *broke your bond!*"

The sorcerer looked to the ceiling, then at us. "Can you believe he still thinks that's a good thing to boast about?"

Callum and I exchanged glances, then Callum said carefully, "Yeah. Seems it might be best not to talk about that. You know, with the sorcerer you stole it from sitting right there."

"I'll talk about it all I want. We're equals now," Walker said, and put a hand on Jones' shoulder. She looked up at him, and he retreated hastily, wrapping both hands around his mug. "You know. In, in lots of things."

Jones leaned forward and pushed the envelope toward Callum with the tip of her finger. "Damages."

"Damages?" Callum said doubtfully.

"Damn straight," I said. "You *both* trashed our office. Which is our home. So that should be double damages twice over."

"Gobs, shut up," Callum said, and opened to envelope to look inside. He was silent for a moment, then said, "This is too much."

"Even for double twice over?" I asked. "Are you sure?"

"It's what we feel we owe," Ms Jones said. Walker muttered something, which kind of gave me the idea he wasn't completely in support of the idea.

"We didn't have anything expensive in here," Callum said. "Besides, we did lose your book."

"*Disposed of,*" I said. "You know, before it tore the world apart."

"You did well," Jones said. "Yes, you got the book stolen, but even if you'd got it back to me there would have been trouble at some point. It was already going feral – you just sped things up a bit. So while it's not the full amount I promised you, it's fair. And enough to buy a decent chair." She tapped the edge of the seat, and a small woodworm fell out, wriggling in fright.

I stalked over to Callum and peered into the envelope. There wasn't as much cash in it as the last one, but there was more than I'd seen in our future for the next month or so. Visions of fresh mackerel and cosy beds danced happily in my head. Along with bear traps. I looked at Ms Jones.

"And?"

"And?" she said innocently.

"No one hands over an that much cash just because they feel a bit bad for breaking some chairs."

She ran her thumb over her lower lip, smiling. "How on earth did the Watch catch up to you, Gobbelino? You're more suspicious than a banshee."

"Young, silly, etc," I said.

"Are banshees suspicious?" Walker asked. "Or is that just a saying, like sly as a dog?"

"Fox," Callum said.

"Dog," Walker insisted.

"No. Sly as a fox. Although you can also be a sly old dog." Callum looked perplexed for a moment. "That's kind of weird."

Jones and I looked at each other. "Did you mention

needing a familiar?" I asked. "I'd be willing to consider it. Depending on the benefits."

"I won't turn you down outright," she said. "But I'll muddle on for now."

I sighed. "Me too. If I have to."

Callum and Walker gave us almost identical looks of disapproval, and Jones tapped the desk with one finger, the nail trimmed short and flat. "Call it a retainer."

"Well, it either is or it isn't," I said.

"You want it or not?"

That was surprisingly difficult to answer. I mean, yes, I did want it. I definitely wanted a new microwaveable bed. But I also wanted to avoid any more plunges into the Inbetween and tussles with reality.

"We need more details," Callum said again, and Jones leaned back, folding her arms over her chest.

"I don't *have* details, exactly. I just want information."

"What sort of information?" Callum asked.

"The kind that a cat in contact with the shadow Watch's lieutenant can get."

"There's no rank in the Watch," I said automatically, which was true only in that no one wore bars on their shoulders. There's always rank. Even woodlice probably have rank, so they know who gets the best, soggiest woodpile. "And anyway, I've never heard of a shadow Watch."

"Well, I am a lot older than you," Ms Jones said. "I imagine I know plenty of things you don't. Your friend Claudia isn't Watch as you know it. She's shadow Watch. She works behind the scenes, acts as a check on the Watch itself if it gets out of hand."

"Well. I'm not sure she's great at that, then," I said. Or someone hadn't been. Holding someone in the Inbetween to get munched was pretty out of hand.

"The shadow Watch is small. They can't be everywhere, and while not all the Watch know about them, a lot of those who do don't approve. They'll keep secrets from them. But I imagine that's why she was keeping an eye on things around here – the actual Watch would probably like to see you slip up again. She won't agree with that sort of treatment."

Well, that was reassuring. "She said the new Watch leader was different."

"From what I hear, she is. Which interests me. But no matter how different she is, the Watch is vast and hard to manage. The shadow Watch is not. If there are changes coming, Claudia is the one moving the pieces."

"So what do you want us to do?" Callum asked. "Gobbelino's not even in contact with her."

"He will be," Jones said, taking a sip of tea. "Some cats just attract trouble."

Well, that was just unfair. A bit, anyway. "You want me to tell you what she tells me."

"Yes."

"Why?"

"Knowledge is power. And since you lost so much of my previous power …"

I looked at the envelope, then up at Callum. I was on my fourth life. I'd run afoul of the Watch in every single one so far, and not all of them had been my fault. But each time had ended worse than the last, and *still* I'd never heard of a shadow Watch. Our Ms Jones was old, powerful, and probably kept tin foil hats next to her sage sticks.

"Sure," I said. "I'm not hunting anything out, but I'll tell you what she tells me."

"You should think about it," Callum said. "This could be risky."

"I'm thinking about a heated cat bed," I said. "One of the ones you plug into the wall so it stays warm all night."

"Are you thinking of the power bill as well?"

"It's a deal, then," Ms Jones said, getting up. The chair wobbled alarmingly.

Callum sighed. "And how long does this particular retainer last? Indefinitely?"

"No. I'll be by to top up. One can't survive on supermarket own brand alone." And she gave us both a dazzling, lupine smile and left, Walker just about bouncing around her like a poodle.

Callum locked the door behind them and looked at me. "Was that smart?"

"Probably not," I admitted. "But I like nice things. I *want* nice things."

"You know how she said she couldn't imagine how you were caught? I can. I know *exactly* how you were caught."

"I would expect no less from Callum London, PI."

"I don't even know why I'm using your name. Have you given me that cat lady disease? Toxoplasmosis or something? Are there worms in my brain?"

I opened my mouth to tell him it'd only be an improvement, and there was a scratch at the door. Callum jerked away from it like a creature from the void was about to leap through, and we both stared. My stomach did an ugly roll, and I could feel my tail bushing out of its own accord. Ms Jones' scent still clung to the office, and I couldn't smell anything through it. I couldn't tell who was out there, who might have been listening in. I mean, I hadn't *done* anything, not yet – other than the whole book incident and messing around with a sorcerer and consorting with a human and introducing said human to other Folk, of course. But Claudia had as good as said she was covering for me.

Hadn't she?

The scratch came again, pointed, and Callum looked at the window then at me. I shook my head. No, I'd take it. Well, unless they tried to shove me in the Inbetween, in which case someone was losing some fur.

Callum crossed quickly to the desk, grabbed the cricket bat, then went back and opened the door.

A stocky one-eyed cat with a broken end to her tail stood there, glaring at us out of one yellow eye. The scar tissue over her missing eye was old and painful looking.

"Um, hello?" Callum said.

She looked from him to me, then examined the office. "Rough," she observed.

"I could say the same about you," I retorted, and she snorted.

"Is that any way to address a client?"

"Client?" Callum said cautiously, not letting go of the cricket bat.

"I've got a missing cat lady," the cat said. "Police are doing bollocks-all, far as I can see. You want the job?"

"What's it pay?" I asked.

"Cat lady's loaded. And dotty. She'll pay you when you find her."

I looked at Callum. He shrugged.

"Who told you to come here?" I asked the strange cat.

"Claudia," she said. "Apparently you're the go-to for crossover cases. She did mention you were a mercenary little peanut, though."

"Gotta make a living," I said, and scratched one of my itchier scars until Callum left the door and bopped me on the nose to make me stop.

"We'll take it," he said to the cat. "What're the details?"

"Come and see," she said, and ambled away.

Callum and I looked at each other. "Legit?" he asked.

"I kind of think so," I said. "And, you know. Two birds and all that."

"I think it's risky," he said, pulling on his wet-dog coat. The snake poked its head out of the pocket to see what was going on.

"Life is risky," I said.

"You coming?" the cat asked, putting her head back around the door. "I haven't got all day, you know."

"Merely conferring with my colleague," I said, and both she and Callum snorted.

"You got transport?" the cat asked.

"In a manner of speaking."

"Meet you downstairs, then." She vanished again, and I peeked out into the hall to watch her slip through the door to the stairwell, then looked back at Callum.

"Hey, you think she likes me?"

"Who, the client?"

"No, you mushroom. Claudia. She's sending us work."

"You should be so lucky," he said, and headed after the cat.

I followed him out the door, and we walked down the stinking stairwell and out into the street, where it was raining. Good, old-fashioned Yorkshire rain with nothing hostile about it, smelling of damp streets and distant fells and land with magic bones. I lifted my face to it and let it soothe my healing scars, and thought I actually was pretty lucky.

I was alive. I had a pretty decent human. And now we had clients, plural.

What more can a cat ask for?

Other than a heatable bed.

THANK YOU

Lovely people, thank you so much for picking up this book. I know there are huge demands on all of our time these days, and I appreciate it hugely that you've chosen to spend some of yours reading about mercenary feline PIs and their scruffy human sidekicks.

And if you enjoyed them, I'd very much appreciate you taking the time to pop a review up at your favourite retailer.

Reviews are a bit like magic to authors, but magic of the good kind. Less tear-a-hole-in-the-universe, more get-more-readers-and-so-write-more-books variety. More reviews mean more people see our books in online stores, meaning more people buy them, so giving us the means to write more stories and send them back out to you, lovely people.

Plus it pays for the cat biscuits, which is the primary reason for anything to happen in life …

And if you'd like to send me a copy of your review, theories about cat world domination, cat photos, or anything else, drop me a message at kim@kmwatt.com. I'd love to hear from you!

Until next time,

Read on!

Kim

PS: head over the page for more adventures, plus a free story collection (which is just a little thank you to you)!

THE ZOMBIE APOCALYPSE
STARTS HERE

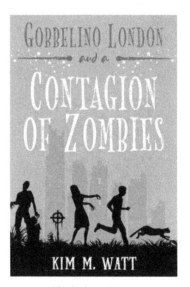

The dead are rising ...

*"Zombies don't exist. You **told** me they don't exist."*
"There's a corpse clawing its way out of a grave over there. I'm
open to the possibility that I may have been wrong."

It all started with a dog and an arm, because of course it did. That's why we have a strict no-dog policy.

But now the dead are rising, and if we don't stop them before the infection spreads any further, we're going to be knee-deep in the zombie apocalypse before you can say *mmm, brains.*

And we'd be all over it, if we weren't dealing with a small case of internal undeadness ourselves …

Grab *A Contagion of Zombies* today and join Leeds' premier magical investigators in a zombie hunt with a distinctly feline twist …

Scan above or use the link below to get your copy now!
https://readerlinks.com/l/2383607/g1pbinis

TALES OF TROUBLESOME
FELINES

Kim M. Watt

The
Cat Did
It

7 Short Tales of
Troublesome
Felines

*Sneaky, snarky, and up to no good ... Get your FREE
collection now!*

Discover seven free tales of cats with good intentions but
bad execution, cats that may or may not be cats, and cats

that could really be a lot more helpful than they actually are (but you try telling them that).

They inhabit some worlds that may seem familiar, or near enough to be only a step away. Others not so much. Or hopefully not, anyway.

But they all share one key characteristic.

They've all got issues with cats …

Scan above or head to the link below to claim your FREE copy! https://readerlinks.com/l/2383609/g1pbirm

ABOUT THE AUTHOR

Hello lovely person. I'm Kim, and in addition to the Gobbelino London tales I also write other funny, magical books that offer a little escape from the serious stuff in the world and hopefully leave you a wee bit happier than you were when you started. Because happiness, like friendship, matters.

I write about baking-obsessed reapers setting up baby ghoul petting cafes, and ladies of a certain age joining the Apocalypse on their Vespas. I write about friendship, and loyalty, and lifting each other up, and the importance of tea and cake.

But mostly I write about how wonderful people (of all species) can really be.

If you'd like to find out the latest on new books in *The Gobbelino London* series, as well as discover other books and series, giveaways, extra reading, and more, jump on over to www.kmwatt.com and check everything out there.

Read on!

amazon.com/Kim-M-Watt/e/B07JMHRBMC

bookbub.com/authors/kim-m-watt

facebook.com/KimMWatt

instagram.com/kimmwatt

twitter.com/kimmwatt

ACKNOWLEDGMENTS

First of all, and above all, thank you to you, lovely reader. Thank you for reading about mercenary cats and rips in the fabric of reality and the dangers posed by wanting things to be too perfect. You are wonderful, and without you there would be no more Gobbelino adventures.

Thank you to my wonderful editor and friend Lynda Dietz, of Easy Reader Editing, without whom my book would be riddled with far too much bellowing. She makes the editing process fun, entertaining, and utterly painless. Plus she laughs at my terrible jokes. All good grammar praise goes to her. All mistakes are mine. Find her at www.easyreaderediting.com for fantastic blogs on editing, grammar, and other writer-y stuff.

Thank you so many times over to my fantastic beta readers, who caught so many mistakes and from whom I learned what colours rats can see and that snakes can't blink. You are all awesome, and I don't know what I'd do without you. I would hug you all, but that would involve flights and me getting over the whole personal space thing.

Thank you to Monika from Ampersand Cover Design, who grasped almost instantly exactly what I wanted from the cover, and was very patient over my dithering about the name. I have trouble with titles. Find her at www.ampersandbookcovers.com

And, every single time, thank you to Mick, without whom I would likely have thrown my laptop out the window very early on in this writing adventure. You provide tea, cake, support, and excellent story setting tours of Leeds. You are amazing.

Finally, and obviously, thank you to the Little Furry Muse, a.k.a. Layla, who may not have lent Gobbelino her name, but she definitely lent him her coat and her attitude. Seriously, I'm glad she can't speak. Or that I can't hear her …

ALSO BY KIM M. WATT

The Gobbelino London, PI series

"This series is a wonderful combination of humor and suspense that won't let you stop until you've finished the book. Fair warning, don't plan on doing anything else until you're done …"

- Goodreads reviewer

The Beaufort Scales Series (cozy mysteries with dragons)

"The addition of covert dragons to a cozy mystery is perfect...and the dragons are as quirky and entertaining as the rest of the slightly eccentric residents of Toot Hansell."

– Goodreads reviewer

Short Story Collections

Oddly Enough: Tales of the Unordinary, Volume One

"The stories are quirky, charming, hilarious, and some are all of the above without a dud amongst the bunch …"

The Cat Did It

Of course the cat did it. Sneaky, snarky, and up to no good - that's the cats in this feline collection, which you can grab free by signing up to the newsletter on the earlier page. Just remember - if the cat winks, always wink back ...

The Tales of Beaufort Scales

Modern dragons are a little different these days. There's the barbecue fixation, for starters ... You'll get these tales free once you've signed up for the newsletter!

CPSIA information can be obtained
at www.ICGtesting.com
Printed in the USA
BVHW041654100423
662074BV00014B/114

9 781916 078093